Prime Minister

Also by John Stewart

Three historical novels
The Centurion
Last Romans
Marsilio

Two biographies
Standing for Justice
A Promise Kept

Two political novels
Visitors
The President

Prime Minister

John Stewart

SHEPHEARD-WALWYN (PUBLISHERS) LTD

First published in 2010 by
Shepheard-Walwyn (Publishers) Ltd
107 Parkway House, Sheen Lane,
London SW14 8LS

British Library Cataloguing in Publication Data
A catalogue record of this book
is available from the British Library

ISBN: 978-0-85683-274-1

Typeset by Alacrity, Chesterfield, Sandford, Somerset
Printed and bound through
s|s|media limited, Wallington, Surrey

I have known gentlemen who have felt that in becoming members of Parliament they had achieved an object for themselves instead of thinking that they had put themselves in a way of achieving something for others. A member of Parliament should feel himself to be the servant of his country, – and like every other servant, he should serve. If this be distasteful to a man he need not go into Parliament. If the harness gall him he need not wear it. But if he takes the trappings, then he should draw the coach. You are there as the guardian of your fellow-countrymen, – that they may be safe, that they may be prosperous, that they may be well governed and lightly burdened, – above all that they may be free. If you cannot feel this to be your duty, you should not be there at all.

ANTHONY TROLLOPE
The Duke's Children, p.99, Penguin Books
(The Duke's advice to his heir)

In memory of
Andrew MacLaren MP

Acknowledgements

My grateful thanks are due to Tommas Graves for the initial prompting and for his unfailing encouragement throughout. Our many conversations were invaluable in shaping and refining the various points and issues. David Triggs, of course, was ever supportive, and my gratitude is due. Again, Bernard White's enthusiastic support was most encouraging. I am thankful to Addie Morrow for his useful comments on the first draft. I am also very appreciative of the considerable help given by Brian Hodgkinson and am grateful for his advice on the various points of principle. Proof reading is an all-important task, and for this my thanks are due to Arthur Farndell. Anthony Werner, my publisher offered excellent advice. For this, and his willingness to publish, I am indebted.

I wish to thank the Librarian of the Garrick Club for his courtesy and the information he generously provided.

The magnanimity of the many subscribers who have backed this publication is gratefully acknowledged and appreciated.

Contents

Prologue

The Rt Hon Henry Blackstone M.P.,
House of Commons,
London SW1A 0AA

Dear Mr Blackstone,

The current crisis is long past the stage when it can be blamed on gloomy journalists. Experts we deem wise, apparently stand helpless; meanwhile the debt mountain creeps yet higher.

All this you know and like me you must be deeply worried, for this peril isn't going to disappear tomorrow. Now, if I say there is a way, please don't dismiss my words too readily. I'm not a crank. At least, my friends assure me that's the case!

We need to ease the burden of taxation. I've heard you say as much. Yet the state is desperate for funds, especially at this time of welfare crisis. Can this be resolved? Not instantly, but we could begin to shift the tax impost from earnings and enterprise to community value. That is, the value that accrues to site location by the collective presence of the community. Indeed, the city skyline is a visual image of this value. So what, I hear you say, but you must agree that any reduction in income tax would be more than welcome at this time

I can send you further information should you want, but better by far would be a meeting. This, I know, is a huge presumption on my part, but I wouldn't be proposing it if I didn't think the matter was important, if not vital.

I can only hope that you can find the time.

Yours sincerely

Alexander Collingwood

Chapter One

Henry Blackstone had just been elected Leader of the Opposition at the age of thirty-six. This was unusual, but Blackstone *was* unusual. He was a handsome man, though not over-smooth, and his stature seemed much larger than his actual size. Many remarked on this, being suddenly made aware of his considerable presence. As well as reading philosophy, politics and economics at university, his understanding of the Greco-Roman world was comprehensive. His father had planted much of this, as the biographies of great men had been a teenage diet. Blackstone's world never had been small.

Blackstone didn't have much time for what was called 'the party line.' He had joined the Conservatives for the simple reason that it was his father's preference. Indeed, one of the politicians that he much admired was Philip Snowden, the inter-war years' Labour Chancellor. Tribal politics was not Henry Blackstone's practice.

The usual Monday morning heap of newsprint lay before him, and what a dismal litany. Mounting bankruptcies, soaring unemployment, house repossessions at depressing levels, strikes and threats of further strikes, the all-too-present fear of violence on the streets, and, of course, financial chaos in the city, with banks shored up here, and companies rescued there – laudable perhaps, but where was the borrowing going to end? And the Pound, well, it was heading for the floor, if not beneath the floorboards. Poor old Bill Jones, the PM, was being savaged daily, but what could he do, indeed, what could the so-called Leader of the Opposition do? The answer, precious little, other than some tinkering here and there, but that was it. Of course, they had their grand designs, but to Blackstone's mind this was mostly window dressing. It would take a brave politician to tell the people that they had no answers. To Henry Blackstone, the truth was simple; they were caught amidst a storm, and all that he or anyone could do was wait until it ended.

Blackstone pushed the papers to the side. The research people would be highlighting the important passages in due time. Now it was the pile of letters. Phone permitting, Blackstone did his best to scan as many as he could before his first appointment. At the very least, all would have to be acknowledged. Even if the letter were nutty, neglecting such basic civility was unwise.

After a period his secretary entered with a welcome cup of coffee. He sat back. The last letter he'd opened was lying on the desk before him. Casually he read it at a distance as he sipped his coffee. Alexander Collingwood, an interesting name, he mused. Why had he thought that? He had no idea. It had simply attracted him. He re-read the letter. 'Another one putting the world to right,' he muttered. Yet, the letter had been written with a certain diffidence. Not the usual self-assertive know-all. Alexander Collingwood, yes, it was distinctive – funny how the mind was drawn to some particular sounds. Should he see him? It was a question he was asking almost hourly as the experts clamoured for his ear, all with their 'must-dos' to halt the current crisis. Crisis! It was a tsunami! Nothing was sacred, and respected trading names were swept aside without a sliver of respect. He was Leader of the Opposition, but what could he oppose? The Government was in freefall and it didn't seem the thing to do to stick the knife in when the PM and his troupe were rushing for the cliff.

He took another sip of coffee and his gaze reverted to the Collingwood letter. Yes, there was something different; it was just a feeling, but he had no inkling what it was. Maybe he should ask around. Who was this guy Collingwood? What made him tick and think that *he* had something significant to offer? An arrogant nutter, determined he was specially sent to save the world! No, dammit, go for it, another thought reacted. Who knows what it might reveal.

He turned to his secretary and handed her the letter.

'Tell him I'll meet him in the lobby by the Gladstone statue – tomorrow or Wednesday at ten-thirty.'

*

Collingwood could hardly believe it. He'd thought the letter was a waste of time, a last desperate, but futile shot. Yet it had worked. The gods were on his side. This was only the first hurdle, though; there were many more to come.

*

4

The central lobby wasn't crowded. The sounds were subdued, yet there was a note of busyness as people went about their business. Blackstone scanned the scene and there he was, tall, trim and grey-haired, a figure naturally exuding dignity. Blackstone knew that he had found his man.

'Good morning, Mr Collingwood,' he said, extending his hand 'Good morning, Sir.'

Blackstone hesitated.

'We'll not have coffee here,' he said almost impatiently. 'Let's go outside.'

'As you wish, Sir.'

Blackstone knew he was acting strangely. There was even a touch of alarm. Even so, something told him he was right. Where would they go, he wondered, as they walked down the steps to the St Stephen's entrance? He hailed a taxi.

'The Garrick Club,' he told the cabbie as if he'd long before decided.

'An old friend took me to the Garrick – oh, it must be twenty years ago. This is quite a treat, Mr Blackstone,' Collingwood began as they settled in the cab.

'It's a pity but I rarely get the chance to use the place.' He looked at Collingwood knowingly. 'This job I've got keeps me fairly busy! What's your profession, Mr Collingwood?'

'A small family publishing house: we have a few fairly successful authors on our books, so we manage. My daughter has now joined me, so that's a great help, but as you probably guess, publishing isn't easy.'

'I can imagine. It's good you have your daughter helping.'

'Yes, she's a blessing. She's twenty-five, and very good with publicity. That leaves me free to select the next manuscript from amongst the pile.' He laughed. 'The one, we hope, to make our fortune!'

The conversation continued on a light note, but not a word was said about the content of the letter. That would happen when they sat down with their coffee.

'That was quick,' Blackstone remarked when the taxi drew up at the entrance. As they got out, a cold wind funnelling down the street brought tears to their eyes.

Inside the heat was welcome.

'There's a chill wind out there,' Blackstone acknowledged.

'Yes, you wouldn't think it was mid-April.'

Collingwood was taken to the morning room, where they selected two comfortable leather chairs. Unsurprisingly, there was a portrait of Garrick above the mantelpiece; in fact, the walls were lined with portraits.

'This is delightful,' Collingwood reacted.

'Yes, it invites contentment. That was Lord Byron's sofa.' Blackstone pointed.

'It is a sofa, yes, yet, when you say it was Lord Byron's, history lends its magic.'

Once they had settled with their coffee there was a pause, and Collingwood knew the moment had arrived. So much could depend on the next few minutes. The major question was: Would Henry Blackstone be receptive?

'Mr Collingwood, your letter talked about easing the tax burden, but you also suggested shifting the tax to what you called location value. What exactly are you proposing?'

'At the moment tax is collected from private and corporate earnings or, if you like, enterprise and also trade, of course. But tax discourages, and few if any sing a hymn of joy when they receive their tax assessment. Indeed, it goes without saying that reducing taxes would be very welcome, especially now. The state, however, is hungry for revenue. Present welfare needs are mushrooming, not to mention the debt burden. So how can we ease or reduce taxation? It seems impossible.'

'It certainly does,' Blackstone echoed. 'Go on, Mr Collingwood.'

'There is a fund that rises naturally in communities. Its value reflects the advantage of location. In the high street, for instance, the location of a shop can reap a huge advantage. Then compare the high street to the side-street corner-shop. Now think of the City of London and the location value there – astronomic! The question is: Who creates location value?'

'I think I know what you're saying, but continue.'

'No one could conclude that the location value of, say a Manhattan or City property, was due to the efforts of a single individual or, indeed a corporation. Clearly the whole community pushes up the value. In the old wild-west town of the movies the saloon and the general store were in the high street, not the middle of the scrub! In other words location is the draw. Why build in the middle of the desert?

'So if the community creates the value, to whom does it belong? There can only be one reasonable answer – the community! In

6

fact, the community creates a natural fund and is therefore self-financing. This is the shift I would propose.'

Collingwood held his peace, and Blackstone sat for some time completely silent.

'I've heard people make fun of this idea, but I've never heard it expounded,' Blackstone said quietly. 'This is a vote killer. Every patch of suburban green will be up in arms, and the property boys, well, they'd go into orbit. It seems self-evident, but, at the same time, a bit too good to be true. For instance, if it's such a good idea, why have all the economic gurus ignored it? To put it bluntly, why should you see the answer when all the experts down the ages seem to have ignored it. I'll have to think about this. It seems right. It doesn't sound like just another theory, another think-tank bubble,' Blackstone continued. 'But, even if we did take it up; how in God's name could we sell it – especially to the party? Mr Collingwood, you'll have to be patient. I need time to digest this, and by the way, I'm Henry!'

'And they call me Alexander.'

'That's that treaty signed! You know, I feel as though I've caught a glimpse of something, but is it a nightmare or enlightenment? There's more to come, I know.'

Collingwood nodded.

'The trouble is I've got another appointment. Could we have dinner tomorrow evening?'

Collingwood hesitated: it was barely noticeable.

'Yes, I can do that...'

'You hesitated, Alexander, is there a problem?'

'I promised to treat my daughter to dinner – a belated birthday celebration.'

'Bring your daughter along.'

Collingwood's face lit up.

Blackstone noted Collingwood's pleasure, but made no comment. Collingwood, though, felt that something needed to be said.

'My daughter Anna and I are close. I know that she'll be thrilled.'

'Alexander, I will have the pleasure of meeting her tomorrow evening. But now, I must be going; otherwise I'll be in my secretary's bad books! She, by the way, will let you know about tomorrow evening's venue.'

They both stood up.

'Thanks for seeing me and thanks for the Garrick. I find these old clubs reassuring!' Collingwood said quietly.

'Father and Grandfather were members; it's a kind of family thing. When I was young, Father and I used to come here quite a lot. You get attached.' He paused. 'Things are bad, Alexander. All these gleaming towers we see, just built: acres of office space, and not a soul inside other than security. And they're still building them! The skyline's crowded with tall cranes. How long before the banks pull out the plug? Alexander, I need to know more, much more!'

Chapter Two

The banking system was teetering, and two major failures on Wall Street were echoing memories of 1929. News reports were bordering on hysterical, and calm words, especially reports of 'green shoots,' were simply not believed. Yet somehow the nation was holding course, reluctant, perhaps, to believe the worst. Collingwood scanned all the main papers. The gloom was universal. And the book trade didn't add much light, he added grimly. The future was bleak. Dear God, how would he provide for Anna?

A crisis cabinet meeting was set for the afternoon. There were calls for the Prime Minister's resignation, but what good would that do? And, if he did resign, what could his successor do? They'd tried all the old tricks. Predictably, militancy was on the increase and the looming threat of strikes was all too real. In the circumstances Collingwood fully expected the dinner with the Leader of the Opposition to be cancelled, but no, a phone call from Blackstone's secretary confirmed the time and venue, a restaurant near Marylebone High Street.

Anna and high fashion didn't mix, yet she had taste and when she did step out, heads turned. Anna was attractive. At times she could appear quite cold. It often was the cloak of shyness, but it also gave aspiring beaus the message that they'd overstayed their welcome. Collingwood had met two of these hopefuls in the past year. In fact, he rather liked one of them. Very personable, he thought, but Anna shook her head. He was very nice, she told him, but all he talked about was rugby. Collingwood suggested that the phase would pass, but she only smiled, and so he let the rather tricky subject lapse. He was concerned, though. Would she ever find the 'right' companion? Too much head, Anna, but he kept his peace.

*

The thought of meeting the leader of Her Majesty's Opposition had made Anna ill at ease, but no one would have guessed, except her father. He knew the signs, and he dared to hope that his attractive daughter might, at last, find someone who could focus her attention. It was a dream, but fathers surely were allowed to hope!

When they arrived at the restaurant, the Collingwoods were shown to a corner table, no doubt selected for its privacy. The restaurant was warm and friendly, modest in size, and the Italian proprietor courtesy itself.

'"The Maestro," that is, Mister Blackstone, phoned to say he might be late, fifteen minutes maybe,' he relayed. Clearly the leader of Her Majesty's Opposition was a regular.

Twenty minutes later Blackstone rushed in.

'Sorry I'm late. The PM's statement caught us on the hop. They're heaping on more taxes. It's completely mad, but that's the government's mind-set.' He stopped. 'Alexander, who is this graceful lady? Methinks we have another Collingwood, and what a tasteful dress!' Blackstone's words had a freshness that betrayed their spontaneity.

'Thank you, Sir,' Anna responded quietly. The beginning of a blush didn't develop.

After ordering pre-meal drinks they took their seats, and right from the beginning it was clear that Blackstone viewed the dinner as a working occasion.

'Alexander, what you said yesterday has been running round my head ever since. Your comments about location value being the community's natural fund are difficult to fault. It all seems so blindingly uncomplicated. So why has no one taken it up? Am I missing something? I know there's part of me who sees the current way of things as simply how it is and I suppose that's the way we mostly think. This isn't easy, Alexander, and it could cause a rebellion in the party. Yet the idea is simplicity itself. The community collects what it creates and stops plundering what it doesn't create, that is, individual and corporate earnings. My sister's cat could understand it!'

'Plundering is a good word. I didn't use it yesterday, for I felt it might sound a bit strong, but that's exactly what happens. Individuals plunder the community's location value fund, and the community plunders the individual's rightful earnings. The trouble is, this plunder has the seal of custom. It is centuries old and, as you've just said, it's difficult to see past it.'

'Take the young bloods from the estates, where petty crime is common. How will it help them?'

'A good question, but not an easy one to answer,' Collingwood said pensively.

'Ah, here's Leo, what do you recommend this evening, my friend?'

'The fish is good, Maestro.'

'Leo never fails.'

'Maestro, the BBC guys say the headman's going to quit. You get ready for the job, eh?'

'You'd lose my custom, Leo!'

'I come and cook for you.'

Blackstone laughed, and Leo beamed.

There was more laughter as they made their choice and ordered wine, and then the conversation started up again.

'Your question about the young bloods,' Collingwood began, picking up the thread. 'If a hundred per cent location value were collected, the tax shift would be near to total. In such a situation all tax on earnings would be greatly reduced, and, one would hope, abolished in most cases. Again, access to sites would be allowed on payment of the relevant location value. This access would be open to anyone, including those in inner-city slums, and would, one would hope, allow people to pursue their natural bents. Getting a "job", no matter how soul destroying, is hardly conducive to a contented society. Such is the broad theory. But, of course, such a total shift from our present situation would be impractical, and, indeed, inhumane. The shift, by necessity, must be gradual, for no one must be rudely ousted from their property.

'Initially, with a small percentage shift, benefits wouldn't be obvious. Politically, it would be difficult to sell on the doorstep, except for one thing – tax reductions on earnings. And, of course, there are the taxes we often miss – you know, you see the price of something then you read, plus vat! And stealth taxes; they're like a plague of nibbling mice.'

'Alexander, you've given me more ideas in the last ten minutes than I've had in a week of crisis meetings! Indeed, it feels as though I've come upon a secret that's been hidden for some time, and I've only turned the key! Ah, here's the wine. I always order the house speciality when I come here. I hope you like it. I find it as good, if not better, than the fancy stuff.'

Blackstone stretched himself.

11

'I must say it's good to be away from that whirlpool at West-minster. Did you have to come far?'

'Richmond – it's quite an easy journey. Just three stops on the fast train to Waterloo – then the Jubilee Line to Bond Street.'

'Yes, but a tedious journey late in the evening. Sid, my tame driver, will see you home.'

'Thank you,' Anna reacted, clearly grateful to escape the late night tube and train.

Blackstone smiled.

'Thank Sid!'

Anna laughed. Her father hadn't seen her looking quite so happy for a long time.

'I have a flat quite close.' Blackstone explained. 'I should move to Westminster, but I like it here. It's a bit like a village. You get to know the local traders and we have a farmers' market.' He paused. 'Alexander, how would your suggestions affect this whole scene? Take the High Street here.' Blackstone continued. 'Say a site was available on payment of location value. What about the structure on the site, the buildings, in other words?'

'Buildings, being the product of human labour, are not subject to location levy. The site owner, or landlord, to use the common term, is generally the owner of the buildings too. If they had a tenant, one might assume they would simply pass the levy on. But how could they? The tenant is already paying the most, for the landlord always takes the most. To take more would be to drive the tenant out of business. All right, due to the tax shift the tenant is enjoying a reduction in general tax, but so is the land-lord! This aspect requires further explanation, but at another time, perhaps.'

'Ah, I see the food is coming. I like it here; it's simple and not out of the freezer. – Damn, my mobile. At this hour, they only ring me when there's something big.'

Blackstone got up and moved to the entrance for better recep-tion. He came back almost immediately.

'The latest gossip is, the PM is resigning. Rumour has it that he's lost the battle with his left-wing rebels and is handing in his resignation. Anyway, let's eat. There's no point in fasting when you don't have to!'

Collingwood smiled and Anna burst out laughing.

The conversation was light and general as they ate, and Collingwood felt the economic questions had ended for the evening. Then in the midst of joking about his latest political indiscretion, another question came.

'Alexander, so far I'm with you, but what about a tenant with a long lease. In fact, what about tower blocks with the myriad of leases and sub-leases. What about the twentieth floor, as it were?'

'Good question. Clearly, there would need to be some kind of referral, like recourse to arbitration. When it comes to a tower block, it's a question of identifying the chief beneficiary of the location, after which the various shares can be calculated. Another method would be to bill the tenant, who would be forced to approach the landlord for a reduction in rent, reason being that the tenant couldn't pay both the levy and his full rent. Again, when required, there'd be recourse to arbitration.

'Someone I know has worked out a computer programme that can cope with all the tower block intricacies. I can forward a copy of his analysis if you like. In fact, a group of us have been working on this whole idea for some time.'

'Ah, there's the telltale bleep again.'

Anna watched Blackstone make his way to the entrance as before. There was something very ordinary about Henry Blackstone, and paradoxically, extra-ordinary. He flaunted no parade of his position, yet a natural sense of presence did it for him. Not a man of rigid attitude, she felt, but rock-hard when the need arose.

She watched him return and there it was again, the ordinariness and the sense of presence spilling from its unassuming source.

'They want me at central office. They're shooting into orbit at the thought of an election. So I'd better go and cool them down. An election is the last thing that the nation wants.'

'The last time this happened, we had a National Government. That was 1931,' Anna responded.

'Yes, but that solution wouldn't be popular with the PM's party.'

'Shades of Ramsey MacDonald, you mean. I always thought that Ramsey didn't have much option.' Collingwood interjected.

Blackstone nodded pensively.

'What can the PM do? His "centre" and his "right" are pressing for austerity and his "left" are blocking him. He can't carry his party, his ratings are below ground and his so-called friends are lining up to stab him in the back. The hard fact is – his tax-and-spend dreamboat has hit the rocks. Well, enough of this. I must be off. It's been both informative and a very real pleasure. Don't forget, Sid will be here in about twenty minutes, so you'll have time to have your coffee in peace. I insist we have another meeting soon.'

His smile focused briefly on Anna, and all at once he was gone.

Collingwood's gaze was quizzical.

'Well?'

'Henry Blackstone isn't just another politician!'

'Did you like him?'

'Yes.'

Collingwood's smile was barely discernible. He'd probed about as far as a father dared.

Anna knew exactly what her father was thinking, but she knew better than to stoke the fires of attachment. The daughters of the manor would be queuing up! Henry Blackstone could pick and choose, and probably had. Anyway, he'd hardly noticed her and the brief smile at the end was a polite formality.

Chapter Three

Bill Jones glowered at the stony faces sitting round the table. Except for the Foreign Secretary and the Chancellor, he trusted none of them. They had failed to back the crisis measures he'd proposed, while talking openly to the press about betrayal of the party's principles. Cabinet discipline had collapsed, and Jones had no option but to seek an audience with the Queen and offer his resignation.

Now the Cabinet was assembled to hear the outcome. They wouldn't relish what he had to say, for there was no shortage of egos panting for his job, not forgetting Chris Crouch, peddling the neo-Marxist mind-set. What had happened to the party he'd grown up with?

The Jones family had been solid Labour for three generations. His grandfather had been a lay preacher, a pillar of the Nonconformist Church. His party principles were Christian principles. That was how he thought. Now all that was gone.

Bill Jones was seventy; the heady days of election-night success were long forgotten. He was tired, and the last months had been a constant struggle. There'd been no fun, just opposition, often bitter, levelled at his person. Again, his rotund figure, largish ears and thinning hair gave sport for the cartoonist. His wife Ellen had been pressing him to retire for ages, but his sense of duty had kept him at the helm. With worldwide chaos in the markets, how could he simply walk away?

'Well, Bill, what's the score?' Crouch burst out, unable to contain himself. As usual, he'd been militantly informal.

'Chris, I have to disappoint you. I haven't resigned.'

'What!' exploded the Home Secretary. 'You haven't got the confidence of the Cabinet or the Party. We want a new man who will honour manifesto commitments!'

'With what?' the Chancellor barked.

'Ladies and gentlemen, Her Majesty wants to form a coalition government. She maintains, and I agree, that it is not the time for either a party or a general election. The situation is dire.

Meltdown is the fear the BoE is facing. We need to make decisions, decisions that will hurt many of us, and we need to make them very soon.'

'We're being sold down the river.' The Health Secretary, Jake Hud, was livid. 'This is another MacDonald debacle. And you're going to lead this gathering of clowns?'

'I told the Queen the country needed someone younger.'

'So what's the next chapter in the nightmare?'

'The three party leaders are to report this afternoon.'

'You've betrayed us and the people,' Hud bellowed. 'Mark my words, that teenager Blackstone will get the job.'

'Well, Jake, you opposed every proposal I made to ease the current crisis. What's more, you persuaded your considerable parliamentary following to do the same. You were vehement and you brooked no compromise. Today is the result of your persistent efforts.'

Hud looked as if he would blow up.

Deliberately, Jones put his hands flat on the table before him, and they watched, waiting, they supposed, for the next revelation.

'Ladies and gentlemen, this is the last Cabinet meeting of this Labour administration and my last appearance as Prime Minister.'

'Prime Minister, we should crack a bottle of bubbly! After all we have been together for some time,' Chris Crouch chipped in.

'Chris, you've actually called me "Prime Minister". I've had to wait a long time, but it's been worth it! Perhaps we've got more in common than we think.'

'What's that, Prime Minister?'

Hud jumped up.

'I've had enough of this bloody pantomime!' he exploded, and gathering up his papers, he strode headlong from the room.

'Prime Minister, you haven't answered.'

'Humanity, Chris, humanity!'

*

The three party leaders felt like schoolboys waiting for the head-master's chastisement, and their banter reflected this.

'This feels like a business lunch,' the Liberal leader Willie Windbourne began. 'Our heads are full of business but no one says a word until the last moment.'

'Cheese and biscuits is the time, I believe,' Henry Blackstone quipped.

Bill Jones laughed. 'Some phone up the next morning!'

'That's really laid back!' Windbourne responded lightly.

The door opened and the Queen's private secretary entered.

'Her Majesty apologises for keeping you waiting.'

The whole process was businesslike and efficient. The Sovereign saw each party leader briefly, then all together, and it seemed that the matter was decided simply by circumstance. Bill Jones being the elder statesman, and not wishing to continue as premier, took the role of deputy Prime Minister. The Liberal leader of the minority party clearly did not have the mandate of the second largest party. He was also constrained by policy directives that he knew he dared not compromise. So it was the young Henry Blackstone that was chosen. Neither Jones nor Windbourne raised an objection, though Windbourne might have hoped he had a chance.

There was little doubt that the Sovereign had received the best advice, but she could also call on her own unrivalled experience.

*

Anna and her father had missed the news the night before. Both had been absorbed in reading manuscripts. Nibbling at the pile was how the elder Collingwood thought of it. Time had simply slipped them by. So the next morning, when she made her routine visit to the newsagent, the tabloid headlines stopped her dead.

'Boy Wonder takes charge.' The large heavy print was easily read. 'The triumph of Inexperience over Incompetence – Blackstone takes charge.' Anna's heart was pumping. This was the man they'd dined with just two days ago. This was the man who'd heard the economic principles that her father held so dear, and he'd been interested. Most didn't hear or want to hear!

She bought the popular tabloids and the heavies and, almost forgetting the milk needed for the morning coffee, she rushed back.

'Father!' she called out. Collingwood rushed into the hall immediately.

'What's wrong, dear?'

'Nothing's wrong father – look at this!'

'My heavens! This is a situation I've dreamed about: someone in government who knows the basic economic law.'

'Shades of Campbell-Bannerman.'

Collingwood nodded.

'And Asquith and Lloyd George?'

'Perhaps, perhaps – Philip Snowdon knew but I doubt if his PM Ramsay MacDonald saw the full significance, but I may be wrong.'

'Henry Blackstone does. He won't forget, father.'

'I think you're right, dear. There's steel beneath that quiet exterior. We'll have to send him our congratulations – or maybe our commiserations. He's inheriting a nightmare. But we mustn't push ourselves.'

*

Henry Blackstone sat back in his chair. He had just seen two of his own party's shadow cabinet. Winston Hughes was now Home Secretary, and Ted Banks, Industry. Ted was a good man, and his job would be crucial. The junior posts were to come, but doubtless some would be disappointed. It was a National Government and all three parties had to be represented. Balance was the key word, and Blackstone was determined to be fair.

'Who's next?' he asked his secretary.

'Mr Jones, my old boss.'

'Jenny, we must show Mr Jones every courtesy. What's his drink? Tea or coffee?'

'He usually has coffee.'

'I'll leave that to you. I can hear him outside.'

'Good to see you, Bill. Thank God you're on board to hold my hand. This job's relentless. And sending disappointed men away is not a job I like.'

'I know, people say you're hard, but, in truth, you never do get used to it.'

'Ah, here's Jenny with the coffee.'

Jenny and her old boss were obviously on good terms. This Blackstone noted, and it ticked another box. Almost immediately Jenny returned with the coffee, when Jones indulged some humorous banter. Jenny was obviously pleased, and after she had gone, the two men immediately began to discuss the placings in the Cabinet.

Time passed quickly.

'Bill, you recommended your Chancellor, James Jamieson. I

agree, for continuity at the Treasury is vital. Is he a man open to fresh ideas?'

'A bit slow to make up his mind sometimes, but I've always found him reasonable. In other words, he isn't rigid.'

'Bill, your friend the Foreign Secretary, would he mind being Leader of the House? I feel we need to give the Foreign Office to our Liberal friend Willy Windbourne.'

'That's all right, my old friend's tired running around.'

'Thank God that's settled.'

'Henry, I've got two rather controversial suggestions...'

A knock arrested their attention. It was Jenny.

'May I take the coffee things?'

'Of course. Oh Jenny, I've been meaning to ask you: could you get Alexander Collingwood on the phone? He's got a publishing house in Richmond somewhere. I think it's "The Green".'

'Certainly, Sir.'

'Now, Bill, these controversial bombshells you're about to drop?'

'One is, the-one-and-only Chris Crouch, and the other is Jake Hud. Hud's not a man I warm to, but he's got quite a following, and I fear he would cause trouble if he didn't have a job. He's an able man. Chris, well, if we didn't have him, we'd have to invent him. He speaks for the folk that everybody's written off!'

'He's a likeable devil. Bill, can we have another chat in the morning? We need to get this show on the road. The luxury of silence isn't one we can rely on! In other words, we need to show the flag.'

'Indeed, it's important to let the people know we're doing something. Something that they feel will help. Henry, you've been very gracious. You know, part of me doesn't like this too much, but another part is very glad the burden's gone.'

'Thanks, Bill.'

Jones stood up, and the ex-Premier and the new Premier shook hands. Then just as Bill Jones left, and, as if on cue, the phone rang.

'Mr Collingwood, for you, Prime Minister.'

'Alexander, I've been meaning to phone you all day, but as you can imagine the Downing Street routine is something else!'

'Congratulations, there's a letter in the post from the both of us. But you phoned, Sir. What can I do for you?'

'We need to meet, and the sooner the better.'

19

'I'm at your service.'

'I hate to say it, but would eight-thirty be all right?'

'Earlier, if you like.'

'Let's say eight. I need to pick your brains on how to introduce the subject of location value and the natural fund. The aim is not to frighten people but to give them hope.'

'Exactly, see you in the morning.'

'Alexander, could Anna and yourself reserve Friday evening for a bite at Number Ten? By then, I'm sure I'll have a bucketful of questions!'

'Anna will be thrilled and I'll be her willing escort.'

'I'll send a car to pick you up.'

'Thank you Prime Minister.'

'See you in the morning.'

Chapter Four

Alexander Collingwood was on the doorstep of Number Ten at eight a.m. and was conducted to the Prime Minister's study. Coffee was offered, and after the normal pleasantries, they immediately got down to business.

'The location levy sounded so simple the other night and I thought I understood it, but when I pondered how it could be gathered, I met a wall of problems. Everyone to whom I speak maintains that it's impractical. I must say my doubts are rampant. Alexander, I can't embark on a wild-goose chase!'

'The principle is simple. What is complicated is our current set-up. A small percentage collection doesn't help, of course, for there's no clean break, as it were. In other words, the old system and the new, of necessity, must run together initially. However, there are people who have made a detailed study of the application and, of course, there are our friends in Australia, New Zealand, America, that is, both the US and Canada, and Denmark also. In all these countries first-hand knowledge is available.'

'But why don't we hear about it, if it's so widespread?'

'It's seen as just another tax. That's why the tax *shift* should be highlighted. We should remember that the application in other countries is partial. Again, the legislation is often repealed. The property-vested interests and house-owning suburbia are powerful lobbies and self-interest triumphs over justice. The projected benefits that natural economic law allows, although far-reaching, are seen as vague and in the future. They are difficult to sell on the doorstep. Whereas "soak the rich" is easy.'

'I can imagine. So, what are we to do?'

'I feel we need to form a group with a strong chairman, one who can control the various firm opinions. I know people who are very knowledgeable and have made a detailed study of application. Some say it's easy, but the proof of the pudding etc, etc!'

'Would you act as Chairman?'

'I think not, you need someone with authority, preferably Cabinet rank. I'll sit on the committee, if you want, as a sort of guardian of the principle. What I said at the beginning I do feel is important – the principle is simple; what is complicated is our current set-up. We need to find the words to make this proposition catch the general interest. Once it's up and running, tax reductions, and their benefits, will be obvious. But getting to that stage will concentrate the best of minds!'

'All right, Alexander, we'll move on this. I'll have to leave you now, but I'm looking forward to Friday.'

'Likewise, Prime Minister.'

*

The Cabinet room was buzzing. Some, including Jake Hud, had only been summoned that morning. In fact, the call had taken him completely by surprise, for he had assumed the inevitable black mark from Jones would exclude him. On one side was Winston Hughes, now Home Secretary, and on the other, Ted Banks, who'd got Industry. 'Sandwiched between two Conservatives,' he joked. 'Do I get danger money?'

'Here they come,' Ted Banks whispered loudly.

Willie Windbourne, and Bill Jones took their seats on either side of the Prime Minister.

Briefly, Blackstone bowed his head, before proceeding.

'Is he awake?' Chris Crouch's stage whisper was clearly audible.

'You are, Chris' Blackstone shot back without the slightest hint of censure. Then he continued. 'Ladies and gentlemen, the task before us is unenviable. Problems loom on every side, soaring unemployment is at heartbreaking levels, and strikes: strikes called, it seems, to cause the most disruption: such blackmail tactics are particularly distressing.

'The hard-working core of the country is angry. Taxed to destruction, the signs of their distress are growing. Ladies and gentlemen, this is dangerous, for if the solid centre cracks, no amount of chatter, whether right or left, will make amends.

'We represent a National Government and squabbling in public is not a practice to indulge in. If we don't display some dignity and discipline, how can we expect respect? This, of course, applies to all levels of society. Common decency must return to lead us. Rules we have in plenty, but it's principles that count, what-is right and what-is-wrong principles.

'I've been Prime Minister for a day, give or take an hour or two, and in this short time I've learned of our bankrupted state. We've been spending when there's nothing left to spend. Mr Jones, I witnessed, battled manfully but without support. Ladies and gentlemen, the problem is still with us and hard decisions must be made.

'There's something wrong in the state of Denmark, if I may paraphrase a well-known playwright, when the rich are still amassing fortunes and the poor are driven further to despair. Democratic parties have been concentrating on the greatest happiness for the greatest number. That is where the votes are. But what about the others who are not within this magic circle? Here we have the haves-and-have-nots, a bitter division. Yet, with all this, we must beware of wreckers who would use our weakened state to undermine the constitution. Ladies and gentlemen, there is a lot to do! Your comments.'

'Prime Minister,' Janet Simmons jumped in immediately. 'You've told us how dire it is. But can you give us some hope?' Janet was in her late thirties, easy on the eyes and right of centre in her views.

'There are no quick fixes, Janet, but we can turn things round. We need a fundamental shift in tax.'

'Tax is crippling us, Prime Minister. Small traders in my constituency are falling like ninepins.' Jake Hud spoke up.

'You didn't say that in the Commons last week.'

'I got it wrong, Prime Minister. The thought of cutting welfare brought the shutters down.'

'Jake, we need a shift of taxes from production, but what I have in mind may recreate the Iron Curtain, never mind the shutters!'

'Prime Minister, I'm good at dodging barriers!'

'I hope so.'

Questions sparked around the table, but no one tried to be too clever or upstage the new Prime Minister. Jones observed all carefully. Henry Blackstone was much tougher than his easy manner betrayed. He could cut you down and do it with a winning smile. This, he sensed, the Cabinet realised, and no one was prepared to put their head above the parapet. They weren't facing poor old tired Bill Jones.

Blackstone spoke briefly with the former Premier just as they broke up.

'Happy with that, Bill?'

'It went off well. No one tried to hog the show. Jake Hud surprised me. But there you are.'

'I'm going to use him. He's got the fire. All we need to do is harness it!'

'Good luck!'

Blackstone chuckled.

*

Blackstone beckoned Hud as they left the room.

'Jake, are you free this evening?'

'I can be, Prime Minister.'

'Half six, if it's suitable.'

'I'll make it suitable.'

'Good, see you then.'

Blackstone was acting on an instinctive feeling. Hud was his own man and he wasn't afraid to speak up or oppose the great and good – a strong mind for a challenging chairmanship. But could he handle the slings and arrows, for both sustained and vicious opposition were assured? A tough post for a tough operator. Yes, Blackstone thought, he would obey his instinct. He thought of Alexander Collingwood. That too had been the gift of instinct, and that had certainly worked.

*

Jake Hud was forty, he was sharp-featured, with a wiry frame, and he still retained a generous head of hair. At half six he presented himself as arranged and was met almost immediately by the Prime Minister. No hanging around. He liked it, and he liked Blackstone too. So far he'd pressed all the right buttons. Blackstone was a big man, not so much in the physical sense, but he was so bloody unassuming that you usually didn't notice that he had this presence thing until it suddenly was upon you.

'I don't normally allow myself a tipple until it's after six. Indeed six thirty is the usual time. Would you like to join me, Jake?'

'Try and stop me if you can!'

'Good man. Come into the office. It's a bit chaotic – some of Bill's stuff is still there – but I like it better than these pristine reception rooms.'

Hud guessed that Blackstone didn't care too much one way or the other. He was just creating an atmosphere of informality.

Hud chose a gin and tonic, and Blackstone poured himself a glass of red. They sat down.

'Jake, I would like you to chair a committee of a rather special

24

kind.' Blackstone began. 'You may see it as a poisoned chalice, but to me it is a most important post. It's all about taxation shift.'

Blackstone then outlined the location value principle in the same simple terms as he had heard it from Alexander Collingwood. He was alerted, though, for in explaining the various points in his own words, the potency of the principle grew more evident. Hud was silent but he was listening keenly; then suddenly he erupted.

'This is bloody dynamite! And you want me to chair a bunch of eggheads who are experts on the subject. I take your point about the poisoned chalice. As my Scottish friends would say, you're a canny one, PM!'

'Do you get the principle?' Blackstone pressed.

'It's the bloody truth!'

'You've got it!' Blackstone sat back in his chair with relief. He had picked the right man.

'It's so simple. The community collects the location value, the fund it has created, and the citizen walks away tax-free. Why has no one ever thought of this before?'

'They have, but it's always been defeated by the vested interest and, of course, first attempts at application are difficult. We could dress this whole idea up in different clothes, like using amenity charges as a measure, thus minimising the use of property terms, such as site location and land. We haven't chosen that option. Our aim is economic freedom, and for that to be accepted in the hearts of men and women, the principle needs to be presented in plain and simple terms, terms that all can easily understand.

'It won't be easy, Jake, but, as my friend Alexander Collingwood says, the principle is simple. What is complicated is our current set-up. And Jake, this is potent stuff. Let's not use the megaphone. We need to move slowly and with caution. The scare-mongers don't need any help. Above all, we don't want to frighten people and debase the principle. In truth there's nothing to be alarmed about; indeed, most people would be better off. Take the farming community: their rating would be low and, with tax on earnings eased, they would feel a new freedom. A farmer is close to the land he labours. His caring wardship has often a devoted nature, and this should be protected from zealot-like officials pursuing the letter of the law. Again, a farmer's son should be encouraged, not hindered from following in his father's footsteps. The principle we advocate is just, and we protect its integrity when we apply it wisely.'

Chapter Five

Blackstone was Prime Minister of a National Coalition Government born out of crisis, and some pronouncement was expected; but what could he say that would convey the hope that Janet Simmons called for in the Cabinet. The truth was he had no idea. The Location Value proposal would take time to implement, and time was not a luxury he possessed. The people wanted answers now. Platitudes, of course, would engender anger, and the government could lose authority before it even started. Better honesty by far, even though it carried gloom. Both Bill Jones and Willy Windbourne felt something needed to be said, but neither had anything specific to offer. His advisors had sheaves of proposals, but these were mostly cosmetic. 'Well, Blackstone,' he muttered to himself, 'you'll have to brave the screen.' In fact, prime time had just been confirmed for Thursday evening.

The speech was skilfully crafted. The redrafts had been numerous but, as far as Blackstone was concerned, it was lifeless. Thursday morning came. Then the hours ticked by until at nine p.m. the producer's finger pointed. Blackstone scanned the first page of the written speech before him. It hadn't changed. It was still bloodless.

The pause was all he could afford. He had to start.

'On Monday last Her Majesty asked me to form a national government to deal with the present crisis. As you will have learned, this is proceeding and will soon be completed.'

He stopped reading. This was hopeless. Launch out, Blackstone, an inner voice was prompting, and he did just that.

'The last time we had a National Government was during the Second World War, so why now? What has brought us to this pretty pass? And, of course, who is at fault? Who is to blame? Well, do you know something? I think we're all a trifle guilty. Many of us have borrowed foolishly, encouraged, at times, by irresponsible finance houses. Government, too, has been profligate, borrowing well beyond accepted norms, forced to, they would say, by irresponsible banking practice. But let's not wallow in past weakness, but rather face the future with resolve. The blame game is completely unproductive.

'Taxation is too high; this is a general complaint. Much of it is raised to aid distress through unemployment, which is often triggered by the burden of that very tax. Ask any employer and he will tell you that he has to find double the amount the employee actually earns! I'm not disputing that all this is not done with the best intentions. But is it reasonable? That's the question.

'The state needs revenue, so taxes in some form are clearly inevitable. However, a lot depends on where taxation falls. In fact, I feel we need a tax shift from earnings, both corporate and private, to the natural fund arising from the presence of the community. Easing tax on earnings is essential. This is the key to regeneration.

'Currently we are forming a group of economists with cross-party representation to research the subject. This will be chaired by Jake Hud, who, as you know, is a member of the Cabinet. An old Labour friend of my father said, and I heard it more than once, that "government will do anything for you except get off your back". Our intention is to unload the tax burden, and do just that – get off your back! It won't be instant, for the complicated system under which we labour will take time and patience to unravel.

'Now, there have been disturbing instances of lawlessness, triggered, it is said, by jobless frustration and exploited by disruptive elements. Frustration is understandable, but lawlessness will not be tolerated. Attacking the rich will solve nothing and only make thing worse. As the saying goes, "you cannot strengthen the weak by weakening the strong". But the strong have a duty to the weak and, when this is absent, strength is soiled by selfishness.

'We need an outbreak of goodwill. We need a reaching out of compassion from those who have to those who're in distress. State-directed welfare is under strain. We cannot leave it all to them and pass by smugly on the other side.

'There are no simple one-off answers to this crisis. Public-sector borrowing is at danger levels and international loans come at a price. We will be funding infrastructure works, but we cannot solve the impasse simply with more handouts. We need to pull together, and we need to help each other. This crisis isn't going to go away tomorrow. But I am hopeful, and I urge you to be hopeful too. Keep going, even when you feel you can't. My vision is not to dumb down to a common level but to dumb up and tap the talent of the people. Here lies the cradle of enterprise and invention. Let innovation start! 'This is a short address. My prepared one is here.' He lifted up the text. 'It was much longer. So you got off lightly! Thank you all for listening and good night.'

The image on the screen faded.

*

Anna and her father sat back in their easy chairs. There were no spontaneous assessments.

'What do you think Father? Did he pull it off?'

'He didn't say much, but then, there isn't anything to say. We've taxed and spent our way into a hole and the world downturn has done the rest. What did you think, dear?'

'Brief, blunt, but shot with shafts of hope. I liked the bit about innovation, and he seemed to be encouraging charitable projects. It's not so much what he said, but how he said it. The man himself came across.'

Collingwood smiled.

'You were very attentive.'

'He's got something, Father.'

'Yes, dear'

'Don't be silly! I'm serious. He sounded genuine and it came across.'

Collingwood's smile persisted, but he made no comment. Instead he pressed the remote.

'We'd better listen to the experts pontificating.'

'That's the last thing you usually watch.'

'We're guests at Number Ten tomorrow night. We'd better know what our host is up against. Here they are. They've wheeled on the heavies. Sim Wells, Hugh Gabbie and Jason West, with Jeremy Winter as presenter.

This was a right-wing anti-labour speech – a real slap in the face to Bill Jones. Someone should tell Blackstone that he's leading a National Government. The man said nothing,' Wells said forcefully.

'What were you watching, Sim?' Gabbie reacted.

'The same sentimental non-speech speech as you. He said nothing! And, Hugh, what's this vague natural fund?'

'Well, he's got you asking the question and I bet that's what he wants. But, Sim, he fingered tax, which is at crippling levels. We can't keep slamming on more. If we do we'll wreck the little business that is left.'

'Tell him to squeeze his friends in the City, but he won't, for that's the sacred cow!'

'Sim, what will happen when you've driven us all away and there's no one left to tax?'

Wells grinned. 'I'd get some peace!'

'The usual dogfight, signifying nothing,' Collingwood grumbled. 'Jason's mostly reasonable.'

'He's yet to come, so keep listening is the order.'

Jeremy Winter was still laughing at Sim's quip, when he turned to Jason West.

'Well, Jason, what were you watching?' he asked reflecting the previous exchange.

'I heard something new: the words "tax shift". It wasn't explained, apart from the mention of a natural fund arising from the community's presence. My ears popped open when Jake Hud was mentioned as chairman of some study group. Now Jake is hardly a right-wing fanatic, so this idea can't be a Conservative hobbyhorse.'

'Good camouflage, Jason,' Wells piped up.

'Maybe. I was also interested how Blackstone used exhortatory words and phrases in a way most politicians would avoid. I mean "helping each other" etc. The hard-nosed bods may double up in laughter, but I wonder. I think he's got a point and, do you know, I kind of believed him. He's that sort of guy.'

'Tosh!' Wells reacted. 'You'll have me bursting into tears! All that stuff is useless. A roll of Twenties in the back pocket is what the average citizen understands!'

'Sim, full marks for cynicism.' Gabbie reacted.

'Realism, I call it. Anyway, the speech was far too short. The people want to hear some substance,' Wells shot back.

'The people want to hear fresh thinking, not the usual flannel!'

'I don't think I want to listen to any more of this. Anyway we've heard the essence. Do you agree?'

Anna nodded.

'Does Sim Wells believe all that?'

'He half does, I suspect. It's a game. He's saying what everyone expects!'

'His cynicism is sheer poison. Has he no conscience?'

'He wouldn't see it like that. It's a play with a familiar script, fired, perhaps, by dreamy projects that he's grown to loathe. And, do you know, Sim Wells would probably be the first to help you if you were in trouble. It's wise to take no one for granted.'

They lapsed into silence for a time.

'Jason West was reasonable,' Anna said quietly.

'He echoed your feeling, Anna, and he got the point about the shift.'

Anna glanced sideways at her father but made no response. Her thoughts had moved on to the following evening.

Chapter Six

No one had anticipated that the outbreak of hostility would be so instant and so vitriolic. Friday morning's *Today* interview had suddenly changed the climate. Collingwood had switched on the radio some way through the programme and by chance tuned into the attack.

'This vile left-wing agenda, led by that militant Hud, will destroy all hope of a recovery.' The chairman of a property conglomerate being interviewed was almost beside himself. *'This is an attack, a direct attack on property, the bedrock of the state's stability. It is what we get when a weak tree-hugging Conservative tries to placate left-wing envy. It's disaster! Why is everybody so complacent? Don't they know that every suburban garden is under threat.'*

'How can you say this?' the presenter protested. *'The committee looking into this has only just been set up.'*

'We don't need to wait to know their game. Blackstone let the cat out of the bag. He said they were shifting tax from income to the community-created fund. This is property, and householders who have spent their lives paying off their mortgage will find their asset taxed and its capital value drop.'

'Are you not being somewhat alarmist?'

'Alarmist! Ask yourself why you're being so complacent?'

'Well, Sir Harold, you have certainly given us food for thought, but I'm afraid we've run out of time,'

Collingwood smiled knowingly. They had started early, he thought. But then, the vested interests never slept. He was lucky to have heard the programme, for normally proofs kept him more than busy in the morning. Anyway, there was one thing sure; Sir Harold Hanwall had got the message loud and clear. But then, those who benefited most from community value usually did.

The phone rang, and his hand stretched out automatically to lift the receiver.

'Collingwood.'

'Henry Blackstone here – Alexander, did you hear that tirade just now on the Today programme?'

'Yes, by chance I did.'

'This could wreck it all before we've even started! How should we tackle this?'

'My advice is, don't! Do nothing. The tirade was over the top. Interviewers are cautious of such people. Let it die on the vine.'

'I doubt some busy journalist will be knocking on the door.'

'Very probably. My suggestion, for what it's worth, would be to tell it simply. That is, that you're setting up a committee to study the matter. And if they press, say any loss in value would be easily balanced by gain. We don't want to say too much at this stage, in case people like Sir Harold set the fireworks off.'

'Thanks, Alexander. I must admit to having doubts, disturbing doubts. Only this morning I woke up wondering if I were kidding myself, for it's a political no,no! Even so, I'm rather protective of the location value principle. Anyway, I'll see you both later. As we arranged, the car will call at six. That, I hope, will cover traffic hold-ups.'

*

Both Collingwoods savoured the luxury of travelling by car. Anna, her father noticed, was wearing an evening gown. It suited her lissom figure, and as usual it was modest. A father hoped for a daughter's happiness. Henry Blackstone was a decent man and he certainly wasn't a womaniser. His daughter was attracted. He knew the signs. But such things were never predictable.

'I feel a bit on edge, father.' Anna confided. 'Dining at Number Ten isn't exactly routine.'

'Yes,' Collingwood joked, 'it's hardly a chippy! Anna, I don't think it's going to be too formal. I spoke to the secretary yesterday, and she hinted that we could be dining in the flat.'

'The Jones' have moved out?'

'A speedy removal is the tradition. It used to be a very sudden affair. You know: 'The King is dead, long live the King.''

The official car seemed to slip through the traffic with uncommon ease. At least, that was how it felt to Anna. They were now in Birdcage Walk and in no time would be there. She had often watched public figures coming and going through the famous door, and in a few moments she would be doing the same. Strange, how it felt so dreamlike.

Anna's excitement was mounting as the car turned into Downing Street, but no one would have guessed from her cool formal expression. They were expected, and, once recognised, both the gates and the familiar door opened as though triggered automatically. The first thing Anna sensed was something very obvious. Ten Downing Street wasn't just a house. It was a nerve centre, in fact, Britain's 'West Wing,' filled with history's rich inventory. And, of course, behind the famous door it was extensive. She hadn't expected the hall to be so spacious, and that old leather porter's chair: there was little doubt it had a history.

The lift whisked them up quickly to the flat, where Blackstone was waiting. There was no leisurely viewing of the past PMs, whose pictures followed the stairs.

'Good to see you both again,' he said warmly. 'Sorry I'm not entertaining you in the more upmarket rooms downstairs. I'll blame my simple bachelor ways.'

Anna smiled but could not think of anything to say. Her nervousness was controlled but it made her awkward.

'Anna,' he added, 'how graceful you look in that lovely dress.'

Anna felt he meant it, but was still too tongue-tied to respond.

'My sister Patricia is cooking. Needless to say, the kitchen is out of bounds to "helpful" brothers.'

'Maybe I could help?' Anna offered. Anything but this silly awkwardness, she thought.

'Let me negotiate!'

Once Anna had retreated to the kitchen, Blackstone and Collingwood were soon busy in conversation.

'Jake and Marjorie Hud are due anytime,' Blackstone began. 'I thought it would be good for Jake to meet you informally. He's busy pondering whom to include on the committee, and your help will be invaluable. Alexander, we need to move as quickly as we can on this.'

'There are people who have spent years, if not a lifetime, studying the preliminary requirements of application, such as land registration.' Collingwood responded. 'Here I feel we've got to watch, for I do believe they grow to love their complications. Simplicity is the key and to marry young able minds to this expertise will be no mean task.'

'Jake's tough and he doesn't court popularity; yet this is balanced by a damned good sense of humour. I think I've picked the right man, but, Alexander, your steady guiding hand will be invaluable. Ah, I can hear the lift. The Huds have arrived.'

Collingwood's first impression of the new arrivals was of a well-matched couple. Jake was sharp-featured and sharp in many other ways, while Marjorie was homely and had the gift, he guessed, of calming troubled waters.

'I'm thinking of putting Sir Harold on the committee. That would liven things up!' Hud joked after the preliminary introductions.

'You'd never get it past health and safety!' Collingwood reacted.

'We're keeping Marjorie standing. Let's sit,' Blackstone interjected.

'Thanks, you must have read my mind, Sir.'

'One of my occasional pastimes,' he responded flippantly. He turned to Jake.

'You were saying that experts were claiming that a national land valuation could be triggered within six months. Further trials would take two years. I'm sorry Jake, but that's hopeless. We could all be out of a job by then and the next government could repeal and wipe our efforts off the statute book!'

'Well, that's what they say, Sir!'

'Even so, I find it difficult to accept that what is true and natural cannot be applied more quickly – Alexander?'

'I know a young man called Tommy Thompson who is a wizard with computers. He maintains that with the right software we could take action much, much quicker.'

'Let's employ him. Jake, we simply cannot wait. I've already mentioned a tax shift. If I say it's two years down the line, I'll lose the plot! I warned you, Jake, this job has no in-built need to swallow hemlock, but it's close!'

'Then, tonight's my last taste of luxury. Tomorrow it's the front.'

'Something like that.' Blackstone smiled knowingly. 'You'd best drink up! – Ah, right on cue, here are the cooks. May I introduce Anna Collingwood and my sister Patricia.'

After the introductions were over, Marjorie Hud took Anna aside.

'You look lovely, my dear. That dress and your blonde hair swept up like that. It's so graceful.'

'You're very kind Mrs Hud.'

'Marjorie to you, my dear.'

'What are you two conspiring about?' Blackstone interrupted.

'I was complimenting Anna on how well she looks,' Marjorie responded.

'And so she does – would that Anna were the glass of fashion that the nation heeded! – Patricia's waving. Time to take our seats!'

Patricia Blackstone was intrigued. Where had he managed to find her? She knew of course, for Anna had told her all. This girl had everything: looks, good taste and intelligence, and from her casual asides, she was well-read. Of course, she was a publisher's daughter.

Patricia watched her brother at the opposite end of the table. Anna was to his right and Jake Hud to his left, while at her end she had Alexander Collingwood and Marjorie Hud. Collingwood had a bearing rather similar to her brother. Both were impressive men, and Henry had that kind of hair that politicians dream about: crinkly and immovable, even in a gale.

Praise for her cooking was forthcoming, even from her brother. She smiled to herself. Henry, whom she'd grown up with, was now Prime Minister. She found it difficult to accept. Yet, at the office in the City it was all too real, as people were forever whispering who she was – the Prime Minister's sister. The anonymity of Patricia Blackstone had gone.

'Alexander,' Blackstone beckoned. 'Jake's off to the front in the morning. What weaponry do you recommend?'

'A thick skin is good basic body armour, but better still a smile and ready humour. That wins hearts and minds! A brigade of laptops making inroads with the Press can frustrate the enemy's recruitment efforts. But, as I've said before, the best weapon, in both attack and in defence, is the conviction that the hordes of braying complications cannot overcome the principle. The principle is the standard, like the Roman Eagle, that holds the legion loyal and intact.'

'There you are, Jake; with a briefing like that you can only win!'

'I'm a cautious man, Sir. I'll take a drop of hemlock with me just in case!'

Easy laughter spilled out around the table.

'How can we meet the soaring needs of welfare, yet keep taxation from erupting?' Blackstone interjected.

'What a question!' Jake Hud reacted.

'It's one that I could be asked tomorrow morning!'

'Taxation is funding essential relief. We can't reduce it!' Jake followed up forcefully. 'But we can shift taxation from production!' 'Exactly, Jake! That's why I need movement on location-value levy. We can't wait. Get those academics moving. Let *them* take the hemlock!'

*

'You're very quiet Anna,' her father said as they glided back to Richmond by official car.

'I had a wonderful evening. Henry and his sister were very kind, and that nice woman Marjorie was such a sweetie. And, Father the conversation was electric. And poor Jake Hud can have no doubt about his priorities.'

'But it was done very neatly and in a way that Jake would understand. Remember, he was the one that was calling for more taxes.'

'Yes, he gave Bill Jones a hard time. Shrewd of Henry to have picked him, but he was taking a risk.'

'Picking the right men is a leader's skill, and I think Henry Blackstone's got it.'

'He's very impressive,' she said sleepily, 'yet he makes no fuss, no fuss at all.'

Yes, my dear, and you couldn't keep your eyes off him, he trought, but he said nothing. Contented, he sat back in his seat.

Chapter Seven

Collingwood was in the middle of editing a manuscript when the phone rang at what seemed the most inconvenient point. For a moment he was tempted to ignore it, but his better part prevailed.

'Collingwood,' he said briefly.

'Alexander, it's Jake. I need to see you. Can I come down to Richmond in the afternoon, say at three? We could have tea in that nice place in the park.'

'Pembroke Lodge.'

'That's it. I'll pick you up at your place. These official cars are a godsend. See you soon.'

Alexander left the phone down and went back to the manuscript. He had put a self-imposed deadline on this book, when there was no need for it. Something wouldn't let him settle and such a mood was not the friend of editing. Then it suddenly struck him: Tommy Thompson, the computer genius, lived in Teddington. He had given Jake his number, but better still that they could meet. At once he lifted the phone and punched in the number.

'Hard and Soft Computing.' It was Tommy's name for his one-man company.

'Alexander Collingwood here – are you free this afternoon?'

'Could be, Mr Collingwood. What's on?'

'I would like you to meet someone. Have you ever heard of Jake Hud?'

'Yeah, some bloke phoned me up this morning. I wasn't in, so he left a message. Said he was heading a committee set up by the Prime Minister. I thought it was some joker having me on, and I forgot it. So this guy's for real!'

'Very much so, Tommy. Do you think you can make it?'

'I'll be there, Mr Collingwood. What time?'

'A quarter to three, Tommy.'

'Right, see you then.'

*

Tommy Thompson bubbled with energy and his chaotic mass of curly hair reflected this. His clothes looked, and probably were, from the local charity shop, but Tommy was oblivious of such concerns. Indeed, his devoted mother often had to tell him when to eat and, not infrequently, when to go to bed. But in the field of software Tommy was a genius.

Tommy met Mr Collingwood, as he always called him, at a class that Collingwood tutored. One evening Collingwood asked three questions: what was location value, who created it, and to whom did it belong? The impact on Tommy was dramatic, for, with the minimum of explanation, he saw the principle right away. After following up the subject, the difficulties of application had intrigued him and he had set himself the task of designing software that might help to solve the problem. The city tower-block complexities, that baffled most, fired him with energy, as if they were an instant stimulant.

'The principle is completely simple,' he had burst out. 'Even my cat could work it out. But we've made things so complicated. If we took a hundred percent, it would be easy-peasy. But no: it has to be twenty per cent or less, to keep the guys, who've had their fingers in the till, from feeling miffed!'

Collingwood could only smile at Tommy's unvarnished honesty.

✳

The May sunshine in a cloudless sky was idyllic and a welcome change from the lingering winter chill. As it was Saturday, Pembroke Lodge was crowded, and they couldn't find a table in the open air. Inside, though, was virtually empty, so they sat close to an open window with the place practically to themselves.

'So you think you can do this, Tommy?' Jake Hud asked, continuing the conversation started in the car.

'Those civil service bods are bright. I've worked with some of them. Just tell them what you want and they'll do it. You ask, how can we separate site and buildings? Easy. Ask the insurance people. Ask the estate agents. Experts abound.'

'It all takes time, Tommy.'

'Just tell the civil service that you want it in a hurry. This idea's been rejected out of hand for years. Every time it's shot to bits before it leaves the ground. We've grown to be like hounded men perpetually under fire. We're too defensive. We're like an army waiting for the day that every boot is polished.'

'My God, Tommy, where do you get your energy?'

'The principle, Mr Hud. It's just; it's true and it's so bloody simple *and* we've got the chance to put it on the statute book. We can't afford to scrape about like hens and miss the bus!'

'Tommy, I couldn't put it better,' Hud responded. 'But I must say that only this morning I had a dozen calls from our newly formed committee members suggesting exemptions.'

'Their hearts are not with the principle!' Tommy reacted dismissively. 'Anyway, a dose of common sense can cure most ills.'

'All right, what about Council property?' Jake pressed.

Tommy looked at Collingwood.

'Your shot, Tommy.'

'Well, Mr C., I remember you saying that Council housing would be largely unnecessary in a just society. If access to a site were readily available on payment of the due location-value levy, and, if people's earnings were the full product of their labour, then you maintained that they would have the natural dignity of a self-sufficient life. Subsidised housing would only be necessary for those unable to help themselves, and as a general "grace and favour" option.'

'I get the idea,' Jake Hud responded, 'but it would sound a bit airy-fairy to the average bloke. Hell, even I find it hard to swallow. Tommy, I'd be laughed out of court! What about the real world, as they say?'

'What people call the real world is the unreal world! The real world is where the state is run in harmony with the natural principles. Someone, not too far away from where I'm sitting, told me that.'

Hud laughed good-humouredly.

'Tommy, you don't give up. I like it. But stop dodging the issue. What about the present situation?'

'The Council would have to pay the levy, either to itself or to the central kitty. This is a designated site subject to planning laws. So the figure would have to be imputed in a rather artificial way. That's the present reality! I feel that all should pay the levy except for sites occupied by, say, churches, government buildings, parks, defence establishments, hospitals – and schools perhaps.'

'Where did you learn all this?'

'Mr Collingwood – he's to blame! Did I make many bloomers?' he added, turning to his mentor.

'You did fine, Tommy. I'm beginning to feel that I'm the pupil now!'

The conversation continued, and after some time Collingwood went to get more tea. This was a successful meeting: more successful than he'd dreamed. Tommy's place on the committee was assured, and with his surety of principle and his grasp of detail, Tommy's fiery energy, would swallow quibblers whole.

They were talking about software when Collingwood returned. Hud was listening and clearly fascinated.

'Tommy, you've given me considerable hope and inspiration, for I know that we can win with men like you on board. And, Tommy, could you manage a meeting on Monday at six p.m? The venue will be the India Room in the Houses of Parliament. Use the St Stephen's entrance.'

'Would they let me in?'

'Come to think of it, Tommy, it might be better if you wore a suit.'

Collingwood laughed heartily. It was clearly time that Tommy pulled himself together

*

When Anna heard her father return, she skipped through to the hallway to greet him.

'How did it go, Father? Did they hit it off?'

'They got on like a house on fire. Tommy was sparking on all cylinders, and Jake Hud loved it. I think he saw himself – you know, his fire-brand youth. The important thing is, Tommy's on the committee. Anna,' he said changing the subject, 'you look animated. Have we landed a big order from the States or some such miracle?'

'No, Father, but Henry Blackstone phoned. He and his sister are going to church tomorrow, and he's invited us to join them. He's making a statement, he says. "The God-is-dead brigade can't win all the shots" were his parting words.'

'And you accepted?'

'Yes. You could do with a day away from proofs,' she chirped. 'He's collecting us. He said he would try and keep the security stuff as low key as possible.'

'Where are we going?'

'Farnham, in Surrey. It's his old family church. We'll also be meeting Willy Windbourne and Henry's sister.'

'All we need is Bill Jones taking the collection,' Collingwood joked.

'He mentioned that. He wants to keep the National government as inclusive as possible.'

'So he's making two statements. One about the Church and one about party cooperation.'

'Father,' she reacted in a tone of mock reproof. 'He's just going to church!'

'Anna, for the PM it's never quite like that. Everything he does is a statement. It's the way it is, and, my dear, the press will almost certainly be there. You can't hobnob with the PM and the Foreign Secretary and remain in the shadows.'

'I hadn't thought of that, but, of course, you're right. There's something else, Father. I do believe that Patricia Blackstone has an eye for Willie Windbourne. She rather hinted at it when we were in the kitchen together last Friday.'

Collingwood chuckled.

'Now, that's what I call taking cross-party relationships seriously!'

Chapter Eight

Blackstone felt like a batsman who'd saved his wicket for the day but scored no runs.

'You're in the same boat that I was in,' Bill Jones sympathised.

'Yes, I need a miracle, like finding oil in Yorkshire!'

Jones laughed. They were in the Cabinet room, where they'd lingered after a specialist meeting on security and where, as usual, more funding was essential. Bill Jones had had the tax shift proposal explained to him, but, then, during his career he'd had innumerable "great ideas" explained to him.

'How's this tax shift idea progressing?' Jones questioned.

'Much too slowly. The experts talk about six months to do this and a year to do that, which, of course, is hopeless in the current situation. But apart from the tax shift can you think of anything we can do that is immediate?'

'There are a lot of unscrupulous people who milk the system, but tracking them down takes time. Also it looks one-sided when the super-rich swan off to some tax haven. But then the non-dom problem isn't simple, either. In the end nothing much is achieved. I've been there, done it, as it were.'

They sat in silence for a while. To Blackstone the empty chairs spaced round the Cabinet table seemed strangely animate, indeed, like witnesses.

'Are you a churchgoer, Bill?'

'We attend the Methodist church in Hinde Street, when we can.'

'I know it well; it's close to where I have my flat. Would you mind if I joined you one day?'

'Not at all!' Jones was clearly surprised, but held his peace.

'I'm attending church tomorrow in Farnham, my old family church. We're meeting Willy Windbourne. My sister knows him. And the Collingwoods are also joining us. We've lost much in the whirl of modern life and I feel we need to reconnect somehow. Get back to our roots. Tap the old principles and let new shoots grow that suit the age.'

'That's quite poetic, Henry.'

'I try!'

They both laughed.

'How about Hinde Street next Sunday?' Blackstone suggested quietly.

'That's a date.'

*

Collingwood scanned the Sunday papers as he waited for the Prime Minister to call. The news was anything but uplifting. Riots in the North ruthlessly exploited by extremists. Only sheer good fortune and the tireless efforts of the police had prevented fatalities. He had already seen the frightening scenes on News 24. With predictable racial overtones, immigrants were being blamed for joblessness and neither side were angels. Anger had sought a focus for its rage, and colour, or the lack of it, was easy to identify. Blackstone had already made a statement urging calm, and extra police had been drafted to the area. Police presence, of course, needed to be handled with care, as sensitivities were raw.

There would be those who would see the PM's church visit as melodramatic or a cheap way to grab publicity in an atmosphere of growing tension. The majority, Collingwood hoped, would assume a simpler conclusion. But whatever the commentary, the situation was serious and it landed squarely on Henry Blackstone's desk. There was no good news, and soon a chorus of frustration would be chanting outside Number Ten. Henry's honeymoon period, if he had one at all, would be brief.

Anna's call, 'They're here,' halted Collingwood's musings, and after the briefest of greetings they were on their way.

'My sister's meeting us there,' Blackstone explained. 'Willie picked her up. It seems they both take cross-party cooperation seriously!'

Collingwood smiled, but neither he nor Anna spoke.

'Things are not good up North,' Blackstone continued. 'And we were lucky, for it could have been much worse. In fact, there's little to rejoice about at present, so some humility before the altar rail is timely! By the way, Jake Hud was greatly impressed by your young friend Thompson, but yesterday's high has been quickly followed by a low. Now it's mortgages. Jake can't see a passage through the complication. We had a brief conversation this morning. That's why I'm up-to-date. Jake's heart is in the right place all right, but there's something missing.'

'Tommy Thompson has great respect for the civil service experts,' Collingwood responded. 'He's worked with some of them, and if Tommy is impressed, they're good, for he's a genius. Jake will be climbing up the walls, and chatting to the fairies, if he tries to penetrate the maze himself. Tommy's right. Give it to the civil service.'

'*Faith*, that's what's missing.' Anna interjected, her sound confident and sure. 'Sorry, I'm interfering,' she added, feeling she had spoken out of turn.

'Don't be sorry! Your intervention is exactly right, and apt, considering where we're going!' Blackstone smiled. He sensed her sympathy and was grateful. Indeed, this morning the crushing weight of his responsibility felt very real. The intelligence reports were frightening. For, with the nation weakened and preoccupied by economic failure, the bad guys clearly thought it was the perfect time to act. The simple logic of these deluded beings was obvious, and they had the prime advantage of surprise. On the other hand, the security services, blamed in turn for over-action and inaction, rarely had a clear line they could follow. For them, certainty was a luxury. It was all too familiar, almost a mirror image when it came to his own situation. There was no straight line to follow. Instead, a forced reaction to the crowding problems left him little time for innovation. He hadn't voiced his doubts, not even to Alexander, but he was far from sure about the implementation of the tax shift. Jake Hud was right to be concerned about the mortgage question and the tsunami it could cause in the city. Was this the time for such a change? It was a real question.

He looked up to meet the gaze of Anna, who'd been watching him.

'Sorry, I was ruminating. Thoughts of a Prime Minister. Would you publish?'

'Too gloomy, Henry,' she responded quietly.

'You could be right. I need more faith, it appears!' He smiled. It was the first time she had called him by his first name, and it seemed so natural, like a soothing balm. Don't be so bloody sentimental, Blackstone, he chastised himself. Yet the truth was that Anna and he were drawing close. She had everything, he thought, looks, grace, taste and the wisdom of someone twice her age. It was hard to believe that he'd only met her a week ago, but then linear time was a deceiver.

'There's the Cathedral perched on its hill.' Collingwood said, as if thinking aloud. 'Soon we'll be turning off for the Hog's Back, with Farnham nestling at the bottom at the other side.'

'Familiar territory for you, Alexander?' Blackstone said in the manner of a question.

'My in-laws had a cottage down this way.'

Blackstone made no response. He so far hadn't mentioned Anna's mother, feeling that it was Alexander's prerogative.

A stab of loneliness kept Collingwood silent. The loss of his wife had been a cruel blow.

✳

Willie Windbourne had a bespectacled scholarly look, which brought maturity to his youngish features. By his side Patricia Blackstone looked vivacious and thoroughly suited to the well-groomed Surrey scene. In fact, the church had generous grounds, but with the security presence, the hovering press and a steady stream of churchgoers, the space was needed.

'They've arrived,' a loud confidential whisper announced, and there they were, their pace impeded by reporters and busy cameramen darting to and fro like swallows.

After kissing his sister and shaking hands with the Foreign Secretary, Blackstone introduced the Collingwoods. But there was little chance of normal conversation as the press, though trying to be respectful in the precincts of the church, found it difficult to restrain their natural hunger for a story.

'After the service, guys, all right?'

'That's a long time, Prime Minister!' one piped up.

'Come to the service!' Blackstone challenged.

'All right, you've got a deal!'

'What's your name?'

'Ed Gray, Sir.'

The Prime Minister's party were given the front pew. The TV cameras were in place and the church was packed. The Prime Minister sat next to the aisle, then his sister and the Foreign Secretary. Collingwood's placing was next and then his daughter. This had been arranged to counter press speculation and shield Anna from embarrassment. Collingwood doubted if it would.

45

Anna was striking, and her dress sense made this obvious. She would attract attention.

When it was time for the address, the Vicar was fulsome in his praise for the famous son of the parish. He had known him as a boy: a good boy, but not too good, of course. Appreciative chuckles followed. Then, to Anna's surprise, he quoted the enigmatic first verse of Hebrews 11.

Now faith is the substance of things hoped for, the evidence of things not seen.

It was a coincidence that could help if Henry were faltering. She knew her father was concerned that he might shelve the tax-shift plan. Indeed, his advisors were bombarding him with difficulties.

They were nearing the end of the address, when Anna was handed a note from one of the secret service men. It was for Henry and she passed it on. When it reached Blackstone, he rose at once, bowed to the altar, and left the church.

Once outside, he focused on the secret service man. 'What's happened?' he barked.

'Rioting has broken out again. Two churches have been damaged and a petrol bomb was thrown at a mosque. They're worried about tonight, Sir. They want to have the Army standing by...'

'Don't send in the Army,' Blackstone interrupted forcefully. 'That's exactly what these thugs are hoping for. Headlines to stir up hatred! Is there anything else?'

'We foiled a terrorist attempt on a complex in the North West, but just in time. Sir, things are bad! I think you need to speak. Somehow, we must arrest this downward spiral. Sorry for speaking out and dragging you from the church, but the situation is incendiary!'

'Just make sure they don't send in the Army,' Blackstone reiterated. 'One accidental death and *they* would be the enemy.' He sighed. 'I'd hoped for a more leisurely afternoon. But there it is!'

Out of the corner of his eye he saw the journalist Ed Gray hurrying towards him.

'I saw you leaving the front pew, Sir.'

'So you went to church. You kept your word!'

'Yes, Prime Minister.'

Blackstone smiled.

'Then I must keep mine. Call at Downing Street on Tuesday morning about nine, if your diary allows.'

'I'll be there, Sir.' To Gray the offer was a gift from heaven.

After phoning the Home Secretary, Winston Hughes, and after reiterating his views about the Army, Blackstone felt he could withdraw a little from the coalface. Winston was a good man, a safe pair of hands, and he was on his way up North. Even so, the Prime Minister had to act, and what was more, be seen to act. So it was post haste, to Downing Street. Meantime, though, he had to extract himself from the current situation. That was not so easy, for the ladies of the parish had laid on quite a lavish reception. He simply could not walk away. The Prime Minister's job wasn't easy. Everything he did, it seemed, was under the microscope.

He was chatting to the Vicar when the secret service man approached. He was clearly agitated.

'There's been another bomb.'

'How bad?'

'Some injuries, but no fatalities reported. We may have been lucky.'

'Right, it's Downing Street immediately.'

Willy Windbourne's car was full. Collingwood suggested going back by train, but Blackstone wouldn't hear of it. Anna could make them afternoon tea, he joked, for he needed to be back in Downing Street without diversion or delay.

This time the motorcycle outriders were very much in evidence. It was a wonder how they cleared a passage through the traffic. Here were the trappings of power, Anna mused, and how easily it could intoxicate. Somehow, she couldn't imagine Henry being affected. He was too ordinary. No, that was just the surface. He was far too much a man of substance to be caught by such trivialities.

Chapter Nine

Anna was making tea, just as Blackstone had jokingly suggested at the church, while Henry, the ex-Premier Bill Jones and her father were locked in conversation. Apart from phone interruptions they had been talking solidly for three quarters of an hour.

'Gentlemen, tea is served!' she announced grandly.

They were full of appreciative words, but the conversation was barely interrupted. This time, though, Anna was hearing more than snatches.

'You've convinced me, Alexander,' Bill Jones was saying. 'What you say makes perfect sense. Location value is the natural fund arising from the collective presence of the community. It's the common wealth of the state naturally generated, and all we have to do is collect it. Yet the state allows this fund to be claimed privately, a custom that the law has condoned throughout history. The powerful use land holding to consolidate their power, and the more advantageous the location the greater the prestige. It's a worldwide practice. How can you reverse this? But I feel we're indulging ourselves. How can we halt this madness raging in the northern towns?'

'Bill,' Blackstone interjected. 'You've just given us a powerful summary, and the questions that you pose could keep us up all night. Your second question, though, cannot wait, for as you know, I'm booked to speak on this at 6.30. The people will expect something. But, being Prime Minister isn't the automatic passport to enlightenment. However, the Home Secretary's up North, so, at least, I'll be briefed before the time. Clearly, we've got to cool it, as the saying goes, but not abjectly. There needs to be a touch of plain speaking. Anyway, we've already mulled this over. But, dear God, haven't we been lucky! One bomb attempt foiled, and a second, only causing minor injuries! These escapes make me wonder. Can they be simply chance?' Blackstone was contemplative for a moment, poised to take his line of thinking further, but he let the matter rest.

'Now, Bill, your first question: this I'll have to pass to Alexander, for, like you, I need guidance. If we start nibbling at real estate, what effect would it have in the City? Would the property pile get jittery and send shares tumbling, and what effect would that have on the pension funds?'

This was the coalface with a vengeance, Anna thought. How was Father going to answer?

'We cannot win against such difficulties by paying court to them. They are the children of our complicated system. I've said this before, I know, but it's important. Nature has given us her principle, and that's the keystone that we build around. The initial levy would be a small percentage. There would be no need for panic, and the City is adept at finding new and better games to play.'

'What about the international connections?' Bill Jones pressed.

'This is a worldwide crisis. What a blessing if the world would start to copy our experiments!'

'Well, Alexander, I'll say this for you, you're holding to your keystone!'

'Bill, we're humans. We all have doubts. But one thing is certain; the principle is true. Of that there is no doubt! Most see it in an intellectual sort of way. Here understanding can be shallow. But for those who sense the true significance, the principle is transforming. There are those, of course, who do not want to know, but for those who do, well, as I've said, the principle is transforming.'

Blackstone stood up.

'It's time for me to go downstairs and face the music. Alexander, Anna, I'm sorry for detaining you so long. But, then, I'm not sorry, for it's good to have you around. You're free to escape any time, of course, but if you would like, we'll set out two chairs so that you can witness this 6.30 trial by fire.'

'We'll risk the hazard, Sir!' Collingwood responded.

'Good, and, Anna, thanks for tea!'

Anna felt a wave of unreality swirl about her. It was all so ordinary, yet this was Number Ten, the cockpit of government, and she was present. It felt as though she'd gate-crashed some exclusive gathering where she was totally and embarrassingly out of place.

After sitting quietly for some time, her mind still tinged

with unreality, her father's familiar voice returned her to the present.

'We're going down now, dear.'

*

The Prime Minister was behind his desk, and all were waiting with an air of tense anticipation for the minute hand to reach half past. But if Henry Blackstone was on edge, he didn't show it. Then that's what Anna expected. Anna sat, as if mesmerised, watching the pre-broadcast activity. Henry was so calm and to all appearances, at rest, and she knew her heart had made its decision.

'Good evening.' The sound was measured. 'We have escaped two terrorist attempts, their vile intent outside the circle of humanity. Such good fortune shouldn't be taken for granted, and I'm certain that religious leaders will acknowledge this. Now that's not all, for I'm angry! I'm angry that this tolerant country is subject to a murderous intolerance! And one that claims divine sanction for its horrific acts. What an incredible arrogance! May I make it plain: our tolerance of intolerance is dead.

'What are the riots in the North about? Jobs, you shout. They're taking our jobs! Well, do you know,' – Blackstone's tone turned confidential – 'I wish that there were jobs to take! No doubt there are agitators, busy people spreading fiction, stirring things and adding fuel to the fire. I suggest you treat such people with a generous dollop of British indifference.

'Being jobless isn't funny. It brings a soul-destroying greyness. To help to combat this, government has various public works in mind, and these are being rushed forward. There is also a committee studying ways of funding a reduction in taxation by tapping the location value, which is naturally created by the community. This, of course, will apply to the uplift in location value created by the public projects I've just mentioned. It goes without saying that much needs to be done, indeed, very much needs to be done – and quickly!

'Protests are understandable, but violence isn't. All it does, at best, is put more pressure on the harassed A&E. At worst it fathers tragedy. So why not take the path of hope. Our history's full of those who shunned despair and triumphed. We are an inventive nation. Why not turn your hand to something new? Something that you've often thought about but never followed. We need an outbreak of enterprise. Stop waiting for a job. Create one! This is the time. Empty industrial buildings abound and government will be standing by to offer help and ease the burden of bureaucracy. *Oh yeah*, you say, and I say, *try it*!

'What can we do to halt the standoff in the North? Apart from more police, the truth is, very little. But *you* can stop it. You can simply walk away. People may go mad in gangs. But as someone once said, they can walk away singly.

'Good night, and let it be a peaceful one.

'Thanks for listening.'

Anna didn't know what to think. The talk was very short, short enough for media repeats. There was one thing, though, a feeling of intimacy, as if he were speaking to the people and not merely making a speech. And he had spoken as a leader, not one trying to prove his credibility. The trouble was he had given the press plenty of openings. Tomorrow morning would be interesting.

Anna's eyes were following Blackstone's every move. He had a word, it seemed, for everybody, but that was the politician's art, though in Henry's case it was more the man himself. Eventually he moved across.

'What did my severest critic think?' he questioned, his affection barely disguised.

'"Stop waiting for a job. Create one," seemed to be an arrow with a target. You were talking to them, I felt, and not just pleasing the rest of us.'

'Well, after clearing that fence, I can face tomorrow's press with equanimity!'

Chapter Ten

The Mercedes-Benz purred along the Embankment with unhurried ease, its driver clothed with Jeeves-like dignity. In the back seat Sir Frederick Kingsway was reading the *Financial Times*. He was very much the popular image of the city tycoon, with his striped suit adding that authentic touch. Freddie, as he was known to his friends, looked as ease, the very image of the chairman of the board: which he was, of course, Chairman of Kingsway Holdings PLC.

Freddie had sold his risky properties three months before the downturn. His timing had been perfect and against the wisdom of the economic gurus who'd advised him. All was rosy in his kingdom, except the spectre of this boy-scout Blackstone, who was fingering the honey-pot. Location value he called it, but Freddie saw the danger to his hard-earned fortune all too clearly.

Harold Hanwall had made an ass of himself by raving on the radio. To the average listener he'd been written off as a disappointed fat cat wailing for his cream. He should have kept his trap shut. This mode of vulgar publicity wasn't Freddie's style. He had a much more subtle plan. Two economic whizz kids who had the Treasury's ear were on his pay role as consultants. His fee would make them quite loquacious.

He was nearing his office, and with due deliberation he folded his paper.

'Freddie, old son, you have it all in hand,' he muttered quietly.

*

Anna was curious to know how the press had reacted to Henry Blackstone's brief address, so she went out early to the newsagent. Some of the papers had only been delivered and were lying on the floor still strapped in bundles, but it didn't matter for she could read the headlines.

'Stop waiting for a job. Create one' was the first tabloid heading she focused on. The heavy print continued. *With what?*

Get real, Prime Minister! Well at least they highlighted Henry's message, Anna mused. Then the next tabloid. *Premier calls for 'outbreak of enterprise.'* *Big deal, PM, why not start with Number 10?* One of the more substantial tabloids was the next one in the row. It had large black headlines covering half the page. *'Our tolerance of intolerance is dead,'* was their message. Then in smaller print – *At last someone speaks up!*

The heavies were already on the racks. They were nearly all politely negative; too busy trying to be clever and saying something positive was tantamount to being naïve!

Feeling deflated, Anna bought her usual papers and headed for home. Once through the door, she found her father unusually excited.

'Henry's on in ten minutes. He's being interviewed by that over-bearing ego, Jasper Jenkins. It's a mistake. Jasper J will only want to add the youthful new PM to his list of trophies: something to joke about with his clever friends.'

'Well, Father, Jasper may get more than he bargained for,' Anna responded as she headed for the kitchen to make a cup of tea. Just enough time before it starts, she thought.

Apart from a few pleasantries, Jenkins launched straight in.

'This National Government you're heading has only been in place for a week, yet already there are rumblings. And last evening's brevity didn't help. "Don't wait for a job. Create one," had a ringing tone except for those who've got to do it. Even in the short time since you spoke, my website and my e-mail have been inundated.'

'Like is drawn to like,' Collingwood muttered.

'Shush, Father.'

'Your claim that we were a tolerant country excited streams of derision. In fact, some were close to calling you a racist.'

Collingwood shifted impatiently on his seat.

'When's Henry going to speak up? This is poisonous!'

'Carry on, Jasper, you might as well get it all off your chest!' Blackstone's voice sounded laconic.

'Now that you mention it, they took extreme exception to the religious stuff. You know, the idea of all these clerics talking to their various gods. Anyway, I can only report what the people said. It is the voice of the people, Prime Minister.'

'Do you really believe all that, Jasper?'

'Well, I didn't invent it!'

'That's not what I'm asking. Do you believe that the stream of negativity you've reported is the true voice of the people?'

'There'll be other views, of course. I've merely reported what I received.'

'You still haven't answered my question!'

'Hey, that's my line. I'm supposed to ask the questions!'

'Carry on.'

'We've heard little from Downing Street, except some promise of a tax shift. This, my economic colleagues tell me, is an old idea past its sell-by date and unworkable in our sophisticated economy. So, Prime Minister, when are you going to do something? That is the general sentiment I've been picking up.'

'Can you be more specific?'

'These public works you mention. We both well know they're only a drop in the ocean.'

'They're a beginning, Jasper, and such public enterprises call on local trades. In other words, it spreads out. Again, this can be a time to gear up and prepare for the future.'

'Tell that to the company with a killing overdraft! Prime Minister the situation is desperate and there's talk of a pension fund collapse. That would be catastrophic. We need action now. When I was coming here, I bumped into an old and respected MP and we stopped briefly for a chat. 'When's that young man going to act?' That's exactly what he said. Prime Minister, that's what it's like out there.'

'Henry,' Collingwood muttered, 'stop him. He's repeating his message. He's getting it across that you're inactive. That's what people will remember! So, stop him!'

'Don't worry, Father, Jasper's going to run upon his sword. He's overdone it, hammering on like that.'

'Here, we're missing this,' Collingwood cautioned.

'Prime Minister, you've just said that the Chancellor is in conference with the Bank of England and the banks, about the pension fund crisis. But how can we have any confidence in that, knowing the catalogue of recent failures?'

'Jasper, I'm going to add another failure, the failure of this interview. I'm afraid I've found the wall-to-wall negativity wearing and wholly contrary to the message of the National Government. Indeed, as the Queen's first minister I find your approach less than appropriate.'

'*The Queen's first minister!*' Jenkins exploded. '*Who believes such medieval rubbish. You're the people's minister!*'

'*Well Jasper, at least we know where you stand and to those who are still listening, my apologies for this premature departure. Good morning.*'

An announcer was quick to indicate the next programme. Meanwhile there was light music to fill the unexpected vacuum.

'You were right, Anna, Jenkins ran upon his sword. What got in to him?

'Henry represents everything he hates. He wanted desperately to pull him down and he lost it, lost it completely. And losing his temper, well, you just don't do that in his trade.'

'I suppose that our closely held ideas will always bubble to the surface. It's a lesson for us all.'

'Is there anybody out there who's for us?' Anna said almost plaintively. 'Judging by this morning's papers and the media people I have heard, compliments are few and far between.'

'There was a complimentary article in one of the papers. I spotted it while you were making the tea – a chap called Ed Gray.'

'Yes, I remember. Henry spoke to him at Farnham, and I'm pretty certain they're meeting up on Tuesday morning.'

'Anna dear, you're pretty fond of Henry?'

'Yes, Father.'

'Well, dear, I'm very glad you've found a man of substance.'

'Nothing's happened yet. He's said nothing.'

'My dear, it's a fact waiting for its time.'

*

The media closed ranks. Jasper had been over-working was the generally accepted line, and Henry Blackstone let the matter rest. But Jasper knew his wings had been clipped. He didn't like it, for a member of the 'silver spoon' brigade had done it. He hated anything to do with 'old money,' but he had to admit a grudging respect for Blackstone. One thing was certain; he wasn't a wimp.

Jasper Jenkins was at his desk and feeling anything but cheerful now that the full import of the morning's fiasco was sinking in. At least it wasn't TV, where his humiliation could be repeated *ad nauseam*.

The phone rang, and his thin sharp-featured face twitched as he lifted the handset.

'Jenkins.'

'What the hell were you thinking about?' It was Jake Hud being diplomatic! 'Why did you attack Henry Blackstone? My God, Jasper, wise up! Listen, I need to speak to you. Let's have lunch: usual place, usual time.'

'When?'

'Today. Henry's pushing me. I'll explain when we meet up. You should bloody well apologise! I bloody mean it, Jasper! Otherwise you'll end up being a bloody footnote.'

'You *are* worked up, Jake!'

'You're bloody right I am. I don't like to see one of my mates making such a damned fool of himself! Yes, and making a fool of yourself on the same day that that clown Sir Harold Hanwall was sounding off again up north. "That militant Hud, and his vile left-wing agenda." Why doesn't he change the bloody record!'

Jake was suddenly gone, but that was Jake. He didn't hang around.

Jenkins sat back in his chair. He couldn't remember the last time he'd apologised for anything or to anybody. It was not his style, and trying to be 'nice' he left to politicians.

✳

'Father, listen to this,' Anna called out excitedly, as she rushed into his study holding her portable radio. 'It's Jasper J. He's apologising!'

'...now apologising isn't an everyday experience for me!' A brief chuckle quickly faded. 'But in this instance, I feel compelled to say that I overshot. I'm making no excuses. I bungled the job. The no-holds-barred stuff can be overdone. That's it, guys.'

The announcer rounded off the news flash, and then it was on to the next item. Anna pressed the off button.

'What do you think, Father?'

Collingwood took off his reading glasses slowly.

'Apologising isn't his thing. In fact, he seems to thrive on controversy and with the PM involved that's pretty good publicity. But you never know. Maybe he did think that he'd overdone it. Age, Anna, maybe he's losing his fire?'

'I doubt if his website following will be pleased. They'll not like him bowing to the great and good.'

'He's a media icon. They'll get over it.'

'A strange world,' she responded quietly.

'Some people call it the real world.'

'Yes, Father, but you trained me to expect more promising possibilities!'

Collingwood laughed.

Chapter Eleven

As expected, Jasper found Jake Hud in their usual hotel, sitting at their usual corner table. The place was never crowded, and they enjoyed all the privacy they wanted.

'The Earth has changed its orbit, for, Jasper, you've apologised!'

'Once I've gutted two more politicians I'll be myself again!'

Jake laughed. They'd got to know each other some years back after they'd had a stand-up shouting match. In those days neither of them took prisoners and the sparks had flown with colourful intensity.

Both were sharp-featured men and both had kept a generous crop of hair. But now, instead of sparks, laughter was their bond.

'So, Jake, why this sudden call to lunch?'

'It's the PM. He wants some movement; the very bloody thing that you were going on about!'

'And where do I come in?'

'Well, that's the point, Jasper – you may not want to come in! We're not looking for votes, so we're not buttering up the people. We want to put an idea across that is less than popular which we think will right long-standing wrongs.'

'I can feel my instincts reaching for the body armour. So what is it? I know, it's this tax shift-thing.'

Jake nodded.

'Jake, you haven't a hope in hell,' Jasper barked dismissively. 'The economic bods don't take it seriously. What's it about, anyway? I know it's about taxing the land ...'

'Jasper, that's exactly what it's bloody not about – well, not in the ordinary sense – It's the value that attaches to land, and that's why we're having this lunch, for I want *you* to tell the people what it *is* about!'

'They're a bit slow with the white wine. I think I'm going to need it!' Jasper's sound was resigned

Jake waved at the waitress.

'You'd better talk me through this thing, for if I'm going to be shredded I want to know the reason!'

'You've heard the term, location value?'

'Yeah, a flat in Mayfair and one in Hammersmith come with very different price tags, and that's location.'

'Exactly. Now, Jasper, who creates these location values?'

'Jake, that's not so easy as it seems, for there are a myriad of factors.'

'And difficult to separate,' Jake prompted.

'Yeah, they're all connected, in a way.'

'And what's the collective term for that?'

Jasper pondered.

'The community,' Jake prompted, his frustration obvious. 'My God, Jasper, this is like pulling teeth. Don't apologise too often: it may have side effects!'

'Hey, all this is new to me. Stop jumping up and down! So you're saying that the community creates location value.' Jasper was reflective for a moment. 'Yeah, I'll buy that.'

'Another question: who should benefit from this value? Are you with me, Jasper?'

'Yeah, I'm with you, but don't crowd me, for if you're implying what I'm thinking. Jeez! ... Jake, this is high explosive!'

'Explain.'

'Just now the New York skyline flashed up. Its unbidden image was sharp and clear, and there was the evidence: location value writ large, writ very large. The total sum must be enormous. And, Jake, this is where the TNT comes in, for those who claim a location, whether it be in the City or the High Street or indeed a suburban cottage, pocket the location value. The law allows it and has allowed it for yonks, but the truth is it's legalised bloody theft!'

'One more question Jasper: how does the state collect its revenue?'

'That's easy, by pinching our bloody wages!'

'Well, my old mate, you've picked all this up remarkably quickly. No wonder the Beeb pay you such a fortune. And, do you know something, I would apologise more often!'

They both laughed heartily.

'So, Jake, you chair the committee looking into all this?'

'Yeah, a bunch of eggheads. The trouble is, it's all so damned complicated. Hold it, the PM always stops us when we say that. "We're complicated," he interjects. "The principle is simple." Jasper, this is where you come in. We need someone to sell this.'

'The Beeb wouldn't wear it. I'd be out the door faster than a rocket bound for Mars!'

'Jasper, you wouldn't have to commit yourself. Just ask questions and with the usual Jasper rapier thrust. Just think the fun you'd have with all those economic gurus!'

'Jake, there'd be no point in putting their backs up.'

'Jasper, what's happened to you? Reformation doesn't come that easy! You're right, of course, and it makes me even more anxious to have you with us. Think about it.'

'I need to know much more. Why do you call it shift?'

'God, I thought we'd got that one across, for that's the selling point! The shift is simply reducing tax on income and shifting it to the location levy...'

'Which is created by the community.' Jasper cut in. 'It's neat. Jake. I'd heard about the tax reduction but hadn't linked it. In fact, I hadn't thought much about it as the experts kept asserting it was fairyland. One was particularly dismissive. "You only have to look at a City high rise with all the leases and sub-leases, to know it's loopy." I had no answer, of course.' Then he laughed. 'Throw in mortgages for afters!'

'A few days ago,' said Jake, 'I recruited a young man called Tommy Thompson. To put you in the picture: he's a friend of Alexander Collingwood, who in turn is much respected by the PM. Tommy comes to our meetings, when he condescends to wear a suit, which almost certainly he picked up at his local charity shop. That gives you the general picture. The thing is, Tommy is a genius and it takes the civil service experts all their time to keep in step. Tommy, though, is not a big head and gets on well with the Treasury fellas, and together they've created software that does wonders. So things are promising in that quarter. Indeed, at first I thought it was our Achilles heel. Now I'm more preoccupied by the political impasse. We have very little support in any of the parties. Some liberals are sympathetic, but we need more than sympathy.'

'Why were you so strongly anti when I mentioned taxing land?'

'Often when I'm trying to explain location or, if you like site value, the reaction is – that's communism – and land nationalisation is assumed. Jasper, we have no intention of confiscating land or indeed simply taxing land. The levy is based on the value that attaches to land due to its location – hence location value.'

'But, Jake most folk will see it as a land tax. It's a generic term.'

'That may be so, but the measure for the levy is location value. In marginal areas there'd be little or no levy, for there location value is minimal. What we are suggesting is a levy on the annual location value that is created by the combined presence of the community.'

'You're certainly banging on about it!'

'You're right I am, for we aim to shift the tax burden from earnings. Jasper, the idea is to set the people free, not burden them with yet more taxes which they're told is for their benefit. I'm not saying that our present system is devoid of merit. It's pursued, no doubt, with the best intent, but it's misguided. And, Jasper, don't be fooled by this – they're-taxing-your-back-garden – stuff. The levy for the average suburban semi would be modest, and, of course, the tax shift would help towards offsetting this. Location, or if you like community value begins to rise, and steeply, as you move towards the central town and city sites.'

'My God, Jake, you're sounding like an old-time prophet!'

'Don't be bloody silly! I didn't sound like one this morning when I rang you up.'

'No, you were fairly Anglo-Saxon!'

Jake Hud chuckled lightly.

'My God, it's just struck me! You know how the rich get richer and the poor keep locked in poverty, no matter what government's in power – well, it's just hit me.'

'Strike me again. I saw diamonds last time!'

'I'm serious, Jasper. The corporate biggies, the fat cats, are gorging on the cream of central sites. The cream's location value; it's so bloody obvious. At the same time the average chap, who's struggling to pay his standing orders, is taxed up to the eyebrows for daring to work. That's if he can find some! No wonder I get so bloody worked up!'

'Jake, this annual location value: how's that relate to capital value?'

'Listen I'm not an economist. I only chair these eggheads.'

'Come off it, Jake. Stop dodging the question.'

'All right: at present, both the annual value – or, if you like, the rental – and the capital value are determined by the market. In other words, the figure agreed between what one guy is prepared to pay, and what another is prepared to accept. I see the freehold owner in our current system, that is, the one who's paid the

61

capital value, as having by far the best bargain, for presently he owns the perpetual rental. I'll leave you to ponder what that comes to!'

'Jeez, Jake, this *is* dynamite!'

Jake grinned.

'Have they forgotten us?' He grumbled. 'I'm getting hungry.'

'It's all right, Jake; they're coming.'

They both knew the waitress. In fact, she had served them once or twice before, so there were jokes and pleasantries.

Jake lifted his knife and fork and then suddenly stopped, his fork hovering like a bird of prey.

'Are you with us, then?'

'Do I have any bloody option?'

Laughter united them.

Chapter Twelve

With the blessing of Bill Jones, Blackstone had sent Chris Crouch to report on the racial troubles. Chris's views were to the left of Lenin, but he was an honest man and, as Bill Jones said, a likeable devil – a live wire without the coating; certainly he was thin enough!

Crouch's appointment was at ten, and Blackstone waited as the clock ticked on well past the time.

Suddenly the door burst open.

'Sorry I'm late, Henry. The traffic was damnable!'

'Would you like a coffee, Chris?'

'Would I hell? I'd love one!'

Blackstone lifted the phone, and spoke quietly. Then he turned again to Crouch.

'Chris, I'm told you had a busy time up there?'

'I listened a lot, and I talked a little. With some of those guys it was difficult to get a word in edgeways. Anyway, they all went home eventually and it rained. In fact, it emptied down. That deterred all but the total nutters, and then even they slipped away.'

Blackstone smiled. He liked the earthy realism.

'Did you make any useful contacts?'

'There was one Mullah who was quiet in himself, a bit like you, Prime Minister. I got on well with him. I introduced him to the local Vicar and they behaved like buddies. The community leaders were OK. But I was someone from London. I just got the party line.'

'Did you try the – Stop waiting for a job, create one – line?'

'Yeah, my quiet spoken Mullah friend was keen on that, and so was the Vicar. I met the Vicar's youth group. Pathetically few, mind you, but they knew how to behave.'

'Keep in touch with your friends up North. Encourage the Vicar and his youth group. Small beginnings, Chris – water the saplings. Could you attend the Cabinet on Thursday and tell them what you've told me?'

'There's not much to say, Prime Minister.'

'Don't worry, Chris, they'll pepper you with questions and that will prompt your memory!'

Blackstone then detailed the public works project for the area, indicating that Chris would have special responsibilities. After this Crouch politely took his leave.

Blackstone smiled as the door closed quietly. Chris Crouch had his trademark take-me-as-you-find-me personality that he used to cover his initial nervousness, but when he settled down another gentler Chris came into view. Bill Jones was right; Chris was a likeable devil.

*

Henry Blackstone's knowledge of the Greco-Roman world was comprehensive, if not intimate. For as a boy the heroes that he read about were almost always Greek or Roman. In his later teens it was Greek philosophy. Not an easy read, but one well worth the effort. Whereas most of his contemporaries shied away from deeper questions, Blackstone picked them up. He didn't follow his enquiry with an ice pack on his head but rather let his inclination surface when meeting someone of a similar will. In this way books were recommended and new directions taken. He dipped into the profound Upanishadic tradition of India, and indeed, the mysteries of Egypt. Then came the modern philosophers, which he studied at University, and after that politics caught him. In the common meaning of the term, Blackstone was well-read, but there'd been a keener edge to his perusings than simply information gathering.

What was the essence of the great traditions when you stripped away the gloss of dogma? Blackstone, suspected, indeed, rather more than suspected, that true religion and philosophy ploughed a similar furrow. Again, the message of these great teachings was the same. In his opinion, Plato's *one,* as described in the *Parmenides,* was the same as *the one without a second* of the *Upanishads.* For him, the words of Christ, if torn from their historical anchor, spoke with a universal voice. However, most glazed over when he broached such matters, and very early in his life he learned the art of tactful silence. Because of his interest in such things, Blackstone was conscious of the empty churches and the lack of spiritual practice that it meant. What could he do? Very little, he concluded, but he could show example. That's why he'd gone to Farnham and that was why he was going to Hinde Street with Bill Jones. Trying to bring justice to the economic sphere was one thing, but, even though it was far-reaching in effect, it was not the only thing to help the nation on its journey. Society needed spiritual roots. Of this he was convinced. Atheism seemed to him to be a giving up of contemplation. And if the crisis deepened, what inner surety could the people hold to when established pillars of the welfare service shook?

He received dire warnings daily – and one day soon, he feared, they would be more than warnings. Strikes, called by radical extremists, hoping to take over in the wake of chaos, could be all too possible. This, and the terrorist threat, stretched national security to the limit and, of course, the cost was enormous. Indeed, the Chancellor kept warning that public spending had reached unsustainable levels. The situation *was* dangerous, but what could he do? Everything seemed to take an age, and even if the tax-shift plan were running, it would be a small percentage. Anyway it was a tax *shift*, not a tax hike, and government desperately needed revenue.

Blackstone could call on advisors from all the areas of government. They were often brilliant men of wide experience, but Henry Blackstone wanted more. He wanted vision. An analysis of the *status quo* was necessary, but he needed people who would see beyond the common practice, and often complicated practice, to a simpler world with rules and regulations that did not need a lawyer to unfold their meaning.

This morning he had sat in on a meeting between the Chancellor, James Jamieson, and a group of senior bankers. It had been an analysis of the present, panic charged, situation. Blackstone hadn't intervened, but the unvoiced assumption that government would act as guarantor for troubled banks was unsettling, if not unsustainable. Those were the gentle words, he reflected. There were many rescue plans. But Blackstone could only see more debt being piled on debt – a crippling burden for the future.

Given it was easy to be wise after the event, he found it difficult to understand why highly paid executives could have allowed a crisis, such as the sub-prime crisis, to develop. Extending loans to numerous clients, who were fully stretched or even over-stretched was, to say the very least, difficult to understand. Of course, share price, backed by expanding profits, was a heady cocktail.

He needed to talk this through with someone who could tune in to his way of thinking. Not the Chancellor, who seemed locked within the orbit of the current system, but someone with the wit to think of something new.

*

Anna turned aside from her computer and back to the manuscript open on her desk. She looked up.

'Father, this budding travel author writes well, and his journeys in the shadow of the Himalayas are most interesting. I think we should publish. He's only nineteen. Some work on the manuscript is necessary, but not much.' She pushed her chair back. 'Let's have tea!'

'You've read my thoughts.'

Collingwood could hear the kettle boiling as he finished off an e-mail to his printers. The phone rang and he lifted the handset immediately'

'Collingwood.' The phone had been left on audio.

The Prime Minister for you, Mr Collingwood.

'Thank you.'

'Alexander, are you busy this evening?'

'No, Henry, there's nothing on the menu except manuscripts!'

'All right, a car will call for you at six. And Anna too, please, if she's free.'

'I'm free,' Anna called out as she emerged from the kitchen with the tea.

'Did you hear that Henry?'

'I did, Downing Street's already perking up! By the way, the subject's banking, but don't tell Anna in case she remembers another engagement!' There was a brief chuckle. *'Be seeing you soon.'*

Chapter Thirteen

The traffic was heavy and, at the pace they were travelling, it would take at least an hour before they arrived. Anna found it difficult to relax and every hold-up added to her agitation.

'The traffic's very heavy, Father.'

'The tubes have been disrupted. Walk-outs, I believe. I'm afraid the militants are flexing their muscles.'

'More trouble for Henry!'

'Yes, but the militants' hard-faced leader and his cronies are not having it all their own way. The public have been barracking the pickets. And a popular tabloid called the tight-lipped union boss "a feather-bedded winger," and other union chiefs have been openly critical. Meantime we have this continuing disruption.'

'Hasn't Henry emergency powers?'

'He would be very loath to use them, for that is what the militants want, and in fact, are often trying to provoke. Then they're justified in "defending themselves" if you get my meaning?'

'Too well! How do we get into such a mess?'

'Anna, I'll not bore you, or myself, by "rabbiting on" about the natural principles and how they've been ignored. The fact is, the battle between management and workers, the "them and us" divide, has been going on for decades – decades of decades.'

'I know, the have-and-have-not divide. You taught me well, Father. Funny, how it all comes down to the same root. Ah, he's turning right,' Anna said brightly, her agitation gone. 'We're going via Pont Street. About another fifteen minutes, I would guess.'

'Agreed, if Parliament Square is not too busy.'

*

Collingwood and his daughter were conducted immediately to the PM's flat. Blackstone was on the phone when they arrived, and he waved a greeting. The Collingwoods waited and Blackstone made no effort to disguise his voice. He was clearly far from pleased.

'Chris, get them round a table. They're just two stubborn men. Tell them to ditch their pride and get to work. Right, Chris ... I agree it's not easy...I know, but if you can't get them back to work, who can? ... Bye, Chris.'

'Sorry about that. We've got record unemployment, and we have a walk out over differentials! Chris I'm sure will sort it out. He knows the language. Well, how good to see you and thanks for coming at such short notice.' Blackstone's smile focused on Anna.

'Saves me making supper!' She joked.

'You mean you're expecting food?'

They laughed.

'You know, it can be pretty lonely in this job, and talking casually about the way you feel is out. Every word and smile is analysed, and the cameras never stop. It's good to be with friends I trust.'

'Henry, we're in the publishing business. *Anna Collingwood Tells All* could be lucrative!'

Collingwood burst out laughing.

'That was my line, Anna.' His daughter had shed her awkwardness.

'Supper, I'm told, should be here shortly, but meantime let's have a glass of something. Once more, I'm sorry not to entertain you in more palatial circumstances below, but the plain fact is, I rather like the informality of the flat, and I hope you like it too.'

'We do!' Anna responded emphatically.

There was a lull in the conversation while Blackstone handed round the drinks.

'I'm afraid, Alexander, you've got to work for your supper. It's the current chaos. We're underwriting this and bailing out that. We're talking in billions, as if there were a limitless supply! Henry, I would like to know your views on money.'

'"Coined liberty." Who said that Anna?'

'Dostoyevsky, I think. It was on one of those calendar peel-offs.'

'Henry, I'm not an expert, but I've a few heretical ideas.'

'Those are the very ones I want to hear.'

'The Bank of England, one might say, is the guardian of the nation's currency. They provide the notes and coins that the high street banks draw on as the need arises. Whereas the Bank of England is an institution, the high street banks are commercial.

For these financial giants, profit, and the all-important share price, are constant preoccupations, as any discernible weakness heralds predatory bids. So CEOs need to keep ahead of the action, as the Americans would say, and in such circumstances something like the sub-prime surge would have been attractive. The sub-prime debt, or, to put it bluntly, dodgy debt – sometimes very dodgy – was parcelled up with other debts of a more substantial origin. Now, these parcels became security, as is the practice with ordinary mortgage debt, for further credit. They were called CDOs or collateralised debt obligations, and, as we know, they became unstuck. Of course, there was a general flouting of mortgage-to-income norms, spurred by soaring property prices. The property spiral was the engine of it all. The question is: Should a nation's currency be in the hands of such raw commercial interest? Clearly not, when prudent guidelines are ignored. To begin with, vigorous self-regulation should be instituted, with a powerful BoE watchdog.'

'With real teeth, I would say, but carry on.'

'There are many areas, like currency speculation, that need to be examined, but for the moment let's take a look at credit.'

Blackstone nodded.

'There are well-practised rules of course, and I must say the banks are pretty careful. However, the question I would ask is this: When do the banks really offer credit and when are they acting simply as sophisticated moneylenders? My view is that things went horribly wrong when banks were allowed to take over building societies, for then they became exposed to, shall we say, "enthusiastic" mortgage lending that was funding the ever-soaring property bonanza. But let's get back to credit.'

'Good, I thought you'd sold me a dummy!' Blackstone said, while turning to Anna.

'You've been very quiet. I hope you don't find this too tedious. But knowing you, you probably can enlighten us!'

'Credo – credere – credidi – creditum – to trust,' she returned impishly.

'Heavens, that takes me back. My Latin teacher told me that I couldn't pass a horse and cart!'

'That was encouraging!' Anna reacted.

They all laughed.

'Now, Alexander, bring us back to the real world that everyone seems to credit.'

'Prime Minister, I've been saved by the bell. Your good house-keeper is waiting.'

Blackstone swung round immediately.

'Ah, Mabel, meet Anna Collingwood and her father Alexander.'

When the introductions were completed, Anna asked if Mabel needed any help.

'No, m'dear, it's all ready, but it's nice of you to ask. And aren't you a picture!'

'Mabel!' Anna reacted with mock severity.

'Right again, Mabel.' Blackstone chuckled. 'Now, Alexander, what is credit?'

'My father told me that, in his day, if you wanted an extension of your overdraft you would approach your bank manager and talk the matter over. For instance, if you wanted to start a new venture, the bank manager would ask you all about it and then decide if you were credit-worthy – in other words, if he could trust you and believe in your project. It was an agreement between two men. However, if I buy something in the high street using bank notes, trust doesn't come into it. I give him a note, and he gives me change. We don't need to trust each other particularly, for we both trust the currency. It's as safe as the Bank of England. Credit and money will end up doing the same thing, that is facilitating exchange, but they are different in origin.'

'So when a mortgage loan is given, by a young man under pressure to increase his sales, credit can be – shall we say – "discredited".'

'Exactly, Henry, and this practice was widespread on both sides of the pond. Property prices kept on climbing and many thought the boom-bust days were past. Again, there was a belief that house-price advances would hike the value of collateral, if borrowers couldn't or wouldn't pay. Now here I'm going to say something that is most unfashionable, for in my opinion the banks are not the primary culprits in this crisis. It's real-property law that spurs the upward spiral of land prices. The banks follow; money follows, reaching for the dizzy heights. We demand it! We all boast about our house price. We think, in some strange way the party's going on forever. We even kid ourselves that boom-bust has been tamed. But how can .it be when all the laws ensuring bust will follow boom are still in place? I'll make another statement. Real estate law allows the rich to get richer, for those who have, have wealth and have the better chance of having more! So the desire, in a property- owning democracy, to join the haves is like a popular movement. It's unstoppable, and the banks must find a way to follow. They do, of course, and then they crash, just like Napoleon's flight from Moscow. It's sudden and devastating.'

'Like now with house prices heading for the floor! So the party's over and reality has come home to roost.'

Collingwood nodded.

'Alas, too true. Now the question arises: can government offer credit, or, more precisely, allow credit for certain projects?'

'That's the very question I've been pondering! For we need to get things moving quickly, otherwise I shudder to think...' He didn't finish the sentence. 'We can print money and throw it at the problem, but inflation is the spectre that restrains me. I questioned a rather bright Treasury official on the subject, but after ten minutes or so I was rescued by a phone call. He clearly wanted to help and promised me a paper on the subject. The truth was I didn't understand half of what he said.'

'Well, you know, Henry, we might just have the dream ticket...'

'Mabel's beckoning,' Anna interjected.

'Over supper, then,' Blackstone concluded.

'Have you been helping at Number Ten for long?' Collingwood questioned Mabel in a friendly, casual way.

'I did for Mr Bob when his wife was in the country and now I'm doing for Mr Henry.'

'A real insider!' Collingwood joked.

Mabel put her finger to her lips.

'I never say a word!'

'Mabel's a gem,' Blackstone said strongly.

She beamed.

'Well, what's this dream ticket? Put me out of my misery!'

'All right, here it is! The Government forms a development bank under the jurisdiction of the Bank of England. Credit is advanced, but purely for infrastructure works which would be extensive and nationwide. There should be no exceptions. At the same time announce a substantial levy on location value. Also raise the threshold for income tax, again substantially.'

'I get it, Alexander. Infrastructure improvements would go straight into location value and that would be collected, at least in part, but, to be truthful, it frightens me. It would have to be checked out by the Treasury boys.'

'I've thought about this a lot and I don't think it's inflationary, for we're increasing wealth. That's why the credit must not be extended to anything non-productive or stupidly grandiose. In fact, I feel that this should be the general rule. But any such changes should be subject to a rigorous enquiry. However, for now let's keep to our present infrastructure projects Heavens, I'd almost forgotten; the credit for these projects would be interest free.'

'The banks won't like that!'

'Yes, not the best of precedents, as far as they're concerned. This exposes the basic problem. The banks are commercial bodies and they're dealing in the national currency. You might say we've privatised currency!'

'People will say that that's the way it's always been,'

'And they'd be right, up to a point but that's not the whole story, for the circulating currency is the national coinage, and the Queen's head on the notes gives the stamp of authority. History records the monarch's head legitimising coins down the ages. So the question of commercial banks and their apparent privatisation of the currency remains, in my opinion, an open question.'

'I can see that this whole area deserves serious thought. But Alexander, what fires me is your dream ticket, for it's the answer to the present crisis. Offer interest-free credit through a government development agency for serious infrastructure projects. This would boost the overall community wealth, which would be reflected in the location value levy. Indeed, it's the perfect chance to introduce the levy, for it seems that almost everyone's a winner. We'd have job creation as well as income tax reduction funded by the levy. We will need to ensure the middle ground is not forgotten. Another thing, with these infrastructure projects we will need scrutiny. Aesthetic and social considerations must not be forgotten: indeed, sensible planning is essential.'

'What about the rich, Father?' Anna questioned. 'Will they not take their wealth and find a haven somewhere overseas?'

'We'll have restored political stability. And in the current climate re-location could be tricky and uncertain. Again the "off-shore" scene may not be so attractive in the future! In any case, there's nothing to stop the enterprising rich from prospering, and prospering considerably, but you're right, it is an area to watch. And, of course, there's the tax shift; taxes on productive activities would be reduced. They could well be better off!'

'And the great estates?' Blackstone prompted.

'I've mentioned this before; I see the great houses and estates as natural cultural centres and parks for the people. In fact, it's already happening. The owners could well exploit this and, bearing in mind the tax shift, their work would not be grossly penalised by taxes. There is no desire to drive people from their family lands. All we ask for is the location value, the natural community fund. Anyway, country estates enclose much farming land, which, of course, is not Threadneedle Street!'

'Thank you, Alexander. Your "moderately" heretical ideas have disturbed my lethargy, and tomorrow I must get moving. I need to gee them up about the self-assessment forms regarding freehold property. I'm told they're almost ready.'

'Henry, it's hard to believe that after twenty years or more of effort, umpteen letters to the press and prominent officials, after all this time something may be actually happening!'

'Not *may* be Alexander, *will* be!'

'Sorry, my pessimism has been well rehearsed!'

Both men found easy chairs while Anna helped Mabel to clear the table.

'The American President is paying us an overnight visit next Thursday. Nobody knows he's coming, except security, and even they are in the dark about the detail. So keep it to yourself. Why am I telling you this? I need a partner for an informal dinner at the Residency in Regent's Park. Willie Windbourne, being Foreign Secretary, is also invited and he has grabbed my sister, so I'm wondering if Anna wouldn't mind tolerating all the fuss and bother. And Alexander, I can't invite you, for I'm not the host! Another thing, there'll be a press presence and Anna might be embarrassed by the predictable publicity. I'd be flattered by her company, of course. But what do you think? Do you know something, I feel rather like a nervous suitor!'

'Henry, thank God, she's found a man and not a mouse. Does that answer your question?'

'Well, I don't squeak!'

They both laughed heartily.

'Anna's been a long time in there.' Blackstone noted.

'Probably helping Mabel with the washing-up,' Collingwood said casually.

'Yes, that's what it is. Mabel doesn't like dishwashing machines,' Blackstone said with a chuckle. 'And another thing, if

73

Anna's made a hit with Mabel, she's made a hit with most of Whitehall!'

Collingwood's amusement was obvious.

'Bill Jones and I are going to church on Sunday, just the two of us.' Blackstone said after a moment's silence. 'It's low profile in a high profile sort of way. I may be living in the past, but I feel we need reminding of the age-old verities. Simple things like what is right and what is wrong.'

Chapter Fourteen

The next day all the negative forces seemed to strike at once. A teenage bomber triggered her lethal load, prematurely killing herself and injuring a score of bystanders. It could have been much worse. Riots had again broken out. Barricades, made mostly of overturned cars, had been erected. Churches and mosques had been damaged. Indeed, one old medieval church had been gutted, and seething anger was the legacy. The situation was explosive. And on top of that, militant union cells were threatening disruption in those sensitive areas where they had influence. Needless to say, police and security were stretched to breaking point and still Blackstone vetoed army intervention.

Both the Home Secretary and Chris Crouch were in the flash-point area, and a meeting of community leaders was in progress, but the news from that was little but a catalogue of acrimonious accusations, with the Home Secretary's interventions almost totally ignored. A breakdown in dialogue was imminent, and the PM, against the advice of security, decided to intervene personally. Accordingly, the meeting was asked to reconvene in four hours' time. It was hoped, the Prime Minister relayed, that community members would make this a priority.

Travelling by car and helicopter, Blackstone arrived at the town hall venue in good time. Security was steel-tight, and some were full of angry complaints at being searched so thoroughly. Observing from an upstairs window, Blackstone watched the scene unfold with Chris Crouch at his side. He also observed the first contributions. All they could do, it seemed, was rant against the other side. Only one man, a clergyman, expressed regret at the damage perpetrated by people of his own religious background.

'That's the Vicar who had his church gutted,' Chris whispered. 'Where's your friendly Mullah?'

'Poor bloke's got the flu.'

Blackstone sighed. Even in the details the tide was running out!

'Well, Chris, I think I've seen enough. It's time to make an appearance.'

The Home Secretary, Winston Hughes, stood up immediately his chief appeared.

'Prime Minister, we are honoured and, indeed impressed, for I know that you are here at no small inconvenience.'

'Home Secretary, many before me work tirelessly in the field of community relations. Such work I applaud. But I'm not here to praise the speeches I've just heard. Not one note of regret, not one note of apology from any of you except one lone clergyman – the man who's had his church burned down! How can you expect the young men rioting in your streets to cease their madness if you cheer them on? You are leaders. Do your duty; *lead*! I want to hear the sound of reconciliation. And have no doubt that, when I said our tolerance of intolerance is dead, I meant it.

'Government is busy rushing forward plans to initiate public works. This is not merely rhetoric for the press. It will happen, and soon. Ladies and gentlemen, unemployment is a soul-destroying thing, and its elimination is the work that should engage your passion, not tit-for-tat abuse.'

Blackstone then took some time elaborating on plans already under way.

'The government is determined to get things moving!' he concluded.

He paused and smiled.

'Remember reconciliation. It is what the nation expects. Show us the way. Be the example for us all!'

✳

For a number of the media familiars, the habit of negativity was ingrained, and Blackstone's words were seen as pompous. The press, of course, used headlines to encourage sales. 'Headmaster Blackstone slams community leaders,' was almost predictable. However, contrary to all expectation, Jasper Jenkins backed the Prime Minister's stance. He was the guest on a popular late-night questions panel. No doubt the producer had seen him as sure-fire left and anti-Blackstone, so surprise added its attraction.

After listening to his fellow panellists for some time, Jasper's frustration erupted.

'What are you saying? Here we have a Prime Minister who flies by chopper to the epicentre of the trouble, speaks to the community workers face to face, and in no uncertain terms, and

still you're gushing with complaints! What do you want? Or are your mindsets stuck in automatic?'

This brought a quick reaction, with the presenter working hard to keep the peace.

Anna was glued to the screen. Her father had gone to bed earlier, but she had lingered on, anxious to hear the reaction to Henry's dash up North, and it certainly was a reaction. This wouldn't do Henry any harm at all. A sudden desire to speak to him rose to dominate but, of course, it was ridiculous.

The phone rang.

Anna lifted the lounge portable on the coffee table.

'Anna Collingwood.'

'The Prime Minister to speak to you!'

Anna could hardly believe what was happening. Was someone up there pulling strings?

'Henry Blackstone here...'

'It's Anna, Henry. Father's gone to bed.'

'What time is it?'

'It's past eleven.'

'Oh, I'm sorry, Anna. I've been knee-deep in paper for the past hour and must have lost all sense of time.'

'Did you see Jasper Jenkins just a few minutes ago?'

'No.'

'Well, he gave you a real plug on that questions programme. Tore quite a strip off his fellow panellists.'

'Which they didn't like too much, no doubt.'

'No, not one little bit! Jasper was quite funny. He told them that their mindsets "were stuck on automatic".'

Blackstone's laughter crackled down the line.

'Ed Gray, you know, that reporter I met at Farnham, has got something in one of the heavies tomorrow. So we're getting there, as it were. But what does my sternest critic, that is Anna Collingwood, think about my foray in the North?'

'I thought it was powerful. The sound was right. Straightforward, straight talking common sense, and the more of it the better. Short, of course, but that somehow didn't matter. So there it is. That's what your sternest critic thinks. But, she would think like that, wouldn't she?'

More laughter echoed down the line.

'Shall I get Father to phone you in the morning?' She asked.

'Yes, please.'

'When?'

'When does your father usually surface?'

'About seven.'

'Any time from then on – did he say anything about today?'

'I hope I'm not speaking out of turn, but I heard him mumbling, "Don't get diverted, Henry!"'

Blackstone laughed again.

'I get the message. Well, Anna dear, I'd better let you get to bed.'

'I think it's *you* who ought to head for bed! You've had quite a day.'

'Yes, ma'am! As you wish.' He chuckled. *'Bye.'*

Getting up, Anna made for the kitchen, feeling as if she were walking on air. Milk and honey might help her sleep, she hoped. For in her present state she needed something. She had often been completely puzzled by her contemporaries when they became attached, and, mostly, to some uninspiring male, in her opinion. Now she was behaving in a similar 'silly' way, but not by any shadow of a doubt was Henry Blackstone uninspiring!

Chapter Fifteen

After a brief word with the Prime Minister in the morning, Collingwood found himself being driven to Westminster Hall to attend a meeting convened by Jake Hud, and being held in one of the committee rooms to the side of the ancient and empty hall.

Collingwood stopped as he descended the steps to the main body of the hall. It was very quiet. There was something special here. He thought of Richard II and his carpenter Hugh Hurland. In its time the hall was claimed to have the biggest single-span roof in Europe.

'It's a kind of brainstorming session, Alexander,' Jake explained when Collingwood arrived. 'We want to cover every angle. Tommy Thompson's fielding questions, as are the other experts who've been working on the project practically day and night. In your trade it would be a sort of final proof-read. To put you in the picture, we intend to issue self-assessment forms to every council tax and unified business ratepayer. If some freehold owner escapes the net it will be incumbent on him to declare his asset. For there's one thing he can't do and that's hide it. As you yourself once told me, you cannot bury land. And again, to echo your words, if someone pretends he doesn't hold the freehold rights, he'd lose them. That's the bare bones.'

'Well, Jake, I hope I'll be able to keep up with it all.'

'You will, you will. Did you see my friend Jasper last night? He really came up trumps.'

'My daughter Anna saw the programme and was full of it this morning. What did you say to him, Jake?'

'I swore at him a bit. I mean, a fair bit, and he kind of got the message. Personally, I think he's enjoying himself. He's got something he believes in! Ah, here's Tommy and his civil service friends. We'd better take our places.'

'Mr Collingwood,' Tommy called out. 'You'll make me nervous!'

'Tommy, I'm the pupil now!'

The power point presentation was sophisticated. First came the broad outline of the plan, then the various areas of difficulty, such as city tower blocks with their complicated leasing arrangements. Even the floor levels had been factored in when calculating the share of advantage accruing to the location.

Collingwood's head was spinning. This was young men's work.

'Will tower block administrators and such people understand the procedure?' he asked.

'Large city blocks teem with people who will understand the software.'

'I'll take your word for it, Tommy, but it seems hugely complicated.'

'Initially there may be problems, Mr Collingwood, but it'll shake down.'

Collingwood still had concerns. For instance, it would take an army of civil servants to administer. He posed the question.

'Not as many as you think, Sir. A guy with a laptop could cover a fair area. I know what you're saying, but computers are made for this sort of thing, and, Sir, the price per square foot is a universal measure. That greatly helps.'

From Collingwood's point of view, a much-needed coffee break was called, before they launched into the fraught question of mortgaged property and, of course, the exercise that applied to all the situations, distinguishing between buildings and the location value.

'Tommy, this is going to take a fair time to "shake down", as you say,' Collingwood said while they both were sipping coffee.

'It's easy-peasy compared with some of the stuff the City deals with. Some tax experts earn a fortune dealing with the complication. And I mean a fortune! The trouble is, the principle is so simple we're puzzled why its application is so difficult. But even that is simple, for the world we live in is insanely complicated, and that's the problem.'

'Tommy, I'm glad we have you on board. What about your colleagues?'

'They're very bright, Sir. To them complication is fun!'

'Have they understood the principle?'

'All understand the theory, and two or three, I think, have got it, you know, inside!'

'Nurture them, Tommy. They're the ones to be relied on.'

For the second period they were joined by three experienced veterans who had studied the principle for years, and who had trawled the muddy waters of application many times. So the questions were uncompromising, but Tommy and his colleagues held their own. It was prudent to burrow into every possible scenario, but there was a time when such exhaustive searching lost its thrust.

Afterwards Jake Hud beckoned Collingwood.

'Why all this concern for the landlord? They've been milking the system for years. The tenant is already paying the most he can afford. Therefore the landlord can't easily pass the levy on. So let him play the bloody levy!'

Collingwood laughed.

'That may be so with a tenant but not with a leaseholder. The leaseholder does reap a benefit. But, Jake, the landlord's not a rogue, for he hasn't broken the law. It's the lawgivers who've transgressed. The landlords have merely played the system as it is, and we can't tie them up at Tyburn for that! This is Britain, not Stalin's Russia!'

'Alexander, why did Henry give me this chairman job, for these guys are away ahead of me?'

'Yes, Jake, on the detail maybe, but not on the principle. Now, I'll ask you a question. If you'd been in Blackstone's shoes, what would you have chosen, a ranting right-winger, or a pinko leftie?'

'Alexander, if I get your meaning, let's put the record straight. I'm no pinko, I'm ruddier-than-the-cherry Hud. At least that's what they used to call me in the old days! If you don't believe me, ask Sir Harold Hanwall. He keeps rabbiting on about my "vile left-wing agenda".'

Collingwood burst out laughing.

'Jake, Henry picked the best man for the job. You understand the location value fund principle. It's more than just a theory, and that's a big percentage plus. You don't let the grass grow under your feet and you don't suffer fools gladly.'

'Alexander, are you free on Monday?' Jake asked, changing the subject.

'Another meeting?'

'Yes, at the Treasury. It's about the self-assessment forms we're sending out. The Chancellor's being bloody awkward. I think he sees himself upstaged by an economic illiterate, which is a lot of bloody nonsense! Now, everyone knows you're one of Henry's closest confidants, so if you were there, he wouldn't be so bloody pompous. He's supposed to be one of my "Honourable Friends"

– in other words the same party, but I get more bloody hassle from him than from all the rest combined.'

'Jake, Jamieson's a careful man.'

'Maybe.'

'Jake, what time Monday?'

'Ten.'

'I'll be there.'

Chapter Sixteen

Just before Blackstone set out to join Bill Jones at Hinde Street Methodist Church, news arrived that militant hot-heads had disrupted fuel supplies to a Midlands power station. Power cuts were inevitable.

This was wildcat irresponsibility at its worst, and it was deliberate. These idiots should be 'inside', he grated, but he knew he daren't touch them, for Union reaction would, most certainly, erupt. Indeed, their sensitivity on the subject was on a hair trigger.

One thing, though, was certain. He was going to church, but he knew the press would be there and waiting to be voluble on the steps. It was inevitable.

✲

The signs of tight security were obvious as the Jaguar drew up at Hinde Street Church. The car door opened, and Blackstone emerged with his usual sense of ease.

'Prime Minister, what plans are there for restoring power supplies?'

'Prime Minister, should you not be having beer and sandwiches with the unions?'

'Prime Minister, send in the army and throw these reds in the slammer!'

'Yes, George, and you'd be the very one who'd be outraged.' Blackstone held up his hands. 'After the service, all right? Questions then. Now I'm going to church.'

Once inside, Blackstone was escorted to the front pew where Bill Jones was already waiting. There were just the two of them, for Bill's wife was in the Scillies. It was quiet, even though the church was full. Outside traffic noise was faint and didn't disturb the peace.

The service proceeded with predictable dignity and the Old Testament reading was from Isaiah 65. It was one of Blackstone's favourites, and the reader was good. Every word was crystal clear.

...they shall build houses and inhabit them; and they shall plant vineyards and eat the fruit of them.

They shall not build, and another inhabit; they shall not plant, and another eat: for as the days of a tree are the days of my people, and mine elect shall enjoy the work of their hands.

Blackstone's attention wandered as the reading continued, for he couldn't help thinking of the current efforts to plant the seeds of economic justice, as the words were strangely apt.

The wolf and the lamb shall feed together, and the lion shall eat straw like the bullock: and dust shall be the serpent's meat. They shall not hurt nor destroy in all my holy mountain, saith the Lord.

What wonderful words, and how inspiring: the image of his school assembly room was there unbidden. Cynics might scorn it all as sentimental rubbish. Well, if they did, they missed the point. This was the healing sound the country needed.

The Minister's address started with acknowledging the presence of both the Prime Minister and the Deputy Prime Minister. This was a powerful gesture and one to echo in every corner of the Kingdom. We needed to stretch out to others, was the basis of his sermon. Them or they, as we called the government, couldn't do everything. That was as near to politics as the Minister felt that he could tread.

Hearing the words of the Bible read in church had always been pleasing to Blackstone. Somehow, the sound of the familiar words in company made all the difference. And today it was the King James. He smiled. Bill had probably warned them of his preference.

As at Farnham, the ladies of the congregation had prepared a lavish spread, and Blackstone didn't have the heart to simply slip away. However, his aides had told him that nothing much would move until the following morning when the wildcat strike committee would convene. The press, though, deserved his attention, as he had promised to answer questions after the service and this he explained to the Minister.

When Blackstone emerged, with Bill Jones at his side, the press swooped on them like a flock of birds. The confusion of shouted questions was like the bidding at some City market. Blackstone picked the one he wanted.

'What is this strike about, you ask? There is no sound reason, I would answer. This strike is illegal, blatantly political and totally unnecessary. Such is the government's position. I have asked TUC officials to a Downing Street meeting this afternoon, when I hope to outline our proposals. Mr Jones?' he added, turning to the Deputy Prime Minister at his side.

'I entirely agree with the Prime Minister. There is no justification whatever for this wildcat action and the TUC, I'm sure, will see it as deliberate provocation.'

'Ladies and gentlemen of the press,' Blackstone then continued. 'There'll be another briefing early evening at Downing Street. Meantime Bill and I must honour our hosts, the ladies of the congregation, who've laid out a generous lunch for hungry ministers of the crown!'

There was another explosion of questions, but Blackstone only waved and went inside.

'Henry, I like your style,' Bill Jones quipped as they climbed the steps.

'You're not too bad yourself, Bill,' Blackstone returned, matching the humour.

'I'm serious. You tell it straight. I like it, and I've heard many say the same.'

'Thanks, Bill, but now let's face the real inquisitors. The good ladies of the congregation!'

'Henry, I'm old hat, but *you're* sure to be a hit.'

They laughed.

*

Sam Redwell, the General Secretary of the TUC and three of his senior colleagues sat opposite Henry Blackstone, Bill Jones and Chris Crouch who had just arrived fresh from the trouble spot.

Sam Redwell's balding head glistened with perspiration. He was always too hot. He'd been designed for a colder climate, he often joked.

'Jackets off, Prime Minister?'

'Of course, Sam,' Blackstone responded easily.

The meeting had not started, and Redwell was busy sizing up the boy Prime Minister, as he viewed him. Blackstone was flanked by Jones, whom Redwell viewed as a lightweight, and the left-wing maverick Crouch. Not an impressive line-up, Sam thought. He'd had such men for breakfast often. There was one sure thing; these blokes weren't going to tell him what to do.

'I'm sorry the Home Secretary can't be with us,' Blackstone began. 'He's keeping an eye on things up North.'

Redwell nodded. He didn't think much of Winston Hughes – another lightweight, in his opinion.

'Well, Sam,' Blackstone continued. 'You're a plainspoken man of much experience. What's your answer to this wildcat problem?' Blackstone relaxed in his chair, his look quizzical.

'I heard what you said this morning, and if you go on like that you'll have the whole trade union movement down about your ears. Prime Minister, you've got to get these guys round the table. Give them something to save face and get them back to work. I've seen a lot of sudden fires being doused like that. You know, these things happen when the local union boss is out of touch and doesn't see the situation on the ground.'

'Well, I've been on the ground,' Chris Crouch burst out. 'I've heard the strikers speak, and they're not what I would call trades union. They're bloody anarchists!'

'You're over the top, Chris!' Redwell said evenly.

'Sam, they want to bring the country to its knees ready for the promised land – their promised land! Bloody nutters!'

'Well, you were like that once.'

'Sam, I was never in their league. Anyway, why do we allow these people to rant on – especially now. The country is in trouble, for God's sake!'

'It's called free speech, Chris,' Blackstone responded. 'Father used to train horses. He had them on a long rein and the horses circled round him, prancing and tossing their heads, but Father always held the rein. He never let it go. Chris, we'll keep these hot-heads on a short rein, which Sam will hold.'

'What are you saying, Prime Minister?'

'That *you're* going to get the power station back in service. What you said was right. If government put the finger on these bods, the whole trade union movement would be up in arms, but you, Sam, are an old pro. And Sam, play it as you will, but no monetary concessions.'

'This is not my job, Prime Minister!' Redwell protested. 'You cannot order me about.'

'That's true, but I can go on TV!'

'That's ... that's ...' Redwell fumbled.

'Sam, that's hard ball, as the Americans would say, and, Sam, think of the PR boost when you succeed!'

Blackstone kept his gaze on Redwell, and after a moment he smiled.

'You're not just a pretty face, Prime Minister.'

Blackstone laughed.

*

After the meeting with Redwell, Chris Crouch had to rush off, leaving the Prime Minister and his Deputy having tea in the study.

'Do you think Redwell will deliver?' Blackstone asked quietly.

'I think so. He liked your style, Henry!'

'Some style!' Blackstone clearly was amused. 'A padded hammer – he could have jumped the other way all too easily.'

'A padded hammer came my way at the Church reception. One of my constituents tracked me down and started haranguing me about the iniquity of the levy. He'd re-mortgaged his house to prop up his business, and in the current climate things weren't going well. "Now you're hitting me with a levy, and the only growth I have is negative equity." Those were his very words.'

'Bill, there's no quick fix, and few pills are without their side effects!'

'Don't tell me!'

'And Bill, the pills of nature's law are no exception. They can be bitter pills, for bad habits are not discarded easily. Society's addiction to real-estate caused the spiralling property values and their inevitable collapse. Ridding ourselves of this addiction *will* have side effects – even withdrawal symptoms! There is real distress out there; mortgage debt, negative equity, repossessions – it's one unholy mess. I need someone to shed fresh light, but, so far, inspiration has eluded me. Bill, we need a policy, we can't just grit our teeth and say, *too bad*.'

Chapter Seventeen

Collingwood arrived at the Treasury at a quarter to ten and was welcomed by Jake Hud. The committee were standing in knots, having coffee, and at five to ten the Chancellor swept in. Seeing Collingwood's soldierly-looking figure, he immediately approached.

'Good to have you on board, Alexander,' he said, extending his hand. 'This shouldn't take too long,' he added briskly. The Chancellor, James Jamieson, had a well-fed look, a man used to dining out. He spoke in a measured tone. Yes, Collingwood thought, a careful man.

'We're agreed,' he began, 'that these self-assessment forms will be posted to all council tax and unified business ratepayers. The forms will also be available in post offices.'

He looked around the assembled committee and received nods of agreement.

'Will we get them back? Will they understand them? And will there not be mass evasion? What's to stop them "forgetting" the odd half-acre, as it were? Enlighten me, gentlemen!' The tone was not that of one who was in tune with the proposal.

Jamieson's less than enthusiastic attitude had antagonised some of the committee and their reactions reflected this. Eventually Jake Hud got to his feet.

'We'll get the forms back. We're a law-abiding lot. Hell, even I am!'

There was a burst of laughter, which the Chancellor acknowledged briefly with a smile.

'Will they understand them?' Jake continued. 'Two neighbours close to my suburban semi fought for months over where the fences had been put, and that was only inches. People know exactly what they own! Will they go down the evasion route? They would be very foolish. For what remains unclaimed can be re-allocated by the community. You can't hide land underneath the bed.'

'I wish I could be sure. The Revenue spend a fortune trying to beat the problem. Evasion's like a national pastime.'

'I'm not surprised, Chancellor, with the mad hat taxes that you levy!'

More laughter followed, but it was obvious to Collingwood that Jamieson didn't like it.

'Chancellor, this is what the location levy's all about. It's about collecting what the community creates by its very presence. It's not about plundering the earnings of the people. Every time they go to a restaurant, every time they have a drink, every time they get in their car, every time they try to fix the roof, you name it, the taxman's there. No wonder there's evasion!'

'Jake, as usual you put your point with vigour. But say there is a plot of land locked away without access to a road. It could be easily forgotten.'

'Not by the neighbours, Chancellor! Remember landholding declarations will be publicly displayed.'

'Well, Jake, there's no doubt about your commitment, but I'm the Chancellor and the buck stops here!'

The buck stops with Henry, Chancellor! But Jake said nothing.

'This is a wholly new departure,' Jamieson continued, 'a step into the unknown, and in the middle of the current crisis, it could be seen as reckless. Income tax is a standard rate across the board. Given the rate and given the wage, you can work it out, but this new impost varies with location. The public are sure to be confused.'

'Chancellor, if they cope with council tax, they can cope with this,' Tommy Thompson interjected.

'Chancellor, I can understand your concerns,' Jake cut in. 'They're natural. But as far as I'm concerned the *status quo* is reckless, in fact, it's bloody daft!'

'Put with your usual deftness, Jake,' the Chancellor reacted with a smile.

'Chancellor, my accountant grumbles that he has to go on regular seminars to bone up on the latest complications. *He* says it's bloody daft! Chancellor, we're simply proposing to take what all of us, that is the community, creates, and leave to the individual what he or she creates. What's reckless about that?'

'Jake, there are plenty out there who'll take great pains to tell us just how reckless it is – from the City corporation to the suburban semi that you mentioned, they'll be screaming. We need a miracle!'

For a moment there was silence.

'Would you like to say something, Mr Collingwood?' The Chancellor asked.

'I've just thought of Victor Hugo's famous words, and I paraphrase: "Stronger than all the armies of the world is an idea whose time is come."'

'Top that!' Tommy Thompson piped up, and all, including the Chancellor, started laughing.

They continued pursuing organisational factors for a time, and then suddenly the meeting was over. The Chancellor beckoned Collingwood.

'The PM suggested you pop round.'

'Was a time mentioned?'

'No. Just when you were finished here, I gathered'

*

It was showery, but Collingwood didn't have to use his umbrella on the short walk to Downing Street. On arrival he was taken to the Prime Minister's study immediately.

Blackstone was on the phone and pointed to an easy chair.

'I know it's difficult Sam, but hold your ground... I know, we don't want ambitious egos using this to snipe at you... Yes, butter them up, get them on your side before you act ... yes, I know, Sam, solidarity is the union's strength, but when it comes to snakes and scorpions, keep your distance and your powder dry ... good luck, Sam ... the road's uphill, I know, but you can climb it' ... Blackstone laughed. 'You're an old pro – go for it, and, Sam, thanks for keeping me in touch.'

'Sam Redwell, I presume.' Collingwood said lightly.

'Yes, Sam's all right. He's a decent sort of chap when he drops that general secretary mindset. Now, Alexander, thanks for coming round. I've just heard that another building society is in trouble. God, it's coming thick and fast. I'm tempted to use a development bank injection to bale them out, but I don't think you'd approve.'

'It's the last thing you should do, Sir. Development funding can only be used for needed infrastructure projects that will raise the wealth and the location revenue potential of the community. Otherwise you're risking gross inflation.'

'I thought that's what you would say. But, Alexander, if this building society goes, it could be like a pack of cards. It could send others tumbling. We can't just let it happen!'

'What about the major banks and the Bank of England? Can they not gather round?'

'They're dragging their heels, and the BoE is reluctant to step in again! It disturbed my sleep last night. That's the first time. No wonder Pitt knocked back the port! It's the building societies that have metamorphosed into banks. Soaring house prices, the easing of mortgage rules, and as you said, using mortgage debt as security, when that debt was far from safe.'

'Well, we can't tell people not to panic. That's the first thing that they'd do. That building society: how bad is it?' Collingwood asked.

'They can hold out, but the figures aren't good and the shareholders are kicking up a fuss – in fact shooting themselves in the foot.'

'So we're on the precipice without a safety net!'

'I'm afraid so. Alexander, another collapse could trigger an avalanche,' Blackstone responded flatly.

'It will, if they stand around like paralysed rabbits waiting for the BoE to bale them out. Why don't they use their contacts, and work something out for themselves?'

'They tried that and got their fingers burnt. I fear that self-preservation has built a wall of caution.'

'Yes, but preservation is best served by cooperation. The trouble is the banks don't trust each other, for they know that toxic debt's a ghost in every boardroom!' Collingwood smiled. 'Prime Minister, I'm afraid you'll have to exercise your famed persuasive rhetoric!'

'What, again?'

They laughed grimly.

'Henry, we can't just keep on borrowing! Thomas Jefferson was pretty strong on this. *We must not let our rulers load us with perpetual debt. We must make our selection between economy and liberty, or profusion and servitude.*'[1]

'Jefferson knew a thing or six! Well, it looks as if I'm going to have to use this rhetoric you say I'm saddled with! Otherwise, it's another Bank of England intervention. That would keep the stopper in the bath but the signals are far from satisfactory – like, don't worry, the BoE will always intervene, and so everything continues in the same old way, *we hope*, until the next blow-up!'

Blackstone was quiet for a time, and Collingwood remained silent. 'Alexander, I'd like to ask you to stay for supper, but the

American ambassador is dropping by for an informal chat about the President's visit on Thursday night. Between that and other things we'll have plenty to talk about. So you'll have to excuse me.'

Blackstone looked exhausted. Even for a young man, the pace had been relentless. One meeting after another, with phone calls in between.

Chapter Eighteen

Anna heard the familiar sound of the letterbox and the thump of the mail falling on the mat. Her father's hearing wasn't what it used to be, and he often didn't hear the telltale sound, even though the sound could be quite loud – which was usually the herald of manuscripts.

After lifting the scattered mail Anna took it to her desk, where she sorted it into various piles. She always opened the hand-written envelopes first. The rest were mostly bills, and communications from printers, designers etc.

The first of the hand-written letters was A5 size and enclosed something that felt like a card. She opened it carefully. It was a post card of the Eiffel Tower. Hardly original, but who was it from? She turned it over.

My dear Anna, I'm here for informal talks with the French President and felt that sending a 'having a lovely time, wish you were here' card might promote a sense of normality for this embattled PM with only thirty percent approval. Tell your father I brought up the subject of Anne-Robert Turgot, the French eighteenth-century philosopher statesman, during the evening meal and I was immediately engulfed by Gallic charm. Turgot is a hero of the President! However, I'll tell you all about it when I return. Love, Henry.

She stared at the card for a moment as if it were unreal. Then she raced into her father's study.

'A card from Henry,' she called out flippantly, failing to disguise her excitement. 'He's been in Paris, for a meeting with the President.'

'Yes, the French are in just as big a mess as we are.' He smiled. His daughter was elated and was looking radiant.

'Father, I'm very excited. It's all a bit childish. I'm not used to it!'

'Anna dear, it's quite natural to be excited. To be invited out to dinner by the Prime Minister is pretty unique. And my dear, you're obviously very fond of each other. Even your father can see it!'

They both laughed.

'I'm worried about being excited on Thursday and letting Henry down.'

'You'll be all right. A little tip: pay attention to the ordinary things like walking, sitting down, taking a glass of sherry from a tray, in fact, all the simple actions; it helps to still the mind. Anna, you'll be fine, and in any case, Henry will look after you.'

He would, of course, but Henry was PM, he had a role to play, and she would have to play her part amongst experienced ladies such as the President's wife. Thursday would be challenging. She wanted to go and she didn't want to go. It was a playground for doubt, and doubt was keen to play. But dropping out was not an option, and when it came to it, of course, the greater part of her was buzzing with anticipation.

*

Blackstone joked with Willie Windbourne about his latest adventures abroad, while alert to the mood of the Cabinet Members as they gathered. Some entered briskly, others with a casual ease, while a good number arrived busy in conversation with a colleague or colleagues. Somehow he felt uneasy. Two 'blimps' from his own party were in earnest conversation with the Chancellor. A strange alliance, if it were an alliance. Normally Blackstone wouldn't have taken much notice of such particulars, but this morning's meeting was crucial and a rebellion in the ranks would be destructive.

He was introducing the 'bread and butter' approach of free credit for public infrastructure works, and location value levy to fund income tax easement. If the figures added up he would also raise the threshold. In the best of days the package would outrage the vested interest element, the 'blimps' being the predictable spokesmen. He certainly expected sparks to fly, but if such a grouping had been plotting to oppose his moves, the imminent Cabinet meeting would be difficult – to say the very least. He would have to fight, for the option of washing his hands of it all and resigning wasn't on. In Blackstone's mind the nation's need was paramount. No one had suggested any other solution to the disaster, except draconian retrenchment, which, in Blackstone's mind, was wholly unacceptable. Indeed, the situation was desperate. It was like the five-minute warning before the rockets flew. He *had* to push his 'bread and butter' job through.

Who could he rely on? Willy, of course, and Bill would back him also. Then there were Jake and Chris. Winston Hughes was positive; he was on his way, but traffic could easily delay him. The Industry Secretary, Ted Banks, was very much on his side and there were three more he could count on. The Chancellor was almost certainly in the anti camp, even though he'd made a show of being conciliatory. He had allies, but the rest hadn't put their heads above the parapet. So uncertainty ruled, just as it did elsewhere. Where was Jake? He was a key spokesman and Bill, but there he was just coming through the door.

'Is Jake out there, Bill?' he called out.

'There's an unofficial protest march causing traffic chaos. The police are doing what they can, but it's clearly been organised to cause maximum disruption. He's probably held up by that.'

'Probably leading it!' Chris Crouch burst out, sparking laughter.

'Where were you hiding, Chris? I didn't see you.' Blackstone interjected.

'I'm pretty thin, so if I'm standing sideways...' Laughter bubbled round the Cabinet table, but the Chancellor only smiled.

'We'll have to feed you up! Ah, here's Jake.'

'Sorry, Prime Minister.'

'It's all right, I've just learned you've been marching.'

'You've got it! An ugly lot, Sir, either to the left of Mao or the right of Genghis Khan, but then there isn't much difference! The police were in pretty close attendance.'

Blackstone looked around the table.

'Well, ladies and gentlemen, this, if we need it, is further evidence of the nation's troubled state. Something has to be done and I'm hoping for your full cooperation on the proposals outlined in the papers you've received.' He smiled, while very aware of the Chancellor's agitated state. It was unlike him, for he always projected a persona of stability.

'You have, of course, heard these ideas voiced before. But often, with the all-pervading press in tow, it is difficult to speak freely. Now we can, for I find it hard to imagine any of you "telling all" to a gossip-hungry press. So let's have your questions, your objections or indeed your endorsements!'

Bill Jones, sitting at Blackstone's side, could only admire the young PM's approach. He was effectively boxing the Cabinet members in with praise, while also heaping on the pressure. The Chancellor was clearly ill at ease, and Bill guessed the reason. He'd been talking to his City friends, and they had pumped him full of doubt.

It was one of the 'blimps' that spoke first.

95

'This location tax is very unpopular Prime Minister. Most of my constituents see it as a direct attack on hard-working people who've built up some capital.'

'William, the location levy, I would suggest, is not a tax, but a duty due. It's like holding someone else's money that you feel you should return. Location value is created by the community. That is simple fact; the bottom line, if you like. You tell me this measure is unpopular, but then the truth often is. And William, do we tell our constituents the truth, or simply what they want to hear?'

'But is it the truth before its time?'

'A good question, and one I've pondered. William, I see no other way and I do believe this *is* the time!'

'Prime Minister, "who dares, wins" may be a fitting motto for the SAS, but is it how the government should be acting?' The questioner, Charlie Cox, was Education Minister. Blackstone viewed him as a man who thought things through; a good man to have on board.

'A fair point, Charlie, and again one I've pondered. I could answer that things couldn't be much worse, but that of course is not the answer. Charlie, I firmly believe this measure to be true, and the truth is not a gamble!'

'All this business about the truth is a turn-off for a lot of people. Your truth, my truth – so what, they say; it's all relative,' the Northern Ireland Secretary interjected.

Blackstone smiled.

'I agree, Jim, it is a problem and one the thinking class, if I may use the term, often labours.' Jim Burns was another interesting man and one to watch. 'While I would agree that caution is obligatory in the sifting of opinion,' the PM continued, 'I would assert that an excess of relativism ends in a *cul de sac*. Plain speaking cuts through all of this, and this is what is needed when explaining the location value measure. *Knowledge is simply recollection.*[1] These words of Socrates I remember from my school days. If we explain location value straight, the people will recognise its simplicity – and, dare I say it, because it's true! Location value is clearly created by the community's presence. If the yearly levy is not collected it becomes a capital asset for the holder, and if this continues the uncollected sum builds up to be a tidy total. This capital value we call house prices – a combination of bricks and mortar and location value. Now we all know that houses need maintaining, so most of the so-called house price is, in fact, location value – the naturally created community fund. In the current set-up this is not collected, but owned mostly by private interests. As we can observe, such assets are greatly sought after and people take on life-long mortgages for the privilege. The banks and money follow. We require it and they are the providers! The question is: do we ignore these facts and simply carry on, knowing in a few years' time we'll once more hit the buffers?'

This isn't a Cabinet Meeting; it's a bloody seminar! Bill Jones thought wryly. Certainly, Henry was holding their attention. He glanced across at James. Jamieson looked much more at ease. Maybe he'd been re-persuaded, by Henry's answers. The Chancellor was like a character in one of his old history books. 'Bobbing John' they called him; some ancient noble who was forever changing sides. Did he keep that book? He had no idea.

Blackstone continued to field questions, when, much to his relief, Winston Hughes appeared.

'Not an easy journey, Prime Minister. Anyway, here I am, back from the troubled North.'

'How troubled, Winston?'

'Simmering. It could blow at any moment.'

'Well, you'll be pleased to know that I've just announced a massive infrastructure project for the area.'

'Thank God for that!'

'Prime Minister,' the Chancellor began. He shifted in his chair with the deliberation of a potentate. 'My officials are concerned at the issuing of such a towering total of free credit.'

'Is not the City a little miffed as well?' Blackstone smiled knowingly, and the Chancellor could do little but agree.

'Inflation is the ghost, Prime Minister. The fear that it will issue forth is real.'

'This injection of credit is being raised by a Bank of England development agency, specially set up for the purpose. It is interest free. There are no capital moguls to reward, and I fully appreciate that the City will be less than pleased. This is credit for practical projects. There will be no grandiose schemes to bolster town hall pride! As you know, the Treasury have been fully informed. But, of course, you're right to bring the matter up. If I may recall Charlie Cox's point, this is indeed another "who dares wins" situation. Ladies and gentlemen, I can see no alternative. Remember real community wealth will be created by these funded projects. They will enhance location value and the levy that we hope to introduce will retrieve much of this value. These are real changes – not rhetorical flourishes to boost our ratings! And, James, we have no desire to "punish" the City. That would be as foolish as throwing the baby out with the bath water.'

The Chancellor nodded sagely. Bill Jones smiled. James had bobbed again!

The questions continued focusing on application. Here Blackstone called on Jake Hud to outline the progress made in this area, and it was obvious that the Cabinet members were impressed. But it was also obvious from the questions that many of the ministers round the table hadn't done their homework and their understanding, though awakened, remained superficial. Maybe Alexander could address them. There was so much to do. Ted Banks was in contact with the CBI, and had done a good job in reassuring the bosses of industry. Of course, the infrastructure projects had greatly helped, but Blackstone knew he had to get involved himself. The PM was the PM, and his presence and attention gave a lift. Blackstone wasn't fooled. It was the office that did it. He had intended seeing Sam Redwell again. The TUC boss had done well to end the wildcat strike. He had thanked him by phone, but he needed to meet up with him, and hopefully, cement the trust. Time, time, there seemed to be so little of it. Then he remembered what his father had told him all those years ago. 'Stay in the present, Henry, and give measure to your thinking.' At once he ceased his reverie.

Jake's address was drawing to a close, and it was time to bring the meeting to an end, but before doing so he needed an assurance of Cabinet solidarity.

'What's that noise?' he interjected.

'The march Prime Minister, they're chanting and shouting at the bottom of Downing Street.'

'As the saying goes, a bit too close for comfort and a reminder just how dire the situation is!'

He paused, his mood reflective.

'We're at the early stages of a National Government, the unblemished stage,' he began, 'but after looking round the Cabinet table at you lot, I pause.'

There was a ripple of laughter.

'Jokes aside, we have a rare window of opportunity, and I believe a chance to do some good. But I need your support or at the very least your acquiescence. Of recent years Cabinets have not been models of solidarity, but in the current crisis such indiscipline would be irresponsible. "Sources close to Government" revelations are out. And should you not agree with Government policy, have the matter out, but in this room.' He scanned the twenty Ministers seated round the table. Is this acceptable?' He smiled. 'You will recall the words followed by that ominous pause. "Speak now or for ever hold your peace."'

There was more laughter, and then unexpectedly a Labour member raised his hand.

'What's the problem, Samuel?'

'I can't live with this plunder of a family's property!'

'Samuel, you're an honest man. We need you, and before you take decisions that you can't reverse, see me personally.'

'Thank you, Prime Minister.'

'I'll get Jenny to phone you, all right?'

Samuel Bennett nodded.

The meeting was over, and Blackstone sat unmoving. The leather-bound ministerial folders were no longer neat and uniform. Some were closed and some lay open, but by the evening they would all be neat again. The room was certainly elegant. He had read somewhere that the Duke of Portland had enlarged Walpole's study and this was the result.

Would the Cabinet hold together? He'd done his best to play the reasonable card and he could only hope good sense would, in the end, prevail. If not, he would have to wield the axe. He didn't want to, but if the need arose, he would. Suddenly he was tired. Then he remembered that the raising of the tax threshold, and the general easing of income tax, hadn't been discussed. In fact, the raising of the threshold could greatly help the marginal areas, but leave it, Blackstone: that was for another day.

'What got into Samuel, Bill?' he asked casually. Jones, like him, was still sitting.

'Yes, he's usually absolutely solid. He was left some rather nice property, and that possibly explains it.' Jones replied.

'It's all so silly. The way that some folk talk you'd think we were taking the lot. In fact, if they but knew it, they'd probably be better off. Well, Bill, we may have carried the Cabinet, but will we carry the Commons? That's the big one, and the vested interests will be rampant.'

'My land, my house are very dear, Henry.'

'I know. We're up against some rather basic stuff.'

99

Chapter Nineteen

Winston Hughes, the Home Secretary, was the kind of man that people turned to naturally as a confidant. He rarely said much and he very rarely gave advice: he simply listened. As an arbiter between opposing forces, he was quietly effective, for people naturally trusted him. Indeed, his efforts in the North had done much to calm the situation. Presently he was closeted with Jake Hud, hearing what was little less than a confession.

'You know, Winston, I was a bastard in the way I treated Bill. I really was. We get on well now, but somehow I haven't made my feelings plain. Winston, I need to apologise, but I haven't found the moment, for it has to be natural, not some crawling sugary thing.'

Winston nodded but said nothing. Jake wouldn't let it pass.

'What do you think?' he prompted, his sharp features full of concentration.

Winston pondered.

'You could make it public. There'll be an opportunity to say something in a speech, and such a statement can be very effective.'

'You've got it, Winston. Yeah, it sounds right.'

They were still sitting at the corner of the table in the Cabinet Room. Sensing it was time to move, they both stood up as if ordered by a single mind. Then the conversation started up again.

'As ex-premier, Bill has never shown any resentment towards Henry,' Jake said plainly. 'Winston, it takes a big man to act like that. And Henry, hell, he's ageless. Maybe one day the people will waken up and realise how bloody lucky they are! These low ratings are mindless!'

*

Mabel had prepared some lunch for 'Mr Bob' and 'Mr Henry' and both men were lavish in their compliments. Mabel loved it.

'It's nice to see you two so friendly like,' she said in a motherly way.

Both men were much amused before continuing with their conversation.

'I think they'll hold, Henry.' Jones said reflectively. 'And that chanting at the end of Downing Street brought things home to us. Things are bad, and the repossession figures are appalling. The distress that must be causing.'

'It's not done to kick a man when he's down, but that's exactly what we're doing with these repossessions. Someone's made redundant. That's bad enough. Then they take their house away! And we're supposed to be civilised!' As you know, we've asked the Council of Mortgage Lenders to suspend repossessions. What would they be doing with the houses anyway?'

'Sell them off to speculators, who'd simply wait until market started to recover.'

'You could be right, Bill. But this time it may not be so easy. This isn't like eight years ago when we had a dip. This is the big one, and they could find they have to wait awhile! My God, what a mess we've got ourselves into. And we can't just let the mortgage companies go to the wall, though, mind you, my sympathy is somewhat cool, knowing some of the dodgy mortgages they were handing out. Then there's the small investor. Bill, it's just struck me: what if we offer Samuel Bennett this nightmare?'

'That's wicked, Henry. It's a poisoned chalice!'

'It came to me, under the radar, as it were. Samuel's a bit of a terrier and he's a decent man. He'd be strictly fair.'

'I'd say it's a gamble.'

'Maybe, but I'll take it. I treat these sudden inspirations fairly seriously!'

Jones chuckled.

'Bill, how do you get on with the TUC boss Sam Redwell?'

'Friendly enough, I've always seen him as a bit of a fixer.'

'He certainly saved the day at the power station dispute. It would be nice if you could encourage him with a thank-you phone call. You know, these gestures can mean a lot. Bill, in my book Redwell's a key man, and I've got Chris nagging him. As you know, Chris Crouch is a likeable so and so, and he and Sam get on quite well. We need to keep a watch on these extremist nutters, and Sam's the man to do it. What do you think?'

'To put it plainly, Sam and I were never pals. Our relationship was cordial – a word that covers many cracks. But, of course, I'll give him a buzz. One thing, it can do no harm. You're concerned about these wildcat outbursts, Henry?'

'Yes, Bill, and the religious fanatics who think they've got God's e-mail. I see them both as nihilists, an accusation they and their apologists would vehemently reject. But there it is. These people pop up in history from time to time.'

They sat quietly eating for a time.

'The US President is due here at Number Ten tomorrow afternoon for informal talks,' Blackstone said breaking the silence. 'Would you like to join us?'

'Thanks for the offer, but I think not, Henry. I'd be unnecessary baggage. No, better not. Anyhow, I'm meeting him tomorrow evening at the Residence in Regent's Park. You'll like him. He's very easy to get on with.'

'I've invited Anna Collingwood as my partner,' Blackstone said quietly. 'Maybe your wife could keep a motherly eye.'

'Henry, Anna Collingwood will have every head turning. She'll be the belle of the occasion. You're a very lucky chap!'

'You don't have to tell me.'

Blackstone noticed the warmth in his Deputy's eyes, and he suddenly felt very close to this man who, only weeks ago, he'd been attacking from the despatch box in the House of Commons.

*

As soon as Bill Jones, left the internal phone buzzed. It was Jenny, reminding him that his Constituency Chairman was due. A few seconds later the phone buzzed again. Sir Robert Cowdrey had arrived.

'I'll come down and collect him, Jenny.' He smiled. Constituency chairmen were best handled with care.

Sir Robert was a former rugby player, in fact, a one time international and when his large-proportioned hand stretched out, gripping it was quite approximate.

After the usual *bonhomie,* Blackstone escorted his guest to the study.

'Tea will be with us shortly, Robert.'

'Good.' Cowdrey scanned the room. 'This place suits you, Henry!'

Blackstone burst out laughing.

'Yes, Robert, and it's rent free!'

Cowdrey's laugh reflected his size.

'So what's the mood in the Constituency?'

'Mixed, Henry, mixed. They're proud of you. Hell, even I am! But this location tax has made them edgy. They're confused. Can't say that I understand all the ins and outs. There are a couple of busy-bodies stirring up trouble. They're calling the Cabinet a bunch of "lefties". And they're saying that Jake Hud's got you in his pocket! They're attacking you openly and canvassing support, but they're too pushy. Nobody likes them much. Anyway, I'm keeping my ear to the ground.'

'Who are they?'

'Ed Semple and Jo Jacobs.'

'Maybe I should pay a "surprise" visit.'

'Great idea. You need to explain yourself, Henry. You're taxing the nest-egg; there'll be nothing for the grandchildren. It's emotive stuff, Prime Minister!'

'Robert, for most there's nothing for the children, never mind the grandchildren!'

'We can't *all* win the lottery.'

'No, but we can *all* win justice. We can *all* win access to the earth, on paying the due location levy.'

'And what is that?'

'The yearly rental value, which is fixed by the simple working of the market.'

'Semple says he can't make up his mind whether its fascism or socialism.'

'It's neither a fascist rant, nor a socialist duvet. As long as they obey the law, men and women should be free to find their own way in this world. Ah, here's the tea.'

'I need it. Even I can see you're on to something big – yes, big!'

For a time they reverted to constituency gossip and laughter was frequent.

'Henry, to return to this location business; what about buildings? What about bricks and mortar? I know you explained it over the phone, but can you indulge me with another run through?'

'Buildings are the product of human labour and are not subject to the levy. So there is no tax on what a citizen creates, but there is a levy on what the community creates by its collective presence, that is, location value. Indeed, we're back to where we started, for with the bricks and mortar we have our nest-egg! Indeed, we all could own our nest-egg while being subject to location levy. Think of it! The haves and have-nots of today would pass away!'

Once more they reverted to routine matters of the constituency, and then Sir Robert began to take his leave.

'Henry, I hope I haven't taken up too much of your time.'

'Never Robert, don't even think it! Your report and questions have been very useful. Robert, you never stop learning in this game. And do you know something?'

'What's that?'

'Every MP should have a Sir Robert Cowdrey!'

'Henry, you're an old charmer!'

They both laughed heartily.

'Henry, I must add a cautionary note. This bod Semple isn't nice. Plausible yes, when he wants something. I've met these sort of guys before. They're always smiling, but when they're promoted to C/O, run for cover.'

Sir Robert had been in Army Intelligence in his early days. He wasn't a fool, and Blackstone took such warnings seriously.

'Thanks, Robert.'

Blackstone was pensive for a time before broaching the vexed subject of party discontent: one that was a constant background worry. Another under-the-radar idea had just struck him, and, faithful to his nature, he decided to act.

'Robert, we're old friends, so I feel I can speak openly, and, of course, I know that you're a clam. The truth is, I'm concerned about party unity. There are two bods – the most active being that south-coast MP, Harbin – who have made themselves the self-appointed leaders of opposition to the levy.'

'Within the party?'

'Yes, I fear a party split. Luckily these guys are not the brightest. Bears, with little brain, if I may paraphrase. But we need to keep the lid on this whole business. A party rift would be very awkward. So far the big hitters haven't signed up, but we can't just let the matter drift. Would you be willing to chair a panel that dealt with MP's concerns? It won't be an easy one, Robert; you'd need all your famous people-skills! Would you be willing?'

'Henry, I'd be honoured.'

'You're a good man, Robert, and a damned good friend. I appreciate your support. As the idea has just occurred to me, I haven't thought of panellists. Probably a "traditional" from the Lords and also a Commons ally. Alexander Collingwood, whom I told you about some time ago, and, perhaps, the broadcaster, Jasper Jenkins, who will no doubt add a touch of humour. I'll think of others I'm sure.'

'You've given me quite a task, Henry.'

'Yes, and one that fits you like a glove!'

*

Samuel Bennett arrived twenty minutes early at Number Ten. It was his nature. He was always early for appointments, but Blackstone saw him immediately. With his glasses, his studious look and his grey hair, Bennett looked more like a professor than a politician. That was the PM's assessment as he watched him enter. .

'Sorry for the early appointment, Samuel, but I'm meeting the President in not too many hours, so, as usual, time is rather scarce. Have a seat.'

'Thanks for seeing me at once, Prime Minister. I'm sorry about causing a fuss yesterday, but I accept...'

'Don't worry about that, Samuel. The truth is I called you in about something else.'

Bennett's face reflected a confusion of emotions, but he still felt that he was 'on the carpet.'

'I don't want to make a fuss, Prime Minister, but I can't honestly say that I'm with you on this location value measure.'

'Yes, Samuel. Now, how much do you know about the mortgage business?'

'Very little, Prime Minister.'

'That may be all to the good. Samuel, repossessions have been growing at a distressing rate. Presently we've agreed a suspension, but that's only temporary. We need some fresh thinking and I'm looking to you.'

'Prime Minister, I've no experience...'

'Samuel,' Blackstone cut in. 'How much experience had you in Transport?'

'Not much.'

'Exactly! You've a damned good mind. Just see if you can see a way to ease this nightmare.'

'It's a complicated world, Prime Minister.'

'Yes, Samuel, and this race for ownership has left us panting and exhausted. Why do men and women commit themselves to crippling debt that lingers till old age? Is this property-owning democracy a golden age or a nightmare? We're all right, Jack! We've got property, but what about the young, with their start-up problems, the negative equity and, of course, at worst the repossession notice? Ask questions, Samuel, you're good at that. I've heard about your sudden inspirations.'

'Prime Minister, I'm overwhelmed. This is coalface stuff. I'll do what I can, Sir.'

'Good.' Blackstone smiled knowingly. 'Samuel, we haven't much time. This is priority!' He bowed his head in reflection. 'Hey, I didn't offer you a coffee! I take it you could use one?'

'Yes, Sir. After what you've said I need it!'

Chapter Twenty

The famous door was opened for him as he approached, and after acknowledging the doorman, Samuel Bennett stepped out into the morning sunshine, turned left and headed for Whitehall. At once he recognised the familiar figure of Jake Hud, who was approaching at his usual vigorous pace.

'Did you get the sack, Samuel?' Jake called out jauntily.

'Jake, you should join the diplomatic corps!'

'It's bloody obvious you didn't get the push. You're bouncing along like a two-year-old!'

Bennett burst out laughing.

'Well?' Jake prompted.

'Jake, I tried to bring the matter up twice ...'

'And he brushed it aside!' Hud interrupted.

'How did you know?'

'Let's call it an educated guess. Now here's another guess; he gave you a job!'

'You're getting psychic.'

'One of my minor achievements.'

'Jake, how would you deal with these repossessions?'

'God! Pull the blankets over my head!'

'And the mortgage lenders?'

'Tow them out to the middle of the Atlantic and pull the bloody plug! My God, it's just struck me. The PM's given you the mortgage problem!' Jake doubled up laughing. Then for a moment, he straightened himself. 'When are you swallowing the bloody hemlock?'

'Dawn!'

This time both men laughed.

'How would I deal with repossessions, you asked?' Jake repeated quietly. 'I'd play with two words: forgiveness and responsibility.'

'Thanks, Jake.'

*

Jasper Jenkins, once an anathema to the Number Ten press office, now found himself their favourite media contact, something that the BBC was happy to exploit. Today was big news day, for the US President, Andrew Crosbie, was making a brief call on Downing Street's new incumbent.

Crosbie was a well-built man with a TV-friendly smile and a generous mop of hair resembling Bobby Kennedy. Jasper had clashed with him at a briefing, but then he'd clashed with most people. Henry Blackstone, though, had turned the tables and left him gabbling at thin air. That and Jake Hud's colourful home truths had, for some unbidden reason, woken him up, and the stream of negativity, that he had thought was clever, now was viewed as simply pointless. Why had he changed? It was still a puzzle, for there'd been no great inner searching. Yet he felt sure that something had broken through the outer wall.

Such were his musings as he waited for Blackstone and Crosbie to appear. But Jasper wasn't good at waiting. He simmered, his energy just within control. He was like a sleek but restless dog, forever sniffing the air and poised for action.

The two leaders were conducting their joint statement inside rather than the fashionable twin lectern setting outside the front door. There was a buzz of conversation rising and falling in volume, then, exactly on time, the two men entered.

Blackstone spoke first.

'Good afternoon, ladies and gentlemen, and thank you for your presence. We are, of course, very pleased to welcome the President to Downing Street. It's not the first time he has entered this old building, but it's his first time to meet a chap called Blackstone. I think he's got over the shock!'

There was some laughter and the President grinned widely.

Blackstone continued.

'We, the President and Prime Minister, are the current representatives of trusted allies, and friendship is easily confirmed. Again, shared interests and common aspirations unite us in natural alliance. Adversity has drawn us together in the past, and presently economic problems beset us both. These we have discussed in detail and much useful information has been exchanged. Indeed, our mutual concern is the welfare of the people and the taming of that ravenous beast called poverty – Mr President.'

'Prime Minister, thank you for your kind words. The American people have a soft spot for Britain, and if we have the occasional tiff, well, it's a family one. But when the chips are down we are together, *and* we are together now. As the Prime Minister said, we had detailed discussions and I was particularly interested in the tax-shift proposals. Listen, I can't say any more, otherwise I'd be accused of interfering in your domestic scene. Of course, when it comes to foreign policy we're like twins. – Prime Minister.'

'Thank you, Mr President, for your generous response.' He smiled. 'I feel we ought to face the music. Ladies and gentlemen, you have been very patient. Your questions!'

'Prime Minister.' The reaction from one of the journalists was immediate. 'You keep talking, but when are you going to do something? House prices don't know how far to sink. They've lost the floor. Repossessions are predicted to hit record levels. Prime Minister, this tax-shift thing won't help!'

'The shift in tax from earnings to a location value levy will, in time, give general benefit. But for those locked in the current system and saddled with repossession some mitigating force is needed. Samuel Bennett was appointed this morning to oversee the matter. As you may have heard, repossessions have been frozen. That, of course, is a temporary agreement with the mortgage lenders. Mr President, you may wish to comment?'

'We have same problem in the States, but I have no magic answer. We all have to share the burden. We all need to show compassion. Our common humanity will see us through, but if we all grab what's our own regardless of our neighbour, we risk the whole show coming down about our ears. Prime Minister, I'm afraid this is one of my things. I'm tired of this outdated fashion that business ruthlessness is clever and that such cleverness delivers.'

'Bravo, Mr President, I wish I'd said that!'

There was general amusement.

'Prime Minister, this self-help is fair enough but you are the government. It's your job to do something.'

'Willy, you've got a point, but beware of the "them and us" factor. "They should do this. They haven't done that. If they had done that, this wouldn't have happened." We are all they; or if you like, we are all us!'

'Prime Minister, the reason for a location value levy is convincing. I for one can find no fault in it, but *will* the House of Commons pass it?' Jenkins questioned forcefully.

'Jasper, the Commons, along with the great offices of state, are the guardians of our liberties. We must respect their will. We will present our case and fight our corner and, trusting in the good sense of the Commons, we hope that reason will prevail. What people really want is security of tenure. There is no threat to that; indeed, the location charge will be minimal in many instances. In any case, the initial rate won't exceed twenty percent. Sudden and dramatic change would be irresponsible. And remember this is a levy on location value; buildings are not included and remain a private matter. The Location Levy isn't simply another tax. Location value arises naturally within a community due to its collective presence. It is the natural fund of the state and, when this fund is claimed by private interests, the state must seek its revenue elsewhere; hence taxes on earnings and production. – Mr President?'

'I never thought that I would ever hear this great principle expounded by an incumbent officer of state. It was my grandfather's life-long message. I grew up with it. It's in my blood. I wish you well; I wish this great country well.'

'Mr President, your words are much appreciated.'

The President smiled knowingly.

'I hope my press officer says the same, but I doubt it!'

The questions then focused on the international scene, an area where the President and Prime Minister were, except for some differences in emphasis, in full agreement. It was also obvious that both men were comfortable in each other's company. In Jasper's opinion, the joint appearance had projected exactly the right impression. The people could have confidence in these men.

✻

After the briefing was over, Jasper Jenkins was whisked away to a nearby venue where two MPs were waiting together with another journalist and, of course, the presenter. There was also a TV link-up with an American network. It was the usual media set piece offering a balance of opinion but almost always ending in a kind of fruitless confrontation. Jasper's thoughts were suddenly arrested. These guys were all in the anti lobby! Was this an oversight or a set-up? It was a good question.

The presenter, Barbara Bentley, first introduced the panel: Herbert Samson, Conservative; Hughie Bell, Labour; Sim Wells,

110

journalist; Jasper Jenkins, journalist and broadcaster and Rick Richards on the screen from New York.

'Mr Samson, maybe you'd like to open the discussion?' she suggested.

Samson nodded.

'The two men were clearly at ease with each other, but my attention was completely caught by the fear that this measure of location tax is going to be foisted on us, with Blackstone using the power of a National Government to do so. This reckless proposal will undermine the banks. It's a direct assault on property, which gives security to pension funds, health insurance and numerous institutions. Need I go on?'

'No!' Jasper interjected, but Barbara Bentley ignored him.

'Mr Bell,' she prompted.

'It's hard to believe, but I agree with Herbert. This proposal is fairyland, and how dare the interfering President endorse it! Let him sort his own mess out. Anyway, this location thing is too obscure. I fail to understand how it can help us in our present situation and I doubt if my constituents do.'

At this stage the presenter brought in Rick Richards, but following a few introductory comments, when he concentrated on the easy working relationship between the two men, the screen went dead. After apologising for technical difficulties, Barbara Bentley turned to Sim Wells.

'Sim,' she prompted.

'It was the usual hands-across-the-sea stuff!' Wells began. His style was pugnacious, full of wit, but never nasty. 'The times I've listened to such predictable gibberish. Is there anything positive I can say? That's a hard one! A substantial US loan would have been useful, but then, they're in as big a fix as we are. As for this tax-shift business – it's too little, too complicated, and a loser on the doorstep. It's pie in the sky, a tree-huggers' budget. It's not saleable. If I were Blackstone, I'd forget it.

'I must say the two men seemed to hit it off. That seemed obvious. There you are, I *have* said something positive!'

'Big deal, Sim,' Jasper reacted.

'Anything more, Sim?' the presenter asked.

Wells shook his head.

'Mr Jenkins,' the presenter prompted.

Jasper smiled. He didn't think that Barbara Bentley liked him much.

'I could say a number of things, like, what briefing did you lot watch? However, I'll subdue my curiosity. Personally, I felt the two leaders were inspirational. Why? Henry Blackstone isn't working to protect some sectional vested interest. He's working to protect the nation and that means all the people. The difficulties Herbert mentions are real enough, but they are difficulties born of our complicated system not of the principle. *It is* simple.'

'Come off it, Jasper...' Bell reacted.

'Hughie,' Jenkins cut in. 'Why don't you have a word with Jake Hud. He'll soon sort you out! And Sim, I liked your "tree huggers' budget". OK, that was funny, but it's musichall. There's more, a lot more, to my old friend Sim than that!'

Jasper had almost taken over, and Barbara Bentley didn't hide her annoyance.

'Mr Jenkins, the chair, please!'

'Madam, I forget myself. My apologies.'

She nodded curtly in acknowledgement.

'Now, gentlemen, most of you have commented on the easy relationship between these two leaders. What benefits will come out of this? Sim, what's your view?'

'Both are preoccupied with their own domestic problems. I doubt if we can expect much.'

'Mr Samson, what's your opinion?'

'Businesses cooperate without the meddling of government, and in the present situation, it's difficult to see what governments can do except make things worse. Something I'm afraid this government is about to do.'

'Herbert's talking nonsense.' Hughie Bell burst out. 'Government can't allow the business world to run around like headless chickens. They've got to act, but not like this deluded government!'

'Well, gentlemen, are there any further points you want to make?' The presenter had pointedly ignored Jasper, but Jasper, being Jasper, didn't let it pass.

'What happened to your question, Barbara? But that's obvious; you're all too busy sniping at the government to answer. Well, whether you want my opinion or not, I'm going to give it! Transatlantic cooperation between administration heads that respect each other can't be bad. There must be beneficial results.'

Suddenly, as if on cue, the TV came to life with Rick Richards in full flow.

'I didn't hear all of that. I could see you all, but you couldn't see me, apparently. Like Jasper Jenkins, I am hopeful. Both Prime Minister Blackstone and President Crosbie are impressive men. We need such leaders at this time and I would say their meeting has been fruitful and fortuitous.'

'I'm sorry, Mr Richards, for the misconnection and also sorry that I have to cut you short as we are running out of time. Thank you all.'

Simon Wells was the only one that spoke to Jasper afterwards. The two MPs left almost immediately, and the presenter busied herself with the technicians.

'Barbara Bentley's the new name, I hear.'

'Yes, Jasper, she didn't seem to like you much!'

'Yeah, and I'm really worried! Hey, where did she get those two bods? They must have picked their minds up at a bloody jumble sale!'

Wells laughed.

'Sim, why don't you give Blackstone a whirl? He's OK!'

'Hell, Jasper, they'd ignore me down the pub!'

Chapter Twenty-One

Anna tried, but found it impossible, to concentrate on the proofs she was reading. So, leaving them aside, she retreated to Kew Gardens, where she spent most of the morning. This evening her relationship with Henry would be public, and being his chosen companion as a guest of the US President was as high as profiles go. Reasonable assumptions would be made, and the press would lead the field. Tomorrow's headlines were predictable. It was inevitable.

Was this the last day she could walk the streets of Richmond without the knowing looks and whispers. 'You're being melodramatic, Anna,' she chastised herself. 'You're not a "celeb" with designer tinted glasses yet!' Even so, this evening with its inevitable photographs would send a message – the Prime Minister had a lady friend. There had been nothing intimate between them, but Anna knew that didn't matter. The die was cast.

Henry didn't seem to worry about any political repercussions, such as tabloid photographs with 'playboy' Prime Minister headlines. Judging by his workload, the poor man probably didn't have the time to fret about such petty sniping. He had planned to pick her up just like 'any decent chap', to use his words, but the talks at Downing Street had made that quite impossible.

She had a sudden impulse to phone her friend Maggie. Maggie had gone native with a Scotsman in the Highlands. Both had fled the city stress, to live the simple life, yet not so simple, it would seem, without mod cons. She pulled out her mobile, but, as she half expected, Maggie's phone was switched off. It was a pity, for Maggie was the only one she felt she could confide in, without an explosion of superlatives.

What of the afternoon? She would watch the TV coverage of the briefings from Number Ten. After that she would dress and wait for the official car. This, indeed, was a defining evening. There was no escaping the conclusion.

Walking out of the gardens, Anna headed for Kew Gardens Station. It was a short and pleasant walk, and quiet. The wind was in the east, and jet noise was absent. The planes would be descending over Windsor. She walked on, enjoying the sun and the refreshing breeze. Then, after browsing in the bookshop near the station entrance, she crossed over to the platform for the Richmond train. It was only then that she noticed the poster. 'Scrap the Levy – Stop the Plunder!' – beneath which was a graphic cartoon of a hand reaching from the sky and extracting a suburban garden. Suddenly it was all very real.

She told her father about the poster immediately she returned.

'We don't stand a chance, Father. Self-interest will win!'

'Don't underestimate the power of reason when its time has come.'

*

She guessed the car was Special Branch. The driver was certainly professional. He had that air of competence and he had a burly-looking companion beside him in the front. This she had half expected, for Henry had hinted that the transport would be 'fairly official'. What she hadn't expected were the motorcycle outriders – three of them!

'We can never be sure of the traffic, ma'am, and you have a rather important appointment,' the driver had explained formally, but he didn't smile. Indeed, it was only when he saw her safely through the door of Number Ten that he showed his warmth. 'Have a nice evening.' The smile was genuine, almost fatherly.

Henry was waiting in the lobby, resplendent in white tie and tails. He looked so very handsome, and any lingering doubts or reservations that she had were swept aside.

He kissed her lightly.

'Anna, my love, you look wonderful, and what a beautiful evening gown, and your cape, too! My dear, you'll completely charm our American hosts.'

'Henry, aren't you exaggerating a little?' she joked, her eyes reflecting her happiness.

'Anna, beauty informed by modesty is a rare thing nowadays. Now, if it's all right with you, I think we can go. The President asked me if we could arrive on the early side. I think he wants to have an informal chat. We got on rather well today. You'll like him, a tall man with a profusion of unruly hair. The First Lady's called Gill; a warm and friendly person. You'll find her easy company.'

This time the security was tight: a car in front and one behind, as well as outriders clearing the traffic. Henry wouldn't say, of course, but Anna sensed there'd been a warning of some sort. Of course, the President's visit was a time of high publicity and a time which dangerous and deluded people could be plotting to exploit.

With the outriders clearing the way, the Jaguar slipped through central London with unhurried ease. Then unexpectedly, or so it seemed, they had arrived. The moment she had thought about, worried about, dreamed about, had come. Everywhere she glanced she saw a camera lens – at least, that was how it appeared. Once inside, however, the cameras disappeared. 'Watch every movement, give it your attention.' Yes, Father, I've remembered. And it was working. She was calm; excitement had not won.

The President was walking towards them with his hand outstretched, while at his side the first lady was taking at least two strides for every ambling one of his. Instinctively she was drawn to them.

'Henry, where did you find this beautiful lady?'

'Mr President, the gods were gracious.'

The introductions proceeded and ended with Mrs Crosbie taking Anna's arm.

'My dear, you gown is lovely, and how refreshing to meet someone who is not a slave to modern exhibitionism.'

Anna laughed lightly.

The two men led the way into a reception room where pre-dinner drinks were waiting.

The President beckoned Anna.

'Henry has just been telling me how you two met up: an amazing story. Gill, you must hear this.'

She drew closer.

'It all started when Anna's father wrote a letter to Henry when he was Leader of the Opposition. It was a shot in the dark. Mr Collingwood wrote about a shift in tax, hoping, with the situation being dire, Henry would respond. Knowing, from my own experience, the mountain of mail that emerges every day, it *was* a long shot. But Henry picked it up and then met Anna's father for a coffee. The two men hit it off, and a dinner was arranged and that's when Henry first set eyes on Anna.'

'What a wonderful story,' the First Lady responded, clapping her hands in delight.

'Yeah, for me it has real appeal,' the President followed, 'for it was prompted by that very principle I heard so much about from Grandfather. You know, I can still hear his voice. I was only a boy then, but I knew it meant a lot to him. I naively brought the subject up in my first term, but it fired a re-run of the civil war!'

'This is your second term, Andrew!' Blackstone prompted.

'Yeah, I got it. No votes to worry about, but, Henry, Congress has!'

'The good horse has been stabled far too long. Show the noble creature his rightful pasture and, when the people see him running in the field, who knows?'

The President smiled, the TV friendly smile that he was famous for.

'Prime Minister, you've got style.'

*

The informal meeting with the President and his lady was soon followed by the main reception. It was a not a large gathering, and those present were mostly prominent embassy officials. There was also an American banker and a few English friends of the Ambassador. The President and the Prime Minister behaved like twins, chatting to the guests in tandem, while Anna and the First Lady circulated in a similar fashion.

If there had been any doubt, there wasn't now. She was the Prime Minister's lady. Her fellow guests assumed it, and their asides would spread. The press, of course, were always hungry for a headline. If they were to know he'd only pecked her on the cheek! But then, they'd never believe it!

As far as any event could claim to be informal in the presence of the President and Prime Minister, the dinner was without official fuss. There were no cameras and the President's after-dinner words were brief. He had 'an early appointment with Air Force One', he revealed, so farewells were sounded at a modest hour.

After a parting wave to the President and his wife, Blackstone and Anna slipped into the back seat of the Jaguar.

'Now,' he said quietly, 'I can leave my lady at her door.'

'How gallant, Sir,' she responded happily.

She wanted to nuzzle close to him, but rather felt it wasn't done. Then he put his arm across and gently drew her to him.

'You were perfect, my love. You charmed the President, and Gill Crosbie, too.'

'The Ambassador was very solicitous.'

'Anna dear, you charmed them all. You even charmed Willie and my sister!'

She chuckled contentedly.

Leaning against Henry, Anna was content and silent.

'Willie was in top form,' she said eventually, but there was no reply and she realised with a knowing smile that he was fast asleep. Poor man, he was probably exhausted. Then she remembered that she'd forgotten all about the poster she had seen at Kew.

*

As his daughter and Henry Blackstone were on the way to Richmond, Alexander Collingwood was watching the late night news panel. He had read that Jasper Jenkins was featuring, and as he was the new dramatic convert to the location value cause, he felt he'd better watch. But he had almost forgotten and had only tuned in over halfway through. He recognised most of the panellists. TUC secretary Sam Redwell, and a reasonably well-known developer: Jasper Jenkins, friendly to the government, and Sim Wells, no doubt chosen for his 'anti' views. It was the usual confrontational set up, and entertaining, if you liked that sort of thing.

The Presenter had just introduced 'the question of the evening' and had called on Hamilton Davis. Davis was a hugely wealthy property developer and his views proved predictable. Indeed, he went into over-drive, calling the tax an attack on liberty, on Britishness and on enterprise. It would cripple pension funds and threaten the banking system. Nothing could be more damaging. Why were we tolerating this nonsense? The Presenter then turned to Sam Redwell.

'As a Trades Unionist, my first duty is to my members, and I know that Henry Blackstone is going to create jobs and it goes without saying that that's good news for my members. You, Hamilton, are not creating jobs. You're cutting back and your duty is to your shareholders. I think I'll go for Blackstone.'

Collingwood smiled. He rather liked Sam Redwell, but he was overdoing it as well. Davies wasn't deliberately cutting jobs. He was trying to keep the show on the road. Both had damaged their argument by being extreme.

The presenter next called on Jenkins, who immediately focused on Davis.

'You let off a lot of steam, but, Hamilton, you're way over the top. Don't worry, your cosy game is still out there. The tax shift wouldn't be much more than fifteen to twenty percent and there would be a corresponding cut in income tax. You're still OK. You can still cream off the community value.'

'I resent this insinuation!'

'And I resent the way you plunder community value. If you're as snow-white as you make out, take your city tower block to the Outer Hebrides. See how many pay your fancy rents out there. Hamilton, you can only charge your rents because of the city community. You may build the building. That is yours, but you don't create location value; the community as a whole does that. If I'm wrong, take your dreaming spires to the Hebrides, as I've just said, and prove me wrong.'

'Outer Hebrides – this is ridiculous,' Davies fumed.

'Sim, maybe you can come to Hamilton's rescue?' the Presenter suggested with studied ease, but this made Davis even more upset.

'I don't need to be rescued!' he barked. 'I need Parliament to waken up and kick out this reckless adolescent.'

'Hamilton, a week ago I might have cheered you on, for I like poking at the mighty and savaging their latest theories. But in this case my "anti" stance was challenged by a friend who's just about as big a cynic as I am. So I had a closer look at what Henry Blackstone was actually saying and, do you know something, he's right! No one man can claim that he created main street wealth. If he did, he'd be the big head of the year. What the PM suggests is sweet reason. I tried to fault it, but I couldn't. Mind you, I didn't like being on the losing side, but then you have to swallow bitter pills sometimes. Hamilton, if I were you I'd have a closer look. I'm glad I did.'

Sim Wells had done the Presenter a favour, and he'd given Hamilton Davis an exit, but Davis didn't take it.

'This panel is packed!'

'Not so, Hamilton: the Beeb didn't know about my change of heart. To put it in grand terms: this is the first time I've gone public.'

'I think we'd better have another question,' the Presenter said diplomatically.

At that moment Collingwood heard the door opening. Anna was back and, by the sound of things, Henry was with her.

'Well?' he called out.

'Father, we had a wonderful evening. Everybody was so friendly.'

'Alexander, Anna charmed them all! Camp David in the Fall is a distinct possibility!'

'So you got on well?'

'We did. Andrew Crosbie is a decent sort of chap. He's twice my age, but that didn't seem to matter. Were you watching the news panel?'

'Yes, not usually my choice, but I noticed that both Jasper Jenkins and Sim Wells were on the programme, so I thought there'd be an entertaining head to head, but I was disappointed. Sim's also joined the happy band!'

'We can thank Jake, for Jake persuaded Jasper and I'd wager Jasper got to Sim. They're friends. Alexander, this won't do us any harm. These men have got fire and they've got a following. So there were no fireworks, then?'

'Oh yes, Jasper clawed at the property tycoon, Hamilton Davis, but Davis wasn't bright enough to reply in kind. In fact, Sim tried to show him the fire exit, but he was too puffed up to take the hint.'

'Alexander, I treat Davis as a kind of accidental ally. His pomposity plays into our hands. But I fear that there are sharper minds waiting in the Commons and I'll have to face them soon. That will be the big one. Defeat would be a disaster.'

'You'll do it!'

Anna had arrived with mugs of tea.

'Henry, do you think the driver and his friend would like a mug? And the outriders too?'

'They'd love it, Anna, but the outriders could be anywhere around the Green.'

When Anna had gone, Blackstone turned to Collingwood confidentially.

'I know we've only known each other a month, but Sir, I feel that your daughter and I should be engaged. Prime Ministers, of all people, should play it straight, especially for Anna's sake.'

Collingwood held his hand out and Blackstone grasped it.

'Henry, as I've said before – thank God she found you!'

'Well, that's that,' Blackstone said as if it were a hurdle cleared. 'Being Prime Minister can be tough, but things that touch the heart take courage too!'

Collingwood's amusement was obvious.

Chapter Twenty-Two

Neither Anna nor her father had expected press coverage the following morning, certainly not to any major extent. So Anna went to the newsagent as usual. She was shocked, for almost every paper had her image on the front page. Indeed, it was a full-length photograph in most cases: the same photograph. The photographer had done well. They must have held the presses back. The Indian newsagent smiled but made no comment. Some customers took furtive glances, while others were stoically aloof. But was this imagination? One way or the other, it was difficult to be certain.

Collingwood joked about it when he saw the photographs, but he didn't talk of his misgivings. His beloved daughter could now be exploited as a pawn to pressurise the government. Kidnap and worse, much worse, were always possible: for one, faith-driven fanatics looking for publicity.

They were still scanning the papers when the phone rang.

'Yes, Henry ... very much so ... I'd love to ... let me out of here, I'm a celebrity ... Yes, I'm off to buy a pair of large dark glasses, you know, the ones the super-models wear. My friend Maggie said it would add the finishing touch ... Yes, he's here ...'

'Henry wants a word, Father.'

'I'll take it in the study.'

'Is Anna still with you?'

'No, she's in the other room.'

'Good. Alexander, this explosion of publicity concerns me, and I fear that Anna will need protection. We'll try to keep it as low key as possible. Need, though, will dictate. So maybe you can break it gently. I'll explain when I see her in two day's time. I've been invited to address a group of top industrialists and their wives attending dinner at a Tower Hill venue. Hopefully we can stem the tide of "anti" propaganda flowing from the property and banking interests. I've asked Anna if she could hold my hand. If you want to come, Alexander, I'm sure my hosts would make you very welcome. Publishers are always popular, for

121

most bods think they've got a book inside waiting for the promised day!'

Collingwood laughed.

'I'll come if you want me to, but I think it's better for Anna to be free of her father now and then!'

'I'd be happy one way or the other, but I'll leave it to you. Now, Alexander, to change the subject; there's been a rather disturbing development in the Wessex area. A series of protest marches, and they seem to be gaining in momentum. A bloke called Semple, who, until he resigned a day ago, was a member of my constituency committee, has been organising it all. My Constituency Chairman, Sir Robert Cowdrey, is fuming. Oh, Alexander, I forgot to tell you; he'll be getting in touch. He's chairing a panel set up to inform MPs about the levy and counter the "anti" offensive in the party led by a rather forceful MP called Harold Harbin.'

'Sir Robert phoned about an hour ago, but I was out. Anna took the call. I remember watching him at Twickenham!'

'That's him. I think he'd like to kick this Semple guy into touch. But he's managing to restrain himself. They all turn up in coaches, and their placards are well printed. There seems to be no lack of cash, and certainly no lack of car stickers and the like. And they eat well in the local pubs.'

'What are they saying?'

'Hands off our back garden. Stop the land grab. That's the gist of it. Alexander, it's damned tedious, but of course it's a legitimate protest, and so far it's been trouble-free.'

'Anna saw a poster saying something similar. Henry, I'd use the protest to expound the principle. Can't you call a meeting?'

'Security would have kittens if I suggested that.'

'All you need is a few selected people attending as an excuse to have your speech reported in the local press. An open meeting would end up as a bear garden. You're right; Security would never allow a general meeting.'

'Alexander, I think I'll put you in charge of my dirty tricks department!'

'Is that a Cabinet post?'

'Could be arranged. Listen, I'm concerned that these placard protests could be hijacked by the vandal element. It could be nasty. Security is watching, though.' There was a chuckle. *'And so is Sir Robert. Now, Alexander, this panel thing: I hope you*

don't mind, but I put your name forward as one who can reassure the MPs and explain the nature of the tax-shift measures. It could be a little windy, especially if Harbin turns up, but I doubt if he will. Anyway, Sir Robert won't stand any nonsense. I've watched him first-hand many times!'

*

Samuel Bennett was a member of the Reform Club and had invited Jake Hud to lunch. It was Jake's first time to enter the impressive atrium, built, he was told, in the manner of a Renaissance palace. When a young man, he'd had the childish notion that such clubs were filled with blood-sucking capitalists counting their ill-gotten loot. Now, watching the other members and their guests in conversation, they all looked boringly like himself!

After the customary pre-lunch drink in the atrium, they repaired to the dining-room, where, with an urgent eagerness, Bennett launched into the troubled subject of repossessions.

'We can't chuck these people out. The debt must be forgiven, at least for some specific time. Jake, you gave me the idea – remember? Play with two words, you said: forgiveness and responsibility.'

'Did I say that?'

'You did. But who, for heavens sake, will take the loss. The banks would flip!' Bennett looked intense.

'I have little sympathy with the banks. They were encouraging dodgy loans and securing them with even dodgier debt!'

'Jake, if we're going to have forgiveness, it's got to be across the board, banks included.'

'But, Samuel, who takes the bloody hit? Somebody does!'

'In a way we all should share the burden. I've lain awake at night on this one. Jake, the banks will have to be supported and those on the brink made national institutions. Jake, we're not a conclave of angels. The only answer that seems to be acceptable is a moratorium.'

'That's all very well, Sammie, me old china plate, but how do you work *that* out?'

'I don't know, Jake, that's the trouble, but I know I'm right! The PM's been very supportive and has encouraged me to trust my "inner prompting", as he calls it. What an amazing man our young PM is. Young? No, he's ageless. Jake, he gets his energy from a deep well.'

'Don't look at me like that! I agree!'

'Now this moratorium,' Bennett continued. 'It's possible that, in the meantime, the mortgagees could pay for something, say only for the bricks and mortar. Again, if this location-value levy were in place the capital value would reduce, but I feel that that's way down the line. The main thing is to deal with the current situation.'

'Ah here's the main course,' Bennett mouthed.

'I need it,' Jake said bluntly. 'Do you know something, Samuel, you look more like a professor every day."

'A nutty one, if this business that I'm dealing with gets worse!'

'So, are you still against the location levy?'

'Jake, I don't know what I'm against, but I'm not so set as I was. To revert to this forgiveness thing: I strongly feel we need to purge this dog-eat-dog back-stabbing attitude, which seems to be the fashion nowadays.'

'Samuel, are you talking about me?' Jake teased.

'No, the PM managed to reform you. I'm serious, Jake, we need a new ... sound, yes that's it, a new sound!'

'I couldn't agree with you more, but, Samuel, allow me to be cynical. We can talk till the cows come home about good business practice, about forgiveness and responsibility. Which is fine, but how effective will it be and how enduring will it be, if it fails to tackle causes?'

'What causes?'

'My God, Samuel, where have you been these last weeks? Every Cabinet meeting, Henry's been hammering on about location value and you still haven't got the bloody message!'

'Location value doesn't seem to strike a chord.'

'Samuel, where is your house located?'

'Sutton.'

'What's it sitting on?'

'Well, land, I suppose.'

'Of course it's bloody land! And what's the difference between those who own their land and those who don't?

'Well, it's the great divide. The haves and have nots!'

'And what's the difference between your little nest-egg and, say, Belgravia?'

'A very tidy sum.'

'But why pay more for Belgravia?'

'You win, Jake – location.'

'And why is the location more expensive?'

'The community's presence and preference.'

'So, if the community's preference and presence creates the location value, to whom does it belong?'

'Jake, do you want a fee for this tuition?'

'Could be useful.' Jake's eyes sparkled. 'Just one more question. Is there any restriction on buying land?'

'Apart from public areas, not really. There's planning permission, of course. But in general, all you need's the cash.'

'So you buy a property and someone wants to use it. What do you do?'

'Rent it out.'

'What would you charge?'

'The most you can get. No wonder Hamilton Davis was so worked up last night! My heavens, it's just struck me; that's why the have-nots are killing themselves to join the haves. And Jake, the location levy would stop the stupid rat-race. People could still buy their house, of course. There's no levy on bricks and mortar. Repossessions! We could delete the word from the dictionary!'

'Samuel, you've got it, you've bloody got it! You've tapped the secret! If this were evening time I'd call for the bubbly! Hey, you're not eating!'

'It's your fault, you're too good a teacher.'

'Say *that* when you get the bill!'

'Jake, I've just remembered!'

'It's your wife's birthday?'

'I don't live that dangerously! No, I've just remembered a speech from Shakespeare. It's amazing how the mind works – all those years ago.'

'Out with it!'

England, bound in with the triumphant sea,
Whose rocky shore beats back the envious siege
Of watery Neptune, is now bound in with shame,
With inky blots, and rotten parchment bonds:
That England, that was wont to conquer others,
Hath made a shameful conquest of itself.[1]

'Our old teacher used to rabbit on about land enclosure. We thought he was nuts, of course. But, it seems he wasn't daft after all!'

'So Shakespeare's on board,' Jake reacted, 'but I fear the "antis" would be quick to talk it down. OK, you've matriculated, but in the meantime, what are you going to do about the repossessions?'

'A moratorium of some workable duration, and, as I've already said, perhaps the mortgagees could pay off the bricks and mortar factor – in other words, the house. But being treated generously, these people must fulfil their revised obligations. Responsibility cuts both ways. The truth is, Jake, I'm at a crossroads with conflicting signs. It seems impossible to craft a solution that's completely fair, for the mess of complication forbids it. Also, the banks will have to be supported. Once trust goes, God help us. The people need to know their deposits are safe. Jake, the whole thing's a nightmare. There are so many balls to keep in the air – and, Jake, the location levy will make it even more complicated!'

'Samuel, that's not going to happen next week. I wish it were, but we're working round the clock. We'll get there! We bloody well have to!'

'You're worried, Jake?'

'Yeah, I *am* worried. It's the phoney war period. God knows what's before us if we fail! Listen, I must get back to the House.'

'And so must I. Jake, who's that young computer whizz kid that you praise so much?'

'Tommy Thompson.'

'Could I have a word with him some time?'

'Hey, hands off, mate! Yes, Samuel, of course. He's under pressure at the moment, but in a day or two – yes, of course. I'm thinking of putting him forward for the bloody peerage!'

Samuel Bennett smiled knowingly. It was typical Jake.

After Bennett settled the bill, they made to leave the dining-room together, but, just as they approached the door, Jake's eye caught the headlines of a newspaper spread out on one of the tables.

'*Unemployment Soars*, the headline read. Jake almost winced. The clouds were gathering. On the right hand side, there was a full-length photograph of a lady in an evening gown. Jake assumed that it was some celeb he'd never heard off. He was about to continue when he suddenly stopped.

'Samuel, take a look at that, it's Anna Collingwood.'

'Alexander Collingwood's daughter – I've never met her.'

Miss Collingwood accompanying the Prime Minister as guest of the President at the Ambassador's Residence in Regent's Park,

Jake read aloud. 'Mind you, Samuel, it doesn't surprise me. I met her at Number Ten and the PM and her were clearly fond. Poor girl, her privacy is dead.'

'Jake, it's a private matter. It's not our concern.'

'I'm afraid the public, with the prodding of the press, will make it their concern. She'll need protection, but, Henry, I'm sure, will take no risks. Funny, I didn't notice this earlier. Though, in a way I'm not surprised, for it's been a mad rush since my old feet hit the floor at the ungodly hour of five.'

They walked round the perimeter of the atrium and down the steps to street level.

'Have you been summoned tomorrow morning?' Bennett asked.

'Yeah, ten a.m. for coffee was the call. See you there.'

*

Sir Frederick Kingsway sat behind his desk, rocking gently in his large luxurious office chair. His two economics consultants were due: both were PhDs, and were very bright. They had different areas of expertise and had proved their worth. Freddie Kingsway didn't quibble at their fees, which were, to say the least, substantial. Indeed, substantial enough for Freddie to expect his whims to be obeyed.

The buzzer made its discreet noise. His guests had arrived, and Sir Frederick stood up, extending his hand in welcome. He could be charm itself when it suited him.

'Welcome, gentlemen. Coffee will be with us shortly,' he said brightly.

The two men responded with appropriate grace and they all took their seats.

'Now tell me,' Sir Frederick began, 'how are things at the Treasury?'

'A little breezy,' the taller of the Economists returned. He was a thin man, with a deep resonant voice and a designer beard. 'This tax-shift measure isn't popular. It simply doesn't fit the Treasury models!'

'That's an understatement, Jack. The whole idea is positively dangerous,' his companion said aggressively. He was a small man, neat and dapper. 'Property underpins so much and you tamper with it at your peril. This government talks of principle as if it were some magic wand to change dross into gold. We're doing

127

our best, Sir Frederick, and the Chancellor does listen, then he goes next door and then we have to start again. His friends in the City are saying the same as us, but he can't make up his mind!'

'He doesn't want to lose his job!' Freddie interjected, 'he's a politician. Anyway, gentlemen, keep up the good work.'

'We're doing our best, Sir Frederick,' the man called Jack responded, 'Blackstone's the problem. Sam and I have submitted papers spelling out the dangers in some detail. We get polite acknowledgements, but that's the height of it. So we keep plugging away at the Chancellor. Will this so-called levy raise sufficient funds? I feel it's wildly optimistic. We want statistics, not dreamy assumptions. And what about the tower blocks? It's a nightmare!'

'Did the Chancellor respond to your statistics probe?' Sir Frederick questioned brusquely.

'Yeah, he looked at me knowingly over his reading glasses. "Simon," he said, "if the total's insignificant, why all the fuss?"'

Sir Frederick nodded.

'It seems James J is not a mug,' he muttered.

They continued on a similar line for almost half an hour. Sir Frederick was frustrated, but he hid it well.

'Well, gentlemen, keep up the good work,' he said briskly, as he showed them to the door, but his thinking had moved on. He needed to focus more on the political side. Harbin was against the levy. He was active, but he was only 'pussyfooting'. He needed a rocket under him, for time was slipping by. Something *had* to be done. Blackstone *had* to be stopped.

Chapter Twenty-Three

Faithful to his nature, Samuel Bennett was twenty minutes early, but this gave Blackstone time to question him in person. He was impressed, for Bennett had approached his repossessions task with diligence. He clearly had been moved by the distress he'd witnessed, and this, the PM guessed, had made his arguments meaningful enough to gain substantial voluntary restraints. These were very useful; nevertheless, Blackstone felt that parliamentary confirmation was required.

'Samuel, have you still got doubts about our tax-shift proposals?' He asked quietly.

Bennett smiled.

'Prime Minister, I had lunch with Jake yesterday and he gave it to me straight. Perhaps I ought to say bloody straight!'

Blackstone chuckled.

'That's Jake. He's worked wonders, and so have you, Samuel. Your support is vital, as I'm certain that the coming battle in the Commons will be toe to toe! The vested interest don't lack allies!'

'*Inky blots and rotten parchment bonds,*' Bennett said reflectively. Then responding to Blackstone's quizzical look he recounted his sudden school days' memory.

'I remember someone suggesting that Shakespeare was hinting at the dissolution of the monasteries, and the resultant land grab, but who knows? Well, well, and we're still reaching for the ladder, as we call it, still straining for our "parchment bond". Samuel, once you see this truth, you see it everywhere! Ah, here's Bill.'

Bill Jones offered his greetings while sitting down gratefully. With his protruding ears and bald head, Jones was not an arresting figure. Blackstone smiled. That was of little matter. Bill was a decent man and one he'd grown to respect.

'The old pins aren't what they used to be,' Jones sighed. 'But enough of that. Samuel, I've heard that you've been working hard.'

'The coalface, Bill, the repossession nightmare – the sum of human misery, is appalling.'

Blackstone could see a real affection between Bennett and his old boss. Such bonds lent strength, and it was what he needed for the looming parliamentary battle. Samuel had been a good choice.

'It struck me, as I was coming here, that all we need is security of tenure,' Jones revealed. 'We don't need to own the earth our house is sitting on, but we can own the house and so be free of rents. We don't need to saddle ourselves with a lifetime debt to buy the site! That's the real debt burden – you're smiling, Henry?'

'Yes, at two of my friends who've caught the bug! We'll need this depth of understanding when the flack is flying in the House!'

'You're still hoping for next week?' Jones asked.

'Yes, if the Deputy PM agrees. Bill, it really doesn't give us time enough to gather in the troops, but we can't wait, for unrest in the country is near to tinder dry.'

'What about Willie and his lot?'

'The family mafia, that is, my sister, tells me that Willie's got his legion in close order. I wish I could say the same for my lot. Some of the vested interests are stone-set!'

'Henry, it's the same in all the parties. The PPPs, or pro private property group, as they call themselves, have pals in every port.'

'But we're *not* anti private property. Houses are private property. My God, you'd think we were going to house the folk in Stalinist blocks like communist Russia! We must rubbish such propaganda!'

'Yes, Prime Minister, the Deputy PM is right behind you on this one.'

'Thanks, Bill.'

'What about the Chancellor?'

'He still blows hot and cold. He's not attending this meeting and I didn't press him.'

'He's being bloody awkward, and you've been more than patient. The trouble is, Jamieson's convinced by the last bloke he's had a chat with!' Bill Jones was clearly annoyed. 'I'd send the so-and-so to the Lords!'

Blackstone smiled.

'Henry, how do you keep so calm?' Jones burst out.

'You know the story of the swan – calm on the surface and paddling like hell underneath!'

'There's more to it than that!'

'Bill, my father was a remarkable man and he told me many things. He didn't lecture, he simply put ideas on the table. "Don't gallop with excitement; watch and be amused," was one of them.'

'Well, I'm sorry, Henry, I'm not amused by Jamieson, not one little bit!'

At that point Winston Hughes, the Home Secretary, and the Industry Secretary, Ted Banks, arrived. It gave Blackstone the excuse to drop the subject of the Chancellor. Bill could vent his frustration, but being PM, Henry Blackstone had to watch his words.

'Welcome, gentlemen. Any word of Jake or Chris?'

'Chris has arrived, but no sign of Jake,' Ted Banks replied, his red hair catching the light.

'What's your latest thinking on the contractor front?'

'Prime Minister, I aim to spread the bounty and avoid it being swallowed up by one big fish. I want commercial reality and service to the common interest to be a natural union: not just the product of watchdogs.' He smiled. 'There will be watchdogs, though. I'm not that naïve!'

'You're waxing lyrical, Ted!'

'I was up all night practising, Sir!'

Blackstone laughed.

'Well, I'm glad you're practising, for we'll need a truckload of Churchillian barbs to win the hour.'

There was a moment's pause, and then Chris Crouch bounced in.

'Chris, where's Jake?'

'He's chatting up the secretaries. PM, Jake's being Jake. He's a just-in-time man!'

'Ah, here he is.'

Blackstone looked at his watch.

'Just on time. Full marks Chris.'

'Jake, every time I see the fire and energy in your eyes, my spirits rise, for I know the opposition will never have the final word. Jake will top it!'

The amusement in the assembled group was real.

Bill Jones was full of admiration. Henry included everyone and made them all feel good. That was obvious, for, once through the door, they soon were grinning ear to ear. Another thing Jones noticed, indeed he'd noticed it before: the PM's easy nature was rarely exploited. There was a dignity and strength; in fact, a presence that naturally evoked respect.

'Gentlemen,' Blackstone began, 'you all should have pumped a cup of coffee from these self-help machines just behind me; if not, there's still time to try your luck.' He briefly scanned the group. 'It seems you all are suitably armed, but before we start I must offer the apologies of Janet Simmons, our embattled Health Secretary. The pressures she is under are enormous, but she sees in our proposals rays of hope. In fact, she understands the essence of it all and is solidly with us but says quite bluntly that current funding cannot meet the growing health care bill. Unpopular decisions must be faced. Indeed, it is yet another area of need where delay is not a luxury we can tolerate.'

'Where does she see the ray of hope?' Chris Crouch asked pointedly.

'A reduction in tax would raise take-home pay and allow a contribution for the minor treatments.'

'That will be popular,' Crouch reacted knowingly.

'Chris, we simply can't go on the way we're going. Be assured there'll be no pruning of essential areas, but there will be changes, and these we will discuss in full Cabinet. Gentlemen, this is a small group, a rather special group that I've called together so that we may hear what's happening in fields of action other than our own. I would mention that Willy Windbourne, being Foreign Secretary, is abroad but should be back in time for the debate. He is solidly behind us. His reports don't make good reading, for this crisis has a worldwide grip. He also reports considerable interest in our current tax-shift proposals, especially from the old commonwealth. So the world is watching, and when I look around this room at the paucity of our number I hear my cynical voice burst out in raucous laughter. "What can you lot do?" it jibes. And I'll shock you by saying that it's right. It's the *principle* that has the power. *It* acts. We are its instruments. This principle is pure reason, and when it awakens in the heart of humankind, the light of reason shines. This is why you've found this economic principle so compelling. When you're speaking in the Commons, the world will be listening. Don't think that you're too small, or that you're doing it – that's even worse. Know that it's the principle that will touch the hearts of men.'

'That's bloody magnificent!' Chris Crouch's stage whisper was just loud enough for all too hear.

Blackstone's smile was enigmatic, but he made no comment. In fact, he was silent for a time, his head bowed in reflection. No one broke the stillness. Then Blackstone raised his head.

'The Deputy Prime Minister said something very interesting before most of you arrived. It was an interesting slant on things, and I think you ought to have the insight as an arrow in your quiver. It could prove very useful – Bill.'

'Well, it struck me when I was coming here, that all we really needed was security of tenure. We don't need to own the ground, the earth, in fact the location where our house is resting. All we want to do is go home, turn the key and walk inside. We don't need to own the ground, but we can own the *house* and thus be free of landlords and their soaring rents. Our home would still be our proverbial castle. In fact, more people could afford their castle! If we have to raise a mortgage for the house, well, that's nothing to the capital requirement for the location site and the life-long burden that it brings. Why do we torture ourselves for a piece of paper that says we own the freehold, when all we need to do is pay the yearly site location levy, which will be offset by the drop in taxes on our earnings. Striving for a freehold title is an unnecessary burden. Just think what we could do if freed from stultifying mortgage payments. For one thing, would we suffer healthcare waiting lists? Imagine someone coming from another world and viewing how we live today; they'd think we're mad!'

'That's good, Bill. In fact, it's bloody good! Why did I give you such a hard time when you were carrying that hellish PM load? Bill, I deeply regret it, but you're a big man and I hope you can accept my apology.'

'Jake, in politics I've often noticed that fierce opponents grow to be firm friends. This view of mine would seem to be confirmed again.'

'Nicely put, Bill. Thank you.'

'Follow that,' Chris Crouch piped up. It was a favourite quip of his.

Winston Hughes looked across at Jake, and nodded. The *tête-à-tête* they'd had, had borne fruit.

Chris Crouch's 'Follow that' turned out to be prophetic, and there were no more contributions. It was as if the group had received enough strong meat at one sitting. So the reports concerning the various areas of activity proceeded.

Ted Banks was the first, giving a comprehensive picture of his survey of contractual requirements for the government-sponsored infrastructure surge. Then he launched into what he called his depressing survey of the stock market and the whole PLC set-up. Nothing could be done, he felt, until there was a rethink. But how could that happen when the tie-up with the global scene was so complete. Yet, grand facades could crumble suddenly – that was the trouble!

Next came Samuel Bennett. It was a good report, Blackstone thought, but he, of course, already knew the essence.

Chris Crouch described himself as the damage limitation expert. Keeping Unions from the clutches of the angry mob he saw to be a full-time job. It was the old story: the militant activists were prepared to attend committees, but the ordinary fellas didn't want to know. So the extremists had an easy run, but there were always the few who stood their ground. Chris had some sympathy with the young bloods. He had gone through the same process and understood their frustrations. But he found the leaders and the bitter oldies difficult. Their rigid views and cold ambition left no entry point for humour.

'I'm not a religious bloke,' Chris said in conclusion, 'but I often feel God's secret weapon is a damned good laugh.'

Blackstone clearly was amused.

'How do you get on with the TUC boss, Sam Redwell?'

'Sam's OK. He takes a swipe at me sometimes, but that's to butter up his troops. He's not in the government's pocket, is the message.'

'Excellent, Chris,' Blackstone responded. 'Few could do what you're doing, and with so much obvious success.'

Bill Jones smiled. Henry wasn't afraid to praise.

Jake Hud was next.

'What am I doing here? The truth is that the state of preparation we've achieved is largely due to Tommy Thompson. That young man's a genius and he knows his stuff. Of course, it's not surprising, for he went to classes run by Alexander Collingwood. Well, we're ready. We could fret forever over detail, and I'm certain that the nitty-gritty problems that will surface when we put the measure into practice will be dealt with then. I've been an MP for six years, and this is the first time I feel I'm actually achieving something. We need to decide the percentage, of course. Personally, I would go for twenty. Gentlemen, we're going to collect in part the value created by the community – that is the location value. We're also going to ease the plunder of the people's earnings. In my book, that's not bad.'

'Yes, Jake, not bad at all,' Blackstone echoed. 'Thank you, Jake, for your tireless work and also pass our thanks to Tommy, and we must remember that, except for Alexander Collingwood's letter, we wouldn't be having this conversation.'

'You picked it up, PM,' Crouch chipped in.

'I wonder, Chris – I wonder.'

Chris Crouch didn't answer. The PM was a deep one.

'Well, Winston, what's our quiet and astute Home Secretary got to say?'

'It's a stand-off in the North, Prime Minister. I have friends in both camps, all good people, but they have to tread carefully, for tribal attitudes are sensitive. Some of these friends I've made are quite remarkable. There's a Christian Vicar, who had his church burnt down. He shows no bitterness whatever and is always quick to talk in terms of forgiveness and cooperation. He has greatly impressed my Muslim friends, one of whom is very friendly with the Vicar. In fact, they often meet. I personally hold this partic-ular Mullah in the highest regard. So it's not all gloom by any means.'

'Is there anything I can do to help?'

Hughes pondered for a moment.

'You could receive these men I've mentioned here at Downing Street. Hopefully this would send a message that we are a nation where the good are praised.'

'Well said, Winston. Yes, let's set it up – anything more?'

Hughes shook his head.

'Bill, is there something more you would like to say?'

'Prime Minister, it's been a most impressive meeting and for this reason – we're all anchored to the same rock.'

'Yes, and that is powerful, perhaps more powerful than we think.'

Blackstone bowed his head in reflection.

'Gentlemen, that's it for this morning. Oh, Bill, maybe you could have a word with Janet, and inform her of the various points we have discussed. She too is anchored to the rock!'

Chapter Twenty-Four

After the morning meeting was over, the PM's day was solid with appointments. Indeed, it seemed that every ambassador to the Court of St James had requested a meeting. The messages they conveyed were friendly in the main, but two were downright angry. All were complaining of trade irregularities that in normal times would have been barely noticed.

'Prime Minister, UK companies have been dumping,' one agitated voice complained.

'Ambassador, my people say that foreign companies have been dumping, too. They shout for tariffs, but that, of course, is not our policy,' Blackstone replied evenly.

'Prime Minister, these are difficult times.' The ambassador had read the hidden message loud and clear.

After six o'clock, Blackstone retreated to the flat, taking the box of letters his secretary had opened and laid out for him. These were the ones addressed to him personally. Alexander's letter, which had set so much in motion, made him careful of such correspondence.

There was the usual assortment, which he laid out in various piles. Some were the work of cranks, some naïve, some too long, and some were saying things of interest. These he set aside for further attention, but all would be acknowledged. Today there was a letter from a twelve-year-old, and it got to him. The innocence had such direct simplicity.

Dear Prime Minister, why can't Dad get a job? He is very worried. I heard him talking to Mum, about selling the house, but he doesn't want to. I'm only twelve. Can you help please? Yours sincerely, Jim.

Jim had written his name, address and phone number very neatly at the top right-hand corner of what appeared to be school exercise-book paper.

He pressed his secretary's number.

'Yes, Prime Minister.'

'Jenny, the letter from the boy called Jim – do you think you could phone the house and say the PM will do his best. This little chap has spirit.' He gave her the number.

Blackstone was soon absorbed in the other letters. The phone rang and his hand stretched out automatically.

'Prime Minister.' It was Jenny. *I've just spoken to Mrs Robbins, Jim's mother. She was flabbergasted. Apparently Jim didn't tell them he had written. The father is a top-flight engineer who's been the victim of the latest cost-cutting round. Now he's left with a mortgage, school fees and the rest. They didn't expect it, for Mr Robbins had a fairly senior post.'*

'My God, how often could we duplicate that round the country? Jenny, tell Mr Robbins to jump on a train. I can see him Friday. And Jenny, it's well past six. Shouldn't you be going home.'

'It's all right, Sir. I'd only collapse in front of the television.'

'Well. don't stay too long.' Blackstone was pensive. Jenny deserved more than that. Dear God, what does it all mean?

It was coming up to seven, and soon Mabel would be here to 'do' for him. Also, Anna was due to phone after her meeting with the jacket designers. Such meetings were often fraught with indecision, she had told him – a book jacket could make or break.

He continued scanning the letters and placing them in different piles until the phone once more arrested him. This time it was Anna.

'It's good to hear your voice, dear Anna. A good day, I hope?'

'Trouble-free, and no fussing over jacket-cover problems.'

'What about the security folk? I hope it's not too tedious.'

'Henry, I hardly notice. They're very discreet and I haven't hidden behind my dark designer glasses yet!'

'You're off the front page, my love, but tomorrow night could put you back again.'

'Fame is the spur!' she reacted.

'Milton?'

'Yes, but also the title of a famous book as well.'

'Trust a publisher.'

Mabel had just come through the door. He waved.

'Mabel's just arrived to keep me in close order.'

'Mission impossible! Henry, these industrialists tomorrow evening: will they be difficult?'

'Could be, but the presence of my lady may promote their moderation.'

'So I'm a human shield?'

'Something like that – now, to answer your question, yes, it could be a little windy. I can't think that the vested interests will let me off the hook.'

'You must find it hard to take. I mean, all this criticism.'

'Anna, I'm shredded every day, by some journalist or another.'

'I know, I read the stuff. What do they expect you to do? Wave a magic wand!'

He chuckled and they chatted on, the timing of their engagement being the subject.

'How about some time after the debate next week?' Blackstone suggested.

'Not too soon, Henry, for they could accuse you of triumphalism!'

Blackstone laughed.

'Not only wife, but political advisor as well! I think I've got myself a bargain. But, my love, we have to win the battle first!'

'You'll do it, Prime Minister.'

'Mabel's waving , so supper's ready. I'll phone tomorrow about transport etc. The venue is a posh hotel near Tower Hill. Bye, dear.'

After supper, and sheaves of reading matter later, the phone rang. It was Bill Jones.

'Henry, I've just heard a most amusing piece of info and "her indoors", as they used to say, told me to ring you. Apparently Chris Crouch and Janet Simmons had a stand-up row in the lobby, just where you pass into the Commons. Janet's NHS proposals were the subject, and Chris went into orbit. Maybe you don't know, but the NHS has always been a sacred cow with him. According to my source, a policeman had to caution them. Then all at once it changed, and they were laughing. Now this is the icing on the cake, for Chris and Janet were seen in a rather upmarket restaurant drinking in each other's presence like long-lost lovers. Well, I thought that that might cheer you up before you hit the sack.'

'That's a real bedtime story. Bill, the whole country needs to hear the sound of hope. I received a letter from a twelve-year-old today. His Dad had lost his job. It sort of gets to you. You know the feeling.'

'Too well.' Sitting in his favourite easy chair at home, Bill Jones recalled the sense of isolation that he used to feel. Even with Ellen at his side he'd felt it.

'Henry, you're doing wonders, and next week we'll crown your efforts with a Commons majority. In the meantime we have the beginnings of a Cabinet romance!' the former PM said brightly.

'Could be. Chris is forty-five and Janet's nearly forty,' Blackstone prompted.

'Yes, but Janet's fairly rightish and Chris is left of left. It's impossible, but I have a feeling that it's on!'

'Both of them have frantic schedules that fill in lonely hours. That's the feeling that I get. We ought to start a marriage bureau! Bill, thanks for ringing, it was damned nice of you. Regards to Ellen.'

He'd barely replaced the handset when reception rang again.

'The Home Secretary for you, Prime Minister.'

'Prime Minister, it's Winston. I've just got word of a freak storm in the Severn valley area. Power lines have been severed in a number of places and large areas are without electricity and likely to be so for some time. Apparently some of the pylons are a tangled mess.'

'That region is already suffering heavy unemployment and repossessions. What do you say if we both visit the area in the morning?'

'I'll arrange that, Prime Minister.'

'As early as you can, I need to get back.'

'I'll try the RAF.'

'Thanks, Winston.'

The line went dead. Winston never wasted time in chatter.

Blackstone put the phone down, looking at it for a moment, as if it were a perverse creature calculating further havoc. He yawned. A busy day awaited him. It was time for bed.

Chapter Twenty-Five

A confusion of emotions vying for attention was the way that Anna viewed her agitated mind. The prospect of marriage to Henry Blackstone fluctuated between fantasy, a kind of a teen dream, and reality. Could she fulfil the role and tolerate the publicity? Did she really want that sort of life? Yet it would be interesting. She would meet so many people, heads of state, all sorts of dignitaries and, of course, the Queen. It was like taking to the West End stage without the benefit of RADA!

Did she really know him? Such a fundamental doubt was like a blasphemy. There were doubts, but they always disappeared when in his company. The trouble was, they never really had the chance to know each other. Courtship, if you could call it that, was conducted in brief snatches and on the telephone. Well, what did she expect? The poor man didn't have a moment he could call his own. The country's crisis state made sure of that!

She would be seeing him this evening when he'd be addressing a far from friendly audience. He was in the West Country at the moment. He'd called her from his car on the way to Northolt and a helicopter ride. Jenny, he told her, would phone about the evening's arrangements: another arm's-length affair. 'Stop it, Anna,' she chastised herself. Yet she did wonder. Even her friend Maggie would find her situation bizarre!

*

The situation in the West was as bad as Winston had reported. A number of pylons were damaged and two were mangled in a most amazing way. Nature was powerful. A tornado, the locals said, tearing up the area like an angry giant.

The Press followed the PM and his Minister, with the local MP and councillors in close attendance. Then, with the backdrop of a mangled pylon, Blackstone fielded questions. They focused almost entirely on what the government would do and the speed with which normal services would be restored.

'I am not an engineer,' Blackstone began, 'but I'm sure that those with responsibility for these matters will not rest idle. Certainly government will lend the help that's needed in the short term. Regarding the long term, we will be placing proposals before the House concerning infrastructure works. These, and a shift in tax from earnings and enterprise to a location value levy, should further help recovery. Your region has been badly hit by unemployment, repossession, and now this disaster. Be assured that we, your government, are not asleep on our watch.'

There were more questions. These Blackstone handled tactfully. A region in trauma needed reassurance. Then it was time to leave. He smiled, a naturally disarming smile.

'Downing Street beckons.'

Back in the helicopter Blackstone turned to his Home Secretary.

'Well, Winston, what did you think?'

'The MPs in the area might be wise to vote for us next week.'

'You're a cynical old soldier, Winston, but you're right!'

The helicopter started up and the noise level rose steadily.

Henry Blackstone was a good man, Winston mused, but he was a politician, and judging by today's performance he wasn't a fool. He had a fight on and if his opponents felt they had an easy target, they were mistaken. The PM knew the wealthy freehold interests were marshalling their troops. Their so-called secret enclaves were open to the sky. The vote in the Commons would be tight, but it was a free vote. The whips would not be watching. Members could vote according to their will and the freer minds could be persuaded by the power of oratory. It was exciting stuff. So much rested on the PM's shoulders, but he'd gathered able men about him, though not the Chancellor. He could cause trouble. Winston didn't trust him. If Jamieson broke rank, Henry would dismiss him. He would know that. But a few lucrative directorships would cover the shortfall. In Winston's view, the Chancellor would sit balanced on the fence and would only act when he saw which way the wind was blowing.

*

Sir Gerald Samsone, chairman for the evening and CEO and Chairman of the Samsone Corporation, knew that Blackstone's silly game would have to stop. Tampering with the property world was madness, and it would hurt too many people in the highest places. He had invited two economics professors and their wives to the dinner. Both were disdainful of location value, which one described as merely land tax in a fancy dress. Unfortunately Hamilton Davis was attending with his cronies and was trumpeting how he'd quickly cut the boy PM to size. Davis was an idiot, but he was extremely rich and difficult to control. How to shut him up was a real problem, for his blustering was doing much more harm than good. He was like an ageing steam train blowing clouds of steam and puffing, yet achieving little. Samsone couldn't bar him from the dinner. That, he knew, would cause a revolution. Perhaps a quiet word might help, but he didn't have much hope. Hamilton's emotions seemed to roam without a master. Yet he was generous, and wealth came to him like iron filings to a magnet.

Sir Gerald went to Tower Hill early. This occasion was too important to leave to secretaries. Casually he bought the evening paper after emerging stiffly from the taxi. He wasn't young any more, and his big-framed body had its share of aches and pains.

The headlines in the paper stopped him halfway up the steps of the hotel. *Prompt PM visits morning scene of chaos after night of devastation.* 'Not bad, Henry,' Sir Gerald muttered. It was bold print, dominating the page. 'It's a pity you have to make this stupid attack on property. Why, for heavens sake?' He grabbed hold of the handrail and hauled himself up the final steps. God, there were police everywhere. Of course, security would be four-dimensional!

Almost at once he saw Hamilton Davis. 'Awh, God', he groaned.

'Gerald, I've hired a suite for the night. Thought I'd do it in style. Come and have a snifter!'

'It's a shade too early, Hamilton. Thanks for the thought. Anyway, I'd better keep a clear head; there's work to do. Oh, and Hamilton, there are two economic experts attending this evening. They've promised to question our errant PM. It would be useful if the attack could be academic and considered.'

'So you want me to cool it, as the young ones say. I'll do my best, Gerald, but when the steam's up, she blows!'

Sir Gerald continued on, covering his misgivings with a smile.

Chapter Twenty-Six

Anna's doubts vanished when Henry was before her in black tie and dinner jacket. As with white tie and tails, he suited formal attire. So many men looked like stuffed pigeons. This comment, said when she was young, had made her father double up with laughter. Henry was clearly pleased to see her, yet something thought it very strange. Here he was, the Queen's chief minister, and yet he seemed enamoured of one Anna Collingwood! She laughed happily as he approached and kissed her lightly.

Traffic was heavy, and security very visible, as they left Downing Street. He took her hand.

'I've had no space today to think of what I'm going to say. The speechwriters have come up with a fit-all text, but it's nothing like the message that I want to give. It's not their fault, for I didn't feed them with the information. What do you think I ought to say?'

Anna didn't respond immediately. She was shocked, for she realised that his question wasn't trivial. Being the girlfriend of the Prime Minister carried a responsibility. This powerful and able man needed her support. She pondered.

'Henry, you're Prime Minister; say something that we ought to hear, not something politically safe that won't disturb our slumber.'

He laughed.

'Do you think I'm playing safe?'

'Don't be silly, Henry! If you were, you wouldn't have listened to Father.'

'So what are you trying to tell me?'

'Something new, something true, something that touches the heart. Henry, I'm struggling. The moral dimension maybe. You know – are the way we do things right or are they wrong? More heart and less statistics.'

He leaned across and kissed her on the cheek.

'You've sparked that inner light where certainty is sovereign. Thank you, my love.'

Anna sensed, but didn't fully understand, what Henry meant. She sensed, though, that he was somehow focused in himself.

They arrived exactly on time. Blackstone turned to Anna, his eyes full of amusement.

'Just on time – Jake Hud's got the patent rites, so we'd better be careful!'

✳

A liveried hotel doorman was in attendance, but it was the security men that opened the Jaguar doors. Sir Gerald Samsone stepped forward. With his large-framed body, well filled out, he seemed a studied image of a Chairman of the board.

Sir Gerald was graciousness itself. Business was business, but when it came to the social things of life Gerald Samsone was a decent man.

'What a charming dress, my dear,' he said warmly.

Blackstone smiled. A likeable man, he guessed.

They were escorted upstairs to a large reception room with windows looking onto a courtyard area. Drinks were offered and they both chose sherry. The room was already full, with knots of people busy in conversation.

Slowly and, with no little charm, Sir Gerald began to introduce the PM and his lady to some of the distinguished guests. First was Sir William Wellbourne, a senior banker in the City. Blackstone knew the man and viewed him as a traditionalist, an upright man.

'Prime Minister, I am rather concerned at the stream of credit you're proposing.'

'And rightly so, Sir William. You will know, of course, that it is strictly confined to infrastructure projects that will add considerably to community value. This value we hope to claw back, at least in part, by means of the location levy. And, Sir William, should you wish to contact me or write at any juncture, your wisdom and experience will always be appreciated.'

Sir William felt it inappropriate to press his point, and in any case he was rather taken by the young PM. Contrary to what he'd been repeatedly told, Henry Blackstone was a substantial presence.

Sir Gerald had caught the eye of the most senior of the economic professors and waved him over. Instantly, Blackstone and the professor were in animated conversation. Sir Gerald turned away and whispered close to Anna's ear.

144

'I'm sorry, my dear, I've lost my wife, I don't know where she's disappeared to. I'm sure you find this business stuff a little tedious'

'You're very kind, Sir Gerald, but it's quite all right. In fact, I find it rather interesting.'

'Good, my dear.' Sir Gerald's attention quickly returned to Blackstone and the professor.

'You two, I see, are behaving like old friends!'

'Sir Gerald, Professor Gilpin was my tutor at Oxford,' Blackstone explained. 'Not his star pupil, I must hasten to add!'

The professor switched his attention to Anna. He was a smallish man with an abundance of greying curly hair.

'I think he turned out fairly well, Miss Collingwood. Being PM is quite a job opportunity!'

They laughed openly.

It was all going well, Sir Gerald thought, but Blackstone was receiving praise, not censure. That was not what he had planned.

'Professor, in the present situation I would clearly value your advice, and if you had the time – a spot of lunch at Number Ten? Obviously I'm showered with expertise, but the words of my old Professor would have an extra edge.'

'I'd be delighted, except for one condition: that you call me Matthew.'

'How embarrassing: it's a deal, but only if you drop the PM business. It's Henry.'

'Done! Well, I mustn't monopolise your time, for I'm sure Sir Gerald wants to circulate.

The other professor was close by. In fact, Blackstone heard a preview of his conversation as they approached. The voice was loud and carried. Land, it said, was just another cost and could be factored in.

'Is this the micro-economic scene?' Blackstone asked.

The Professor swung round, answering 'Yes...' But the sight of the Prime Minister startled him.

'Sorry to gate-crash, Professor.'

Sir Gerald helped in the exchange of pleasantries, and then Blackstone pressed his question.

'For the shopkeeper in the high street, surely the rental is a major cost?'

'It's still a cost, Prime Minister. You add the figures up and you're either in business or you're not!'

'Well, you're in illustrious company, Professor, for Keynes' hugely influential book *General Theory of Employment, Interest and Money* only mentions land four times, and briefly!'[1]

'Indeed.'

'I must say it's rather strange, for economists are greatly engaged by the current government's tax-shift proposals.'

'That's rather different, Prime Minister.'

'I'm sure it is and I'm sure you could tie this amateur up in knots. Ah, Sir Gerald has another victim lined up.'

General amusement followed, and then the Prime Minister moved on.

'I've no one in mind; I just wanted to protect you from Hamilton Davis!'

'Is that possible, Sir Gerald? For when Hamilton gets you in his sights, you're done for!'

'Prime Minister, you're avoiding me!' It was Hamilton, in full cry.

'Hamilton, how could I avoid you with your sat-nav on!'

Davis guffawed.

'What's all this rubbish about taxing land? Is this a sneaky backdoor way to nationalisation?'

'Hamilton, how could you get it so wrong? This is *not* land nationalisation. May I repeat, it is *not* land nationalisation! It is a levy on location value, or, if you like, the value of the land where your premises are located. *The Earth is the Lord's.* Have a look at the top of the Royal Exchange. It's written in stone. Hamilton, I'll give you a task. Every time you hear the silly words, "land nationalisation" refer the speaker to the wisdom written in the centre of our City.'

'I'll be busy, Henry.'

'You will, but it'll be worthwhile work!'

'Hey, I came to give you a hard time!'

'Well, you haven't done too badly!'

There was another guffaw, and Sir Gerald encouraged the Premier forward.

Anna was full of admiration. Henry seemed so focused in himself, and so very much at ease with those he met.

The period of reception was over, and Blackstone and Anna were given the use of a suite, to freshen up, as Sir Gerald said.

When they were alone, they kissed.

'You're my secret weapon, love, for when the people catch a sight of you, their best parts rule!'

146

'Henry, you're OTT, but it's nice that you should say it. You yourself were masterly. How long before the dinner starts?'

'About ten minutes – Sir Gerald will collect us.'

'Well, you ought to have a rest.'

'Yes, dear,' he returned, with mock obedience.

They both chuckled.

*

The top table was on a low platform, which gave sufficient elevation to scan the sea of circular dining tables, and it was a sea. The place was packed as the Prime Minister and Anna took their seats. Sir Gerald called for order, and then someone said grace in Latin and the meal proceeded with Sir Gerald and Blackstone busy in conversation, the subject the crucial importance of the following week's Commons debate. Anna, on the other hand, was kept fully engaged by Lady Samsone's interest in Anna's publishing activities.

At last it was time for the Prime Minister's address. TV cameras and all the paraphernalia had been trundled in, and all was ready.

Sir Gerald stood up and began by welcoming the Prime Minister and the delightful Miss Collingwood, who had stolen his heart. He recalled buying the evening paper and seeing the headline, *Prompt PM visits morning scene of chaos.* 'That was this morning!' he emphasised.

'Fellow members and guests, I give you the Prime Minister.' Sir Gerald had totally forgotten to mention the general misgivings concerning the government's programme.

'My Lords, Ladies and Gentlemen, may I first thank Sir Gerald for a most courteous and warm reception and for the invitation to address this distinguished gathering. Indeed, the sum of experience and commercial expertise present in this room would be hard to duplicate, but I'll not embarrass you with superlatives.

'At a recent Cabinet meeting one of the ministers was complaining about the inflexibility of the labour market. Now we all know what that phrase means, yet something jarred. Is labour a commodity? What does a free market in labour mean?

I extended my introspections. What is the money market? What does it do? Is this a free market? Is money a commodity? How could a medium of exchange be a commodity? The free market in goods and services didn't pose a problem, but with labour and money the questions lingered.

'Now if I were you, I'd be muttering: why's he banging on about obscurities when everywhere the country is in crisis? A fair question and a necessary question, and the answer – your PM is searching for causes. For if we fail to find the causes, what is presently afflicting us will return again.

'Next week we will be laying tax-shift proposals before the house. These have been fathered by a study of causes. A gathering of this calibre will have understood the thinking behind the proposals. Some see the collection of a location value levy as an attack on property. They see their privileged interest being eroded, and none of us, if we are honest, find that comfortable.

'As Prime Minister, I cannot serve a sectional interest. This is further emphasised by the fact I head a National Government. Is land a commodity? Is a free market in land valid? This is a profound question, even spiritual, but, I will also add, very, very practical. How we address this question is crucial. Some would keep the *status quo*. But I say a vote for that is a vote for a divided nation.

'Preposterous, you might say, but stay, ponder a little. Why do so many struggle to get on the ladder? Well, you can answer that. The haves and the have-nots – the right side and the wrong side of the track. Such language has been with us for a long, long time. This *is* the divided nation. People stand equal before the gifts of air and sunshine. With water there are restrictions and service charges, but no one can stop a person collecting what falls from the heavens. The fourth gift is claimed with title deeds to prove it: *Inky blots and rotten parchment bonds,* as Shakespeare wrote. We have civil freedom. Our Common Law we've given to the world. But have we economic freedom? Take a young man full of enterprise, who lives on the wrong side of the track. He works hard, gathers up some capital, but the rent he's being asked to use the run-down shack he wants is crippling. Say he makes a go of things and his little business flourishes. Again, I don't need to tell you, for you know too well. The taxman cometh! Now. *you* employ experts to cope with such inconveniences, but our young hero can't.

'This rather naïve sketch may give you some idea of the government's thinking. We tolerate a very strange system. We allow location value, such as city-centre value, which is clearly a communal creation, to be claimed privately. And then we tax the enterprise of the individual, and indeed the company, for 'daring' to produce. In fact, the more enterprising, the more the taxman loves it.

'Of course, I'm not criticising the tax authorities. They are merely carrying out the law. What I'm questioning is the law itself. Is the current system right, or is it wrong? This is a moral question and, I believe, much more important than the bottom line of private or sectional interest.

'So to return to the beginning – thankfully we have a legitimate free market in manufactured and agricultural produce. This is still holding, despite protectionist pressure. Next we have the land market. This, of course, is perfectly legal. Personally, I question both the private and public right to say "This land is mine." Instead, I'd say we are the guardians with a duty to maintain the site we hold in good condition. Neglect should earn the censure of our peers.

'I don't know about you, but I find the term "labour market" quite repugnant. What right have we to talk about our fellow human beings in such terms? Also, ask yourself the question: Are human beings a cost of production or the means of production? Just consider for a moment. How would you react if your boss looked on you as an unfortunate but necessary expense?' He smiled. 'My job description, you might say!'

There was a brief burst of laughter.

'Now, we have the free market in money, or a money market as we know it. Here I will repeat. Can a medium of exchange be a marketable commodity? This, to me, is a real and fundamental question. We are in the middle of a financial crisis, triggered, many say, by irregularities in trading practices. What were they trading? Debt! Is debt a commodity? And, finally, are these practices moral?

'We may be clever, but are we intelligent? That's the question.

'I hope these brief comments will prompt discussion, and, of course, your questions. Thank you for listening.'

Sir Gerald stood up and led the applause with obvious enthusiasm. His liking and admiration for Blackstone had completely overcome his reservations.

'Prime Minister, that was a *tour de force*. You had my poor old head spinning. What a range of questions? Now, we'll have a break of, say, ten minutes, when we'll resume for questions.'

Blackstone accompanied his host to freshen up, as Sir Gerald told the ladies, and by the time they had returned the interlude was up.

Sir Gerald tapped the microphone.

'Your questions, please.'

Professor Gilpin was the first to speak.

'Prime Minister, I'm told you're issuing free credit to fund certain projects. This sounds like the Keynesian solution.'

'I cannot be sure of the model or if there is a model. All I know is that strict instructions have been issued that the credit can only be used for valid infrastructure projects. Grandiose mayoral projects are not on! The projects we propose will enhance the wealth of the community.'

'Thank you, Prime Minister.'

'Prime Minister, how can you sanction a stream of unsecured credit?' It was the other professor, exploding in frustration. 'Credit must be secured; that is the basic rule.'

'Professor, your concern, I'm sure, is valid, especially in the light of recent banking irresponsibility. The Bank of England monitored project you're questioning has the security of the actual project – the infrastructure. That won't vanish into thin air, but will enhance community value, which we hope to claw back, in part at least, by the location levy. Indeed, there'd be a yearly pay-back.'

The professor took his seat, but with a show of disaffection.

Three questions followed, all voicing concern that the security of property ownership was being eroded. Indeed, one question was more of a lecture. Here Blackstone concentrated on the inequity of such security. Many on the wrong side of the track had no such security, and little chance of acquiring it. The current tragedy of soaring repossessions illustrated the bitter price of failure.

'For the haves, property security is a pleasing mantra.' Blackstone concluded. 'The question is, is it pleasing for the rest of us? Is the burden of a lifelong mortgage worth it? For, in the end, the overall price is a divided nation: those who have and those who do not have! Of course, our current proposals only cite a twenty percent levy at most. So, for the haves, worry is somewhat premature.'

'It's the thin edge of the wedge, Prime Minister. What MP could vote for it? Their constituents would be in rebellion!' The speaker made no secret of his incredulity.

'The levy will not stop us being a property-owning democracy. Indeed, many more will be able to own the house they live in, for they will be relieved of the crippling mortgage needed for the freehold deed. The levy deals with site location, but the house, the bricks and mortar, are untaxed. For the "haves" there'll be some sacrifice of privilege; even Cabinet members will be subject to this, but it's a sacrifice for the common benefit. In terms that this meeting will understand, it's an investment which will in time return a rich dividend, not only to the few, but too all.'

An angular-looking man stood up without being called. Clearly his frustration had driven him to his feet.

'Why are we wasting our time on this nineteenth-century idea? This is the internet age, where someone with a laptop can make a fortune trading from his garden shed. How would you tax him?'

'I wouldn't!' Blackstone replied laconically. 'The habit of taxing labour is ingrained. It *is* nineteenth-century! – Pitt, I believe, introduced income tax to finance the war against Napoleon. – May I press the principle behind the tax-shift proposal? That is, what a man earns is his affair, but what the community creates is *its* affair. At the moment the community does not collect this self-created fund. We hope to move towards this. Of course, taxes on production can't be abandoned overnight, so, no doubt, the chap with a laptop in his shed will be taxed like the rest of us. The happy state where a man's labour is wholly untaxed is, alas, somewhat distant. Another point: should your hero earn a fortune, then his fortune, almost certainly, will propel him or her to a central site, and guess what, location levy.'

Another hand shot up.

'What about the man, who, just as he's managed to pay off the mortgage on his modest terraced house, finds himself suddenly stricken with disability? His only income is an assisted pension – this levy you're proposing would destroy him! How would you answer that, Prime Minister?'

'Such persons would not be harassed during their latter years. Indeed, insensitive treatment of such people would not be tolerated and would be contrary to the spirit of the measures we're proposing.'

A heavy-looking man rose ponderously to his feet.

'Sir, say I found oil under my few acres in Surrey; how would your Utopian system respond?' Sarcasm was thinly disguised.

'First of all, the Chancellor would rejoice!' Blackstone quipped. An explosion of laughter erupted.

'Seriously, if such a fortune occurred, planning considerations would be obligatory. Obviously, such a find would attract considerable interest and competition for the pumping rights would be keen – to say the least. This, of course, would hike the location value. You, as the incumbent, would have first refusal, as it were. The principle would remain the same as any other site. I'm answering your question as to the Utopian system, as you put it – that is the total levy. A partial levy would be a modification of this, but you will probably agree that any detailed analysis would have to await the leisure of another occasion.'

Knowing smiles were numerous.

Another explosion of questions followed, which focused mostly on application anomalies. It was clear to Blackstone that many either did not understand the tax-shift proposals or had imported misconceptions. So he took the opportunity to, once more, spell out the simplicity of the principle.

'Dr Harwich,' Sir Gerald called out.

'Prime Minister, are you trying to tell us that a location levy is actually practical? I do believe I understand the theory, but the complications are unending. Growth, surely, is what we need, and urgently. President Kennedy, I believe, used the image of *a rising tide that lifts all boats*. Indeed, it seems to be a generally accepted notion, and one that does appear to be confirmed by history. I'm sorry, Sir, but I find the location value measure complicated and impractical, whereas the rising tide analogy seems so simple. Can you help me here?'

'Thank you for raising the issue, Dr Harwich. It so happens that I was handed a paper a day or so ago, which referred to this very subject. Apparently US government statistics indicate that from 1960 to 2005, GDP per capita more than doubled, but the real median household income, of say middle and working class families, rose only by a modest percentage. In fact, it was said that they had essentially stagnated.[2] So what had happened to the rising tide?

'I looked up *Progress and Poverty*. What did Henry George have to say? Mind you, I didn't expect to find the answer right away. I opened the book at random here and there, and suddenly there it was. So, knowing I was coming here, I photo-copied the passage – just in case – and here it is!'

Casually he pulled a paper from his inside pocket and held it up for all to see.

'A likely story, you may think, but, then, some likely stories happen to be true!'

'Anyway here is what George says:

The growth of population, the increase and extension of exchanges, the discoveries of science, the march of invention [etc] have all a direct tendency to increase the productive power of labour – not of some labour, but of all labour...

But labour cannot reap the benefits which advancing civilization thus brings...

Blackstone stopped and scanned the hall.

'Why is this? George explains that the benefits are *intercepted*. How?

'He continues:

Land being necessary to labour, and being reduced to private ownership, every increase in the productive power of labour but increases rent – the price that labour must pay for the opportunity to utilise its powers; and thus all advantages gained by the march of progress go to the owners of land, and wages do not increase.[3]

'This, I suggest, gives an explanation of why the rising tide appears to be selective. In other words: some boats are more equal than others!

'To summarise, growth increases wealth; in so doing it increases location value, an increase labour must pay for access. Few landlords fail to charge the going rate.

'Dr Harwich, the principle of the location value levy is simplicity itself. What is complicated is our present system. This I have repeated many times. We've had a committee working constantly on this, and the computer models that they have created are quite amazing. Like you, I have had my doubts, but what has sustained me is the certainty that the principle is true. This has been my candle in the dark. You might ask, is it a truth before its time? Well, I do believe it is the time. Dr Harwich, the old model has failed us; it's time for something new. *We would simply take for the community what belongs to the community – the value that attaches to land by the growth of the community; leave sacred to the individual all that belongs to the individual.* What beautiful simplicity. These are the words of Henry George. *The teaching of George is irresistibly convincing in its simplicity and clearness. He who becomes acquainted with it cannot but agree.* And these are the words of Count Leo Tolstoy.'[4]

Dr Harwich was on his feet again, but a blustering wine-befuddled voice arrested him

'This is nineteenth century hogwash, a commie fairyland, it's – it's medieval. Get real, Prime Minister! – I'm all right!' the man protested as his friends tried to subdue his outburst. Then, all at once, he slumped back in his chair. The room was silent, and Dr Harwich, still on his feet, cleared his throat. Then he spoke as if there'd been no interruption.

'Thank you, Prime Minister, I am humbled by your careful answer. If, tonight, I came to scoff, I certainly have remained to pray. Thank you, Sir.'

The dining hall was perfectly still, and Sir Gerald took the opportunity to bring proceedings to a close.

Chapter Twenty-Seven

Sir Gerald was almost tearful when he waved the Prime Minister and Anna off. It had been a great occasion. Indeed, he felt privileged in being host to such a striking couple.

'I think Sir Gerald fell for you, my dear.'

She snuggled up to him.

'You were magnificent, Henry. And Dr Harwich, well – was that story that you told the way it was?'

'Yes, it was as if someone had planned it all. Anyway, I'll sleep tonight. It's been a long day.'

'Why don't you drop off at Number Ten...?'

'Not on, my love! I must take my lady home.'

'The whole thing went so well,' she murmured.

'It did, remarkably so.' Too well, he thought. But he didn't say that to Anna. There were dark unsmiling faces in the hall; men who didn't take it lightly that their interests were being threatened. The battle wasn't won by any means. The real opposition hadn't revealed itself. That, he feared was yet to come, and anyway the hard core 'antis' wouldn't broadcast their intentions. He was puzzled, though; why was the opposition so muted, when the event was being televised? It was a perfect opposition platform. Sir Harold Hanwall was there with his rather gracious wife, and Blackstone had fully expected the usual outburst, but not a word, in fact; Sir Harold looked positively benign. Perhaps he felt the measure didn't stand a chance – many felt that way!

They sat contented and silent as the Jaguar glided quietly along the Embankment.

'I'm meeting the father of the twelve-year-old, tomorrow. He's been checked out, of course; a competent engineer, I believe.'

'Will you be able to find him employment?'

'Hopefully, the infrastructure projects and the necessary credit proposals should pass with little difficulty. The debate is on Tuesday. Winston, with Chris at his elbow, are looking after this.'

'Do they get on? They're at the opposite ends of the spectrum!'

'Winston's fairly near the centre and Chris has dropped his left-wing class-war thing. He'll have to, if he's walking out with Janet!'

'"Walking out." That *is* really old-fashioned, Henry!'

'I'm an old-fashioned kind of guy.'

She chuckled and nuzzled closer.

They were silent until the car turned off at the Hogarth round-about, for Richmond.

'I'm thinking of heading off for Great Missenden on Saturday.'

'Great Missenden?'

'Chequers, dear.'

'Of course, where else?' At times, her situation still felt dream-like.

'You will hobnob with Prime Ministers! Yes, it would be good if both you and your father could come for the weekend. We'll probably return late Sunday. I'm certain your father would do much to stiffen up our thinking for the fight next week.'

'He'll be thrilled. His sense of history will be stimulated, and he loves the country. We'll confirm with him when we arrive.'

'Will he be still up?'

'Oh yes, he'll have watched it all on tele, and, of course, the machinations of the experts. My heavens!' Anna exclaimed, as the Jaguar came to a halt. 'There are four security people now.'

'Maybe they're changing over, love.'

'Maybe.'

Alexander Collingwood opened the door as they approached, and they went inside.

'A wonderful evening, Father!'

'Yes, I saw it all. There you were, Henry, and my beloved daughter on the box! A damned good speech, Henry! Excellent.'

'Thank your daughter, Sir; she gave the clues – "something new and something true". Those were the magic words!'

'Your speech was pretty comprehensive. It should have sparked a revolution, but no! And that reply to Dr Harwich. There was something very powerful there. I was quite moved.'

'The whole dining-room was, Father.'

'Come in, come in. You'll have some tea before you go, I hope.'

'As the saying goes, I thought you'd never ask!'

Anna busied herself with the tea things, and the two men sat down to talk.

'Just before we came in, Anna noticed an increase in the security detail. I suggested it might have been the change-over,' Blackstone said quietly.

'No, they've been doubled. There were some suspicious goings on, and they asked for back-up.'

'I haven't mentioned any of this to Anna, of course, but I'm uneasy. Tonight, for instance: why did it pass so smoothly? There was resentment present, bitter resentment; I could read it in the upturned faces, yet nothing happened. That is, except for the drunken outburst.'

'I'd say that gave the opposition bad publicity and may have put a stop to further "anti" outbursts.'

'Maybe.' Blackstone remained pensive.

'Henry, who knows? Dr Harwich certainly was impressed. You know, I've seen men change mid-sentence when the penny dropped. Ah, here's the tea!'

'Father, Henry has invited us to Chequers for the weekend. You've nothing on, I hope?'

'Nothing but a waiting pile of manuscripts!'

'Bring one or two with you. You'll be employed, of course, for there'll be meetings with the so-called kitchen Cabinet. We need to brush up for next week, and your input would be valued. How should we counter a concerted attack?'

'Henry, I wouldn't wait until next week! I would act now! I'd try and find out who the opposition are. That panel chaired by Sir Robert Cowdrey wasn't so revealing as we'd hoped. Many kept their real opinions under cover?'

'Yes, that was what Sir Robert told me. So we need someone to infiltrate the enemy.'

Collingwood nodded.

'Can I use your phone?'

'Of course.'

Blackstone punched in numbers automatically. It was clearly a familiar number.

'This is your beloved brother, sister.' There was a crackle of laughter down the line that was just audible to the Collingwoods. 'It's not late, not by your standards! ... All right, all right, I apologise. Where's Willie? I need him urgently...

Tomorrow morning – good – get him to phone me... A compliment from you, Patricia, is a real brownie point!' More laughter crackled, and Blackstone put the phone down.

Collingwood and his daughter were clearly amused.

'That, as you will have gathered, was Patricia. PM's don't impress her. No doubt you will have guessed my thinking. Willie and his party will be my Vauxhall Cross!'

'Who's "M"?' Anna joked.

'Willie!'

*

Following an early morning phone call Willie Windbourne arrived at Downing Street at ten, where he found the PM and Bill Jones leisurely enjoying coffee.

'Is this a rest home?' he enquired jokingly.

'Yip, for redundant party leaders!' Blackstone returned. 'Can I get you a coffee, Willie?'

'It's all right, Henry. I'll pump this flask. LDs are quite catholic in their skills.'

Willie took his seat, holding his cup carefully. He was a tall man, slim in build, with a shock of fair hair and a naturally pleasant demeanour.

'Willie, we want to know the mood in the House. Not just the official stuff, but what is really going on. To put it bluntly: who's for us and, who's against us. Do you think your folk could keep their eyes open?'

'If we're going to be the CIA, do we get paid in dollars?'

'Straight from the Fed! Willie, there's nothing very special about this. Bill and I have our feed-backs, but we felt you could be more...'

'Independent!' Willie completed. 'Henry, we're just as tribal as you lot! But I know what you mean. I have a funny feeling that it's all too quiet. Is there someone out there busy gathering votes and making promises?'

'Exactly, Willie.'

'I think you'll find that it's the new money that is set against us,' Windbourne continued.

'Willie, there's a fair amount of old money not too happy either!' Bill Jones said wearily.

'You would think we were going to crucify them!' Blackstone interjected. 'We really need to put the point across, both loud and clear, that the levy isn't draconian, and that the old lady living in a large house on her own will not be driven out. Indeed, in such special cases there'll be recourse to arbitration.'

'Henry, what about the landlord who tries to pass the levy on to his tenant. What's to stop him?' Bill Jones queried.

'The landlord is already taking the most and you cannot take more than the most, for the tenant will move, or close shop.'

'But, Henry, the landlord knows that the tenant has received a reduction in income tax. Would he not try and take advantage of this?'

'There could be some upward pressure, but I doubt if this would be a factor of significance, for there would be downward pressures, too.'

'Your reasons, Henry?'

'This is not a tax on land, but a levy on the value that attaches to the land, due to its location, which varies and reduces on moving out from the highly valued site.'

'Henry, I know what you're saying, but people still see it as a tax on land,' Bill Jones interjected.

'Yes, I've found that, too. We have to keep chipping away. It's a levy on location value, which, by its nature, is a diminishing charge as we move towards the margin. It is not a flat rate charged willy-nilly. The burning question is, can the landlord pass it on?'

'Yes, that's the question,' Willie Windbourne emphasised.

'Central-site landlords would find it very difficult to pass their substantial levy on. The sums could put their tenants out of business. Indeed, they would probably relocate. Anyhow, the "acres" of empty office space, which would be subject to the levy, would make landlords pause, before pressing their increase. This applies to the average high street as well. Empty sites will be levied, so landlords will be cautious.

'Because the levy will be partial initially, say twenty per cent, if we're lucky, land holdings will change little, and new enterprises at the margin will still be faced with rent: reason being that all land is enclosed and subject to the law of real estate. In fact, due to the bounty of the levy, some help may be offered to start-up businesses. The landlord will try but, for reasons already mentioned, passing on the levy will not be automatic. Certainly, the margin will always be attractive to new enterprises; and, as such areas are extensive, a landlord cannot put his rent up excessively. If he does, his valuation will increase, and so will his levy. Anyway, the margin will almost always offer a selection of alternative sites. The landlord's scope is limited. Again, we should remind ourselves that the levy is only on the location value, but

159

not on the buildings. If a landlord wishes to increase his income, he should develop his site to its full potential. Remember, the trend will be to reduce tax on enterprise.

'We can't cross all the bridges in advance, or think we can anticipate every eventuality. That would be arrogance. As long as we don't compromise the natural principle, all will be well.'

'Henry, I think it's beginning to get through.' Willie Windbourne's tone was reflective. 'The landlord's already charging the most that he can get. How can he ask for more than the most, when he knows that the tenant is already paying the most that he can afford? If he tries to pass the levy on, he'll lose the tenant. But the bottom line remains: he pays the levy!'

'Some tenants would be desperate to retain the site location,' Bill Jones cut in.

'They may be, Bill. But if the bank manager taps on their shoulder, desperation will be wearing different clothes!' Willie returned.

Jones nodded.

'On the domestic side, there are a surprisingly large number of empty houses,' Blackstone continued. 'Their location value would be subject to the levy, and doubtless many would enter the market and put a downward pressure on the capital value and the rental. Yes, passing on the levy would be difficult. My friends, I put a virtual ice bag on my head when looking into this.'

Bill Jones sighed.

'Henry, I think I get the drift.'

For a time they lapsed into silence.

'Henry', Willie started forcefully, 'the taxation reductions on income and production due to the tax-shift: how can we stop the landowner absorbing these in rents and hiked capital value? We haven't really answered this.'

'Yes, we've rather dodged that one,' Blackstone admitted. 'The law of real-estate rules, OK,' he added, nodding pensively. 'Or does it? What do you think, Bill?'

'I think the same downward pressures would apply as we've just mentioned. There are a lot of derelict and half-used sites that would be forced onto the market because of the levy. And another thing, there are a lot of fixed term agreements out there. So upward pressures would be slow to manifest. John Stuart Mill and Co were adamant that the landlord couldn't pass the levy on.'

160

'Bill, you're a lot more upbeat than me!' Willie reacted. 'The property boys will squeeze the market for every penny!'

'Yes, but it's not the old game any more. Owners, who were prepared to spend little on their property, knowing they could make a killing on the freehold when the time was right, will have to think again. I think you'd find a lot of stuff coming onto the market, and that, of course, would put a bridle on the rent increases. But what excites me is the hope that many young bloods, encouraged by the lower taxes, may branch out on their own. This we must support.'

Blackstone nodded.

'Every brick and every tile belongs to the owner, but the element land, which is the gift of nature, is not for man to claim as being his own.' Blackstone spoke as if he were thinking aloud. 'He can have the use of land by paying the location value levy relative to its area and position. The trouble is, we are still subject to real estate law. The levy we propose is only partial, for we cannot race beyond the people's will. And, because of this, free land at the margin would not be possible, that is, in the general sense. One further point: the valuation Jake's been rushing to complete will be repeated annually, we hope. Now that the mechanism has been established, this shouldn't be too difficult. So, if the landowner pushes up his rent, he could be liable to a reassessment. To put it another way: bells would start ringing in the levy office for the landlord would have signalled an increase in his valuation. Again, if he were daft enough to pass the increased levy on, he'd lose his tenant, and "hey ho" he'd still be saddled with the levy! And, do you know something, if the levy were so easy to pass on, why are there so many hard against it? Why all the fuss? As Bill said, it's not the old game any more. And I suspect we'll not have to search for anomalies.

'The landlord, of course, is not a criminal. He's the friend next door, simply trying to earn a crust. It's the system that's lopsided.'

'Landlords for bricks and mortar, but not for land, I say!' Willie intoned.

They laughed.

'The property owner's getting a tax reduction on his earnings as well,' Blackstone said quietly, 'and by the instrument of the market he's angling for the tax break of the tenant, too.'

'Henry, it's like what you said last night to Dr Harwich. That's

161

why the rich get richer and the ordinary guy keeps struggling,' Willie said forcefully. 'Yeah, some boats are more equal that others!'

Blackstone smiled. 'Well, we aim to have the rising tide lift *all* the boats.'

Chapter Twenty-Eight

The police officers shook hands with both the Prime Minister and his Deputy and then filed out. Their report on inner-city lawlessness was sobering. More police on the street meant more funding, but where was it to come from? Day after day there were departments clamouring for funds. In any case, throwing money at the problem didn't seem to work.

'What do you think, Bill?'

'I'm sure more policemen on the streets would help, but we've been saying this for years. Our plans for infrastructure work will inject some hope, but we need something else. Henry, in the words of the Psalmist: *The fear of the Lord is the beginning of wisdom.*[1] But imagine saying that on *Newsnight!*'

'Bill, you don't go to Hinde Street for nothing!'

'Don't look at me like that! I'm not Gaunt's *prophet new inspired!*'[2]

'Maybe not, but you could chair a committee. We need fresh thinking. I was speaking to that rather intelligent Indian Deputy during the break. He quoted from his tradition, something not dissimilar to the Psalmist. A candidate for the committee, I would say.'

'So you're serious about this committee?'

'Oh yes, and its distinguished chairman, too!'

'I see,' Jones said with mock resignation, his amusement obvious.

'Bill, I'm meeting Mr Robbins, you know, the father of the twelve-year-old I told you about. He's due in about fifteen minutes. Do you want to meet him?'

'I think I'll skip it. These things are better one to one. And I might get landed with another job!'

They both grinned.

'Anyway, I'll see you at Chequers.' Jones continued. 'I can't get out of that one, for Ellen wants to come!'

The good humour was obvious, and Bill Jones took his leave.

*

Hugh Robbins was a stocky man, a perfect rugby front-row forward, Blackstone judged. Yet, as it was so often with such men, he had a gentle manner.

'Pleased to meet you, Mr Robbins,' Blackstone said as he stretched out his hand. 'You've been having a difficult time.'

'Yes, Sir, and your phone call was a miracle!'

'Well, you can thank your son.'

'And you, Prime Minister. You responded to the letter.'

'Mr Robbins, we have no idea why things happen, but there it is. Now it's after twelve and Mabel, who does for me, as she says, will be preparing something, probably soup and a sandwich. I ate rather well last night. Now, I'm sure Mabel can add your name to the soup pot.'

'That's very kind, Sir.'

'Right, let's go up to the flat.'

Robbins followed in a semi-daze. This wasn't happening. It was all so normal. Yet Robbins wasn't fooled. The PM's easy manner masked a very sharp intelligence, and he had a tangible presence. He was very 'there'.

He was introduced to Mabel, who called the PM Mr Henry. In her way an influential lady, for, if she sensed that someone wasn't up to scratch, she'd find a way to let the PM know her feelings.

'Mr Robbins, may I call you Hugh?'

'Of course, Sir.'

'Hugh, who is the most important figure on a construction site?'

'A good agent, or site manager is everything: his influence runs through the whole site. His orders are clear. There's no dithering, and instances of indiscipline and shoddy work are dealt with immediately. He's not a tyrant, but he's not a fool.'

'Did you watch the TV last night?'

'I did, Sir, but I didn't think it was my place to lead the conversation.'

Blackstone liked it. Robbins was good.

'You have my permission to lead at will,' the PM returned good-humouredly.

'Well, Sir, I thought your reply to the younger of the two professors very apt. It rang true that the credit was secured by the infrastructure.'

'Yes, the professor, of course, had a point about the need for credit being secured. Too much credit has been raised on the very questionable security of debt packages. In fact, the general lack of integrity has been difficult to *credit,* if I may over-use the word! Tell me, did you understand the tax-shift business?'

'From the beginning, I've understood the idea of location value, but I simply saw it as another tax. Having other concerns, to put it mildly, I hadn't given it much thought. But your answer to Dr Harwich yesterday evening alerted me to its deeper significance.'

Yes, Robbins was good.

'It won't be easy to sell, Sir. Yesterday, we got a leaflet through our door headed, "Taxing your back garden. The attack on private property." And that corporate boss, Sir Harold Hanwall, keeps holding meetings in my area. He's passionate and pretty persuasive.'

'He was at the dinner last night, but he didn't say a word. His wife was with him. Maybe that deterred him.'

'I doubt it, Sir. I've met him. He's not a softie, but he's honest. You could depend on him. What he said he did.'

'Interesting, Hugh.' Blackstone was intrigued, but he let the matter drop. 'Yes, the opposition aren't asleep,' he continued. 'Next Thursday's debate could be a near-run thing.' Blackstone nodded. 'This country seems to specialise in such things!'

The internal phone buzzed and the PM's hand went out automatically.

'Send him up, Jenny, thanks.'

'Chris Crouch is joining us.'

'Chris Crouch! The last time I met him was on a site and it was 'Seconds out!"'

Blackstone smiled, and they were silent for a time.

'Chris is very likeable,' the Prime Minister said quietly. 'And here he is!'

'PM,' Crouch acknowledged.

'Chris, I think you two know each other.' Blackstone said with amused anticipation.

'Hugh, I wondered if it was the same Robbins, and there you are. God, the last time we met it was toe to toe! It's all right, Hugh. The PM has reformed me!'

They shook hands warmly, just as Mabel arrived with the soup. Crouch immediately kissed Mabel on the cheek.

'Mr Chris, you are the naughty one!' She was clearly pleased.

Blackstone was fascinated as he listened to the two men joke about their experiences: Chris from the point of view of a one-time Union official and Hugh Robbins as the harassed agent.

'Gentlemen, it looks as if the Tuesday vote is in the bag. For, as jobs are on the line, what MP would dare to vote against the credit issue? Such a negative move would mean very bad publicity in their constituency newspapers. So you're on, gentlemen. Chris will be checking on the job-creating effectiveness of the various projects and you, Hugh, will have an overall brief on site management. You will both report to the Home Secretary and, Hugh, I feel you ought to try and have a word with Winston Hughes, while you're here in London. Maybe, Chris, you could help with that, for I've got a date at Lambeth Palace. The subject: youth crime, in case you thought I was on the carpet!'

Easy humour united them.

'Hugh, before you go, have a word with Jenny, my secretary. She has a gift for Jim, your son. As I said before, we don't know why things happen. All I can say is, that I'm very pleased Jim posted his letter. Sorry, I must go, or I *will* be on the carpet!'

Hugh Robbins found his situation hard to believe. He shook his head.

'Chris, three days ago I was a no-hoper. Now this. The Prime Minister is a remarkable man. He's so ordinary, so easy in his ways, yet, so very extraordinary.'

*

Sir Frederick Kingsway's business empire was vast. The downturn in trade was troublesome, but most of his wealth was in property and he had reserves in plenty. He could easily wait a year of two, buy up some nice sites from desperate sellers and wait for a recovery. Property always bounced back. His only problem was Blackstone and his damnable government. They could wreck everything.

A leaflet drop would descend on the country over the weekend. It was costing a fortune, but if it spiked Blackstone's plans it would be worth every penny. Indeed, Kingsway was determined to use guile, and any trick that he could think of. There was far too much at stake to be restrained by scruples. He had primed some pumps in the press and media. They were performing well, but apart from a few passionate advocates of property rights, many MPs were cagey and equivocal, and the Chancellor was a wimp. The passionate advocates, though, were persuasive. Then there was the inarticulate anger of the many. These people were outraged that their hard-won property had been targeted. For such folk, protest marches had been organised and Sir Frederick had funded the publicity. These protests were to take place at the weekend in all the major cities. Surely, this would push the dithering MPs off the fence.

His aides told him that the figures were good, but he wanted them better than good. He wanted certainty. Also he was suspicious that his people were telling him 'good news' to keep him happy.

It was Friday and he was waiting for two of his MP allies to arrive. Both Harold Harbin and Dan Draper were their own men. They would tell him straight the way things were, and from the telltale noises sounding in the outer office, he guessed the MPs had arrived.

'Where's the coffee, Freddie?' Harbin boomed. Harbin had only two modes of speaking, loud and louder. He was a tall man with a distinctive crop of grey hair. His friend Dan Draper had a similar growth and was about the same height. In fact, they were known as 'The Twins', but Draper's voice was soft.

Kingsway pressed his secretary's buzzer twice. It was the code for coffee.

'What about Tuesday, Harold?' he asked at once.

'Blackstone's sewn Tuesday up. Let's not waste our time on that.'

'I agree.' Draper's soft voice contrasted with Harbin's harsh unyielding sound. 'Tuesday's about jobs, and we can't attack that. Thursday's the one where we have suburbia on our side. The leaflet drop was brilliant, Freddie.'

'Yeah, but will suburbia clog the Beeb with e-mails, or harass their MPs?' Kingsway barked. 'They may be whingeing, but are they organising a petition?'

'Hamilton Davis is!' Harbin interjected. 'And on a big scale too.'

'Hamilton does more harm than good.' Draper reacted.

'Don't worry; I'll get my guys on to it. We'll shower Blackstone with petitions. We want more prime-site billboards and full-page ads in the nationals. The local stuff is useless! What about the MPs? We need to lean on these guys!' Kingsway pressed.

'They know what side their bread is buttered on. We're a property-owning democracy. Can you picture an MP saying that he voted for the government?' Harbin asked harshly.

'After, Blackstone has spoken, I can. The PM's persuasive.' Draper's quiet voice seemed to emphasise the point.

'Yeah, we need to cut him down to size,' Kingsway barked.

'Freddie, have you got something up your sleeve?' Draper asked.

'I know where to hurt him, but you guys best be in the dark.'

Harbin saw Kingsway as a hard-hitting, business role-model, but Draper wasn't so trusting. The Tycoon was ruthless and, like most ruthless people, the end would always justify the means. Draper was outraged by the attack on family property, but there were boundaries to his protests beyond which he would not stray.

The coffee had arrived, and Draper pressed his point once more about the effectiveness of Blackstone.

'Don't fret, Dan, I'll have that bod fettered. No matter who they are, guys always have a weakness!' In Kingsway's eyes there was the glint of steel. 'And what about the CBI? They're issuing press releases no one understands. Dick James always waffles. And that guy Hanwall didn't open his mouth at that Tower Hill dinner! Hell, he sat with a grin on his face! Jeez, Dan, Harold, do something, get them moving!'

When Draper and Harbin left, Kingsway sat strumming with his fingers on the empty surface of his large expansive desk. Then impulsively he snatched his private phone from its holder and punched in a number.

Chapter Twenty-Nine

It was Saturday morning, and a knock on the Collingwood door revealed someone canvassing for anti-location-levy signatures. Anna was alerted by the methodical nature of the canvasser. This person wasn't an activist, for an activist would have known to skip the Collingwood house. In fact, the woman seemed indifferent when Anna declined to add her signature. Puzzled, she approached one of the security people.

'Some PR firm is organising it, Miss Collingwood,' the officer revealed. 'There's a whole tribe of them knocking on doors around The Green. For most, I'd guess, it's anything for a crust. Times are hard. This is not the only lot. They're all over the place apparently, and not just in London. Costing a pretty penny, I would say.'

Anna thanked the officer and went inside. Immediately she phoned Downing Street and was put through to Henry instantly. At once, she told him what had happened, and the comprehensive nature of the canvassing.

'I expected something like this but not on such a scale. Anna, my love, you're the first one to tell me, and it's very helpful, for we can counter quickly.'

'But what can you do, Henry?'

'Activists are part of the democratic process, but engineered canvassing on a large scale is sure to be distrusted. The people need to be informed about the nature of this canvass. After that it's up to their good sense.'

'If they're anti, they'll still have their prejudices.'

'Then, it's up to us to laud the merits of our case. The phoney war is over and battle has been joined.'

'It's not going to be easy, Henry.'

'No, dear, a photo finish, I would say, and for the country's sake, I hope we edge a nose in front!'

'What about this afternoon? Will this business alter things?' Anna asked.

'No, it's Chequers as planned. A car will collect you and your

father. It may be me, but I doubt it. In fact, I think I'll ask Bill to collect you. I had thought of Willie, but he has got his hands full at the moment. Well, my love, I'll see you very soon, and thanks for the call. If you go on like this, Vauxhall Cross will be clamouring for your services!'

Suddenly he was gone, and a sense of unreality rose like mist about her. 'I'll get Bill to collect you,' he said. 'Willie has got his hands full.' In other words, the Prime Minister probably wouldn't make it, and the Foreign Secretary was busy. So the Deputy Prime Minister would be calling. This was fairyland! It wasn't happening!

✳

The ramifications of Anna's phone call were uncomfortably numerous. But central to it all was someone who had wealth in plenty. Some fat cat, Blackstone assumed, for corporate action was cumbersome and slow to move. Anna's source was as good as it gets, yet the facts would have to be confirmed. A Prime Minister dared not act, and certainly darned not speak publicly, on uncorroborated information.

The phone rang, interrupting his reflections. It was Jenny, announcing the Foreign Secretary.

'Send him in, Jenny.'

Willie Windbourne's tall, rather languid form draped itself over a chair. Although very different from Chris Crouch, he was equally likeable.

'Coffee, Willie?'

'I was just about to steel myself to ask.'

'You shy thing!' Blackstone joked, while placing the request. 'So what's happening. Have we got *any* votes?'

'A fair number, but they're mostly coming with a protest. Henry, they're afraid of losing their seats in the next election. Suburbia have no love for the levy.'

'Willie, it's the bitter pill problem. They're good for you but who likes taking them? Burke says some telling things about *leaders* [who] *choose to make themselves bidders at an auction of popularity.'* [1]

'I'll leave you to say that, Henry!' Windbourne said knowingly.

'So, Willie, how are we going to stiffen them up?'

'Not an easy one, Henry. I've raised the subject with many MPs and not just the Lib Dems. Most get it in an intellectual sort of way. They nod sagely, but who's to say they wouldn't change their mind the following day. Some glaze over. Perhaps, the principle hasn't any relevance to their sectional interest. Then there are those who actually see the full significance. That's uplifting. It's a heart thing, Henry, as if, in Emerson's words, they're *admitted to the right of reason.*'

'*The Essay on History* – a wonderful opening. You're a dark horse Willie, I've never heard you speak like this before. It seems my beloved sister's picked a winner.'

'I'm not a bloody horse, Henry!'

Both men burst out laughing.

'Seriously, I feel the only way to get this principle across is to focus on the moral angle. Henry, this *is* a moral question and it's the way to win the House.'

'Thanks, Willie, thanks for that.'

They sat silently for a while.

'There's another thing, Willie. Anna phoned me.' Blackstone then went on to detail the goings on at Richmond.

'It's hotting up. You'll need corroboration. I'll make a few phone calls. The LDs are good at picking up this kind of info. Then we can let the press office loose!'

'And if necessary I can do an interview on Monday – a one-to-one – that sort of thing. Thanks again, Willie. You called at the right time!'

'Well, the coffee was good.'

'Yeah, we get some things right.'

Willie quickly left, and Blackstone sat back in his chair.

A repetition of the same wouldn't work on Thursday. Willie was right: it was a moral question, but saying only that wouldn't raise the temperature, and certainly wouldn't move the House. He needed something simple – what is right and what is wrong, simple: something that would awaken conscience and wrench the mind from obfuscation.

Willie was good, Bill was good, and Chris and Jake were good. Again, there were Ted, Janet and Winston and more besides. Except for the Chancellor, whom he'd practically written off, he had an excellent team. The circumstances were uncommonly propitious. The need was pressing and the time was ripe. To miss the hour would be a tragedy. This unusual National Government was poised to act in equally unusual circumstances. To lose the chance would be unthinkable.

What was he going to do with Jamieson? The Chancellor worked hard, was conscientious, and did all that was required of him, yet he had the uninspiring nature of an ageing disappointed clerk. One moment he was for the tax shift, the next immersed in doubt. He had asked him to Chequers, but it was doubtful he would come. He had always some 'valid' excuse. All said he was sitting on the fence, but even if he were, he hadn't broken rank. He hadn't used the airways or the press to voice dissatisfaction. That had to be acknowledged, and when it came to personal relationships, James Jamieson was always courteous.

He sat quietly for a moment, letting the various tensions drain. He was tempting fate, he thought knowingly. It couldn't last. Then, as if to prove the point, the phone began to ring. It was Chris.

'They're trying to get at Jake, PM. There's an article in one of the early freebees, reporting on innuendos that's been written in a blog.'

'About what?'

'Marital infidelity.'

'Rubbish! Jake and Marjorie Hud are devoted. It won't stick. It's simply not Jake's style.'

'It's very cleverly written. We couldn't lay a finger on them.'

'Has Jake reacted?'

'Yes: Either accuse him straight and face a writ, or shut up.'

'That's Jake's style! They're trying to damage us, but they've chosen the wrong man.'

'Muck clings.'

'I know. The nasties play on that.'

Chapter Thirty

The weekend at Chequers was the first time Henry Blackstone and Anna were in each other's company for more than a hurried interlude. Their happiness was a joy for all to see, but there was no comment or banter. The Prime Minister was the Prime Minister. Blackstone made it clear that the weekend was informal and an opportunity for ministers to discuss the problems of the hour amongst themselves, so, except for lunch and dinner, there were no fixed schedules.

Anna was in heaven, but she was perceptive and knew to be silent when Henry was reflective. The man she adored was Prime Minister with responsibilities that seemed too much for human flesh and blood. Henry only smiled when she touched on this. He made no comment, but she sensed that he was listening to some deeper prompting. Then he spoke as if responding to her thoughts.

'Anna, my dear, I don't know who or what I wait upon. My classical training says it is the One, or in the words of Plato's *Timaeus: that which always is but never becomes.*[1] My Christian upbringing would say it is the Lord. *Rest in the Lord, and wait patiently for him.*[2] But, my love, I do wait, and when the inner voice, or feeling, or the surety of knowing, comes to mind, I act. Don't ask me to explain this process, for when the knowing comes, there is no doubt.'

Blackstone knew that he was more than fortunate to have found a companion of such beauty and intelligence. She was young yet free of girlishness, or silliness, as she herself was wont to say. Her mother had died young, and her father's influence was clearly discernible; nonetheless she was very much her own person and wasn't the parrot of common or fashionable opinion. There was no doubt whatever that when strolling with her in the grounds, he was in the company of his future wife.

Blackstone, of course, was very much aware of what was going on about him. Janet Simmons and Chris Crouch clearly enjoyed each other's company, though not in any slavish way. Bill and his wife were obviously enjoying a rest, while his sister and Willie were a magnet for quick wit and laughter. The surprise of the weekend was the attendance of the Chancellor and his wife, and while Jane Jamieson attached herself to Marjorie Hud, her husband sought the company of Alexander Collingwood. Their conversations were absorbing; at least, that was how it seemed to Blackstone.

Although Blackstone had been wearied by the Chancellor's dithering and had discounted him as a meaningful supporter, he had been careful to treat him with courtesy. The Chancellor was the Chancellor, and his support or lack of it was bound to have an impact. Of course, to sack him would be stupidly inept, making him an instant enemy and an obvious focus for the discontented. However, the prospect of James Jamieson coming on board was heartening, but Jamieson's propensity to lapse made Blackstone cautious. Jake Hud had also noted the *tete a tete,* but was caustic when he spoke to Blackstone.

'PM, I'm not reaching for the bubbly until James says something solid in the House!'

✳

After having a lengthy conversation with Samuel Bennett on the vexed subject of repossessions, Collingwood felt like a rest; so, spotting a secluded garden seat, he headed for it straightaway. He had just sat down when he saw the plump, well-fed looking figure of the Chancellor bearing down on him. 'Gird your loins, Collingwood,' he muttered to himself, just as the Chancellor sat down heavily beside him.

'Alexander, I've been trying to catch you all afternoon. Your soldier-like figure is always easy to spot amongst us pampered politicians, but you were always deep in conversation.

'First of all, may I say how charmed I've been by your daughter. The PM's a lucky man, Sir.'

Collingwood smiled and nodded, adding a brief, 'Thank you.'

'I'll be frank, Alexander, I wasn't going to come, but my wife persuaded me. I was being stupid and isolating myself, she told me. So I said, "Yes dear", and here I am.'

Collingwood's amusement was obvious. This side to Jamieson he'd never seen.

'Well, James, I know the PM's very pleased that you are here.'

'Alexander, it's an open secret that I've been blowing first one way, and then the other. Being Chancellor, I've got the best brains in the country at my elbow, PhDs by the busload! When I bring up the subject of the tax shift, they listen politely, then they shower me with the difficulties and the danger to the property market, the pension funds and a whole raft of institutions that are funded by land holding. Treasury computer models have been built up and refined over the years, and tinkering with these, they emphasise, is dangerous.'

Jamieson looked at Collingwood, soliciting a response.

'I'm not without sympathy for their point of view. Our modern world is extremely complicated. Indeed, it's little wonder that the best minds freeze before its sheer complexity.'

'So what's the answer, Alexander? In such a sea of shifting sand where can we get a foothold? That's my problem. Every minor adjustment seems to breed a host of unexpected problems. And this tax shift – need I say more?'

'James, if you or I peer under the bonnet of a modern car, the sheer complexity bewilders us. But the designer and the skilled mechanic see a different picture. Indeed, the real expert sees simplicity. It's from simplicity that the complication can be altered and refined with confidence.'

'So...'

'We need to discover the economic simplicity that's hidden by complexity. And how do we do that, we might ask? By looking to nature and, in fact, to human nature. By applying reason, and, dare we say it, its divine simplicity.'

'Don't stop, Alexander. Apply your reasoning to the tax-shift theory!'

Collingwood smiled.

'Let's try another tack, and I'm sorry to embarrass you with a rather childish story. Say you want to start a newsagent's shop. You rent a vacant site half way down a street. Trade's indifferent and you hear about a corner site that's up for renting. So you shift your business, but you notice that the rent is higher. Even so, your increased trade covers that. You're an enterprising fellow and, hearing that a high street shop is vacant, you decide to take the risk. Again the rent increases, this time considerably, and even with the increased business you're struggling just as at the corner site. The other thing you notice is the floor space. All three sites are somewhat similar. What does that suggest?'

'That you're spelling out location value.'

'Can you elaborate?'

'As the floor space is similar, you're implying that the site and not the building accounts for the rental increase.'

'Now, who creates this value increase?'

'The community with its amenities.'

'Do they collect this value?'

'No, the freeholder or in some cases a long leaseholder.'

'But Chancellor, you need revenue. So what do you do?'

'Tax earnings.'

'What effect has this taxation?'

'One thing, it takes a fortune to collect. Also people spend real money in avoiding it, and it's complicated, my God, it's complicated! There are volumes of the stuff, and as Chancellor I'm adding to its complication every year. What's more, tax consultants earn huge fees trying to interpret it. Alexander, I think I understand the tax shift now! I think I've tapped its potency.'

'I'm sorry, James, to have subjected you to such a kindergarten catechism.'

'It's all right, Alexander. It won't be on *Newsnight!*'

'As usual, fame eludes me!'

'But, Alexander, we can't ignore the present complication.'

'The location-value levy principle is not complicated, but our current system *is,* and that is where the trouble lies; it does not spring from principle.'

'Alexander, I've tried the three questions, you know: What is location value? Who creates it? And to whom does it belong? But people often fail to see the significance. It's viewed as a limited measure, indeed sometimes, as if it were naïve! How can such a simple thing have any real effect, they say? Our current tax take is so huge.'

'James, this simple measure takes away the props that under-pin monopoly.'

'Explain, Alexander.'

'Where does the aspiring monopolist seek security?'

'In size, getting bigger. Often they swallow companies, strip them of the dross and ... my God, yes, they keep the real estate, and so they tap the bounty of location value. Of course, there are laws against trading monopolies.'

'True, but not against the growth of a real-estate portfolio.

Churchill warned that land was *the mother of all other forms of monopoly.*'[3]

'Alexander, we'll have to move carefully!'

'That's an imperative, yet not too carefully. One thing: we must adhere strictly to the principle. The principle is natural, and if we obey its law all should proceed naturally. But you're right; we can't rush at this.'

They lapsed into silence, captivated by the mild and sunny weather.

'Despite my sitting on the fence,' Jamieson began, 'Henry has always been polite and considerate. My touchy *prima donna* isolation he ignored, and I'm still the Chancellor.'

Collingwood made no comment, and Jamieson continued.

'I like this place, dates back to the mid-fifteen hundreds, I believe. It's been extensively altered, of course. Here, I feel that Monday morning always comes too soon, and especially at the moment with the desperate pleas and dire predictions. Next Thursday's debate has excited a barrage of negativity in certain quarters, and it's persistent. Sometimes I think they're trying to wear me down. "Chancellor, you're the only one who can save us from this madness," they repeat. There are two special advisors, professor types, who are particularly persistent. Of course, I can dismiss them or tell them to shut up, but I feel obliged to listen.'

'Have they a consistent theme?'

'I suppose they have: pension funds and the property market – a deathblow to development, they maintain. Upsetting both these areas could be catastrophic, and I think they've got a point. My blowing hot and cold is not without a reason.'

'James, under a system that collected location value, development would mushroom. It's speculation that would suffer. That's what the fat cats fear! Pension funds – now that's another matter. Fund managers control huge concentrations of wealth, and exercise enormous influence, even in the boardrooms of the most prestigious companies. All this you know, and you may well share my concerns regarding such large concentrations of wealth. James, this whole area needs investigation, for I can't see how our present system can go on without some reformation.'

'You're right Alexander, I am concerned. A committee has been set up in conjunction with the pensions ministry. Let's say, so far I haven't been inspired! Mind you, they're good people, but we need something – like a couple of sixes over the boundary rail!'

Collingwood laughed.

'It seems that Henry's not the only one that's blest with style!'

Jamieson smiled, sighed and sat back on his seat. Then both were silent for a time. The Chancellor was the first to speak.

'A week ago I visited a large industrial site – an endless vista of workshops. Last year they were humming. Six months ago they went on short time, and now the factory's silent. So large and yet so fragile.'

'James, the mass production line's a greedy animal, and when the orders stop these mammoths die. What's more, they're geared to "just-in-time". There is no slack. They cannot ride the natural rise and fall of trade made violent by the mushroom climb of real estate and its precipitous fall. But let's stretch our legs for a while.'

Both men walked in silence, savouring the elements. It was a very pleasant afternoon: not too hot and not too windy, and except for the elegant outline of Chequers, nature's green abundance dominated. City slums were distant and poverty grotesque. How could mankind condemn itself to such a state? Henry George, that amazing American, had asked a similar question and, with unblemished clarity, had pointed to the remedy. Why were we so heedless?

'Alexander, I suppose you could say we've nationalised this patch of land we're walking on.' The Chancellor joked.

'We could, but I would question your assumption!'

Jamieson looked across at the tall, dignified figure of his companion.

'Your meaning, Alexander?'

'Leviticus 25, verse 23, and I quote: *The land shall not be sold for ever: for the land is mine; for ye are strangers and sojourners with me.*'

'It's not every day I meet an Old Testament Prophet!'

'Perhaps I'll grow a beard and boost the image!'

'Alexander, you questioned my allusions to nationalisation?'

'Yes, James, this "prophet" can be argumentative!'

'Maybe, but I'm still waiting for his answer!'

'James, if I claimed the ownership of the sunlight or the air, you'd rightly laugh at me. But when it comes to water and land, you might say I had a valid claim. Now, here is where I don my prophet's mantle to proclaim that air, sunshine, water, and land are nature's gifts to all mankind. To claim the first two as private property would be ridiculous. Not so with the third and fourth, and here is where the seeds of conflict lie. All the community can claim, in my opinion, is the location *value* created by its own presence. In a way, the location, the site, the land, belongs to no one. We are the guardians, as it were, of nature's gift. James, perhaps I'm being a purist, but I'm uneasy with the concept of ownership, even when applied to the state. So easily it can mutate to institutions and a tedious bureaucracy; and again, so easily it can transfer to private holdings.

'James, as you well know, the demographic picture of the modern world has altered greatly even since our fathers' time, and the practical difficulties facing us are posing questions that few of us are willing to confront. Are our current arrangements sustainable? This is an uncomfortable question. James, there is no doubt that a shift from taxing income to collecting location value will reform the demographic landscape. But I have no crystal ball. I only know the principle that we're introducing stands the test of reason. It is right and true and what grows from such a verity will reflect these qualities.'

'Alexander, there are so many things that are far from satis-factory.'

'Too much change too quickly is a dangerous thing. We are fixing the keystone of reform, and from that the structure of a fairer world should naturally arise.'

'But the principle can be eroded!'

'Yes, vigilance is an imperative.'

'The international scene worries me, Alexander. Will the levy prompt the multinational interests, as well as lesser mortals, to disappear abroad?'

'If taxes on production are reduced – say corporation tax –would they be so keen? If they were investing in real estate as an earner, then, quite honestly, I wouldn't shed too many tears. But, yes, there is a re-location danger, or, at worst, a mini-flood of companies leaving for the promised land. Out-sourcing, as they call it, and re-location has been happening for some time. James, this is speculation, and realities on the ground often trip us up. Say taxes on production are reduced, and the levy does not fall directly on the *entrepreneur,* such people may well choose to hold their fire; and, James, this is a global problem – the promised land is also in crisis, and if taxes on production are reduced by a significant amount, the promised land may come to us!

'My heavens!'

'Yes, James?'

'It's just struck me why Henry keeps going on about the principle.'

'Well, as Henry is also wont to say, don't keep me hanging out there!'

'The principle's the key. If you hold to the principle, you're presented with the answers.'

Chapter Thirty-One

The battle was joined. That was the unreported message of the Sunday Newspapers. One used the nationwide leaflet drop as a leader: another the numerous petitions. The leader columns were almost all against the government; one of the radical papers was particularly negative. Some headlines were colourful, and the 'serious' papers generally predicted Blackstone's nemesis, as all expected him to lose the vote. Indeed, one leader column was quite dismissive. *Anyone proposing a property tax in a property-owning democracy is either politically naïve or completely out of touch.*

Almost every article was anti, and many of these were scathing. Blackstone's proposals were ill-advised, ill-thought-out, and even a proper valuation had been sidestepped. Only Ed Gray and Jasper Jenkins supported the government position, but they were isolated, crying in the midst of an unheeding wilderness.

It was the most conservative newspaper that attacked the orchestrated nature of the petitions. Such appeals should be spontaneous and not conducted by indifferent members of a PR firm. The article even named the billionaire tycoon Sir Frederick Kingsway as the shadowy figure who'd financed it all.

'Freddie Kingsway won't like that!' Blackstone reacted, when Anna pointed out the article.

'Why, Henry?'

'Freddie Kingsway likes to keep out of the headlines. He's a pretty ruthless operator. Of course, when you meet him he oozes charm. Hamilton Davis isn't a softie, but he's a teddy bear compared with Freddie. Kingsway's corporation owns a fair amount of high street property and shopping centre stuff as well, so it's not surprising that he isn't overjoyed about the levy!'

'He's creaming off location value – namely rent, and the high street shops are squeezed for every penny!'

'Yes, Anna, and it's perfectly legal. There are the buildings, of course: in my book, rent for those is quite legitimate, but, as we know, the location value is the community's natural fund, and that's a tidy sum – a very tidy sum!'

They were sitting in adjacent easy chairs with a large coffee table heaped with the Sunday papers.

'The papers are pretty gloomy, Henry.'

'Yes. I find it strange, though, that a right-leaning paper has given us support and where I had expected backing – not a word. Why have the radical element rejected this idea?'

'It's not in their rule book!'

Blackstone laughed.

'There may be more truth in that than we may imagine!'

'Henry, the papers don't give us much chance, and some are pretty rude in what they say, but you seem so calm about it all.'

'I'm playing the *If* card?'

'Your meaning, O sage?'

'Kipling's *If*. You know: *If you can meet with Triumph and Disaster and treat those two impostors just the same.* Boyhood stuff, but adult, should you put it into practice. Don't worry, my love, we'll leave no stone unturned.'

He leaned across and patted her shoulder.

'You're so incredibly nice, and if we don't go for a walk, I'll not be able to control myself!'

'Then I'll not move!' she teased, delaying slightly before getting to her feet. 'When do we leave for church? – Great Missenden, I believe,' she added.

'No, my dear, St Mary's, Thame: the Security boys are playing games.'

Anna made no reply, but she guessed that it was more than games. Destructive forces, it seemed, were gathering, but as she walked with Henry in the grounds such thoughts soon fell away.

*

'I escaped the press this morning. Just one mention on an inside page,' Anna mused as they sat together on the way to Thame.

'You're slipping!' Blackstone joked.

She made no reply, sensing Henry was preoccupied, and what a range of problems was crowding in on him. Certainly security was very tight, in fact, a lot tighter than usual, and the games that earlier Henry had alluded to were, doubtless, all too real. Anna guessed there'd been a tip-off.

Henry left the burden of his thoughts aside. At least, that was how Anna sensed it. He leaned across and kissed her on the cheek.

'You'll find St Mary's a magnificent old church. Lord Williams is buried there. He was the keeper of the young Princess Elizabeth in the reign of Mary. So the place is rich in history. The poor Vicar will be at sixes and sevens, for we weren't expected, but sometimes the unexpected works out rather well.' He smiled. 'Like replying to Alexander Collingwood's letter!'

At that moment the car phone rang. It had to be urgent, for casual calls were not usual on such occasions.

'Blackstone.'

'Prime Minister, it's Winston. Sorry to disturb you, as I believe you're on your way to church, but I think you ought to know. Riots have broken out again up North. Two young men are in intensive care. It could be worse, but it's very far from being satisfactory. I'm leaving for the scene immediately. Naturally, I'll keep you posted.'

'Thanks, Winston. I can speak prime time, if that were useful. But no doubt we'll be in touch.'

'Prime Minister, before you go: I believe Chris Crouch is with you.'

'Yes, he's probably at the church already. Janet Simmons put the thumb screws on!'

Anna could just hear the faint crackle of laughter.

'Well, Sir, the news for him isn't good. Unofficial Tube strikes have been called for both Tuesday and Thursday. It's diabolical!'

'It's certainly deliberate. It won't hurt the MPs much, but as usual the commuters suffer. We'll speak later.'

Blackstone replaced the handset, and turned to Anna.

'It's hotting up. Unofficial Tube strikes on Tuesday and Thursday.'

'That's diabolical!'

'That's what Winston said!'

'Is there anything we can do?'

'Call the TUC boss, Sam Redwell. That's about it. The Official Union in question faces fines etc., but, if possible, that's best avoided. I have a feeling, though, that the hard-faced militant who's stirring things may have gone a bridge too far. The timing of the action is blatantly political, and the ordinary chap doesn't like that.'

'Isn't there a march in London today?' Anna asked.

'Yes, they'll be gathering in Hyde Park about now. In fact, there are protest marches in most of the big cities.'

'It's a property-owning protest, so the nasties may think it's not their scene.'

'I hope you're right, but I doubt it. These nihilists, as I see them, think their hour has come.'

The Jaguar had been steadily nosing its way towards Thame, and they were almost there. Suddenly the powerful structure was before them.

'Oh, Henry, isn't it magnificent?'

'It reminds me of the saying: four square on the deck, and it's as near to eternal as you get in this shifting world.'

'My heavens, look!'

'What, dear?'

'The media – they're here in force!'

'That's pretty sharp, for we only told them half an hour ago! Stay close. You don't have to say a word. Just smile. Remember the thousand ships that Helen launched!'

'Henry!' she said in mock reproof.

The car doors were opened, and at once a chaos of questions began.

'Quiet, fellows, we're in the shadow of the church.'

'Prime Minister, everybody seems to be against you. Why?'

Blackstone caught Anna's hand and held her close.

'When we were children, and when our parents gave us medicine, we turned our heads away. It was to make us well, our parents would have said. Yet still we turned our heads away. You are not children, so I would study closely what the government has said. Remember it's a national government without a sectional bias. We *have* the nation's welfare at heart. So I would urge all of you to study the government's proposals closely. I'm told there's little opposition to the vote on Tuesday. That is good, but Thursday's vote is in the balance and that is not so good. Just before and over this weekend there's been a nationwide campaign funded by the corporate property-owning interest. The tax-shift we propose is in *everybody's* interest.'

Unobtrusively Anna squeezed his hand, and the boost in confidence was immediate.

'Can anyone tell me what is wrong if the community collects the value it collectively creates, and can anyone tell me where we are in error, if we ease the burden of tax on income? Ponder these things; literature abounds, and let your MP know your mind.'

'Now, ladies and gentlemen of the Press and Media, it's time for church.'

*

Tommy Thompson arrived at Chequers soon after the Prime Minister returned from church. Tommy had, at last, graduated to a suit, and Collingwood was quick to compliment him. Collingwood also observed a new social confidence as Tommy chatted to the various members of the inner Cabinet. The Prime Minister had invited him, and that in Tommy's book meant ordered. He was awed by Henry Blackstone, but didn't quite know why. Still, he wasn't over-awed, and his air of independence was very much intact.

No formal meeting had been arranged. It was simply suggested that he mix and familiarise the Cabinet Members with his various programmes, especially those designed to speed up the initial valuation. Tommy had been driven down by official car, of recent times a not unusual luxury, for both the Premier and Jake Hud viewed him as special; special enough to warrant the interest of security, but not high profile lest it focus undesired attention.

Tommy and Jake Hud were particularly close. Jake and Marjorie Hud didn't have a family, and Tommy was to them an unofficial son. Tommy had a doting, though somewhat infirm, mother, but she didn't mind the Huds' attention. Jake in fatherly mode added to the emphasis on security, something Tommy, with his free and easy ways, didn't much appreciate, yet he went along with it.

Tommy Thompson had a busy afternoon, especially with the Chancellor' who prodded repeatedly to discover, just how Tommy could deliver valuation quickly.

'It's not so difficult, Chancellor. Surveyors and estate agents know the valuation differentials instinctively. Site value doesn't fluctuate all that wildly, and you get to know the pattern. Even so there are many anomalies. It's not an easy task, but we have an army of redundant estate agent employees filling in the map. It's been 24/7 for a month, and if we get the OK on Thursday there won't be too frustrating a delay, we hope. There will be errors. These, of course, can be credited against the next levy.'

'But you can't surely survey everything?'

'Key points; the rest is filled in by the programme. Of course, we have the freehold declaration forms. Almost all have been returned, and in the main people have been honest, almost to a fault. You wouldn't think it if you read the papers, but it's true what Mr Collingwood told me years ago. We are a law-abiding country. I doubt if there's been any cheating worth a mention, for common sense tells most you can't hide land.'

'It's difficult to picture it all.'

'The detail of the application may seem baffling, but the principle is simple. It was one of the first things Mr Collingwood told me. If a principle is true, he stressed, the detail will fall into place.'

The Chancellor smiled; a virtual boy was lecturing him. A month ago his ego would have blown a fuse. Today he didn't seem to mind.

'You have a great respect for Alexander Collingwood. How did you get to know him?'

'He runs classes on Economics and Philosophy in Richmond, and I went along. I'm amazed I stuck it, but Mr Collingwood always tells it straight. There's no waffle. I know he kept me on the straight and narrow, for God knows the mess I would be in, if I hadn't met him.'

*

In the afternoon, the news from London was disturbing. Militant elements had hijacked the march and had attacked the police, provoking them to retaliate. Extremist spokesmen, of course, were condemning police aggression.

'Who believes this bloody rubbish?' Jake Hud burst out.

'As you well know, Jake, it's a game. We all go through the motions, and hopefully we can all retire without too many broken heads.'

'I'd bang them up in the slammer!'

'That's what they want. The more headlines the better. So, to use the modern term, we'll play it cool.'

'How do *you* remain so cool, Prime Minister?'

'Tommy gave me the software!'

Jake burst out laughing. The PM was way out front.

Half an hour later *News Twenty-Four* reported a downpour in central London, while screening a deserted and windswept Trafalgar Square. Nature had played her trump card.

Chapter Thirty-Two

The Monday morning papers weren't encouraging. *Blackstone Dead in the Water* carried the general message. But was it the message of the people, or the 'story,' the accepted journalistic line followed with a kind of lemming fatalism. The vital question was: how would the MPs react? It was certainly the question that focused Blackstone's thinking. Would the MPs see beyond the self-serving interest of the suburban property owner? Or would they feel obliged to support it? Would they, in the manner of Burke, be members of parliament, or merely constituency delegates?

Both Tuesday and Thursday's debates would be followed by a free vote, and Blackstone felt that coercion or any heavy-handed persuasion was out. Yet stating his position and intent was valid. One thing was certain: the opposition were not constrained by such considerations. Consequently all three main party leaders agreed to reiterate the government's case. In the final analysis it was up to the individual MP, the only influence being the power of rhetoric on the day of the debate. Blackstone was under no illusion; the outlook was far from sunny.

*

The mood in Sir Frederick Kingsway's penthouse office was confident. All the signs pointed to a government defeat. Freddie Kingsway was pleased with himself. He had acted with his usual speed and resolution, and the dividends were rolling in. The morning's headline was right: Blackstone was dead in the water. That, of course wasn't good enough for Freddie. He wanted Blackstone prostrate on the ocean bed.

The 'Twins' were due; not the brightest pair around, but what they lacked in grey stuff they filled in with ambition. Their confidence was a hollow puffed-up thing and they sought promotion well above their worth; but were much too dull to know it. In the meantime Kingsway found them useful.

Harbin's loud voice was like a herald. They had arrived.

'Freddie, you have a great view here!' Harbin boomed.

'Yeah, and this office viewing platform costs a fortune!'

The two MPs snorted with amused appreciation.

'Well, gentlemen, what about the Commons?'

'Everyone I've spoken to is set against it!' Harbin grated harshly. 'Who dare go against the people's will?'

'Hell, you guys do it all the time,' Freddie Kingsway teased.

'I'm serious, Freddie. The leafy streets of suburbia are solidly anti-Blackstone!'

'Have we still got the Chancellor in the bag?'

'His experts have been nagging him. Yeah, I think he's with us!'

'Dan, you're very quiet,' Kingsway prompted.

'I'm not as confident as Harold. Jamieson was at Chequers; I don't like that. You know, a lot of members button up, and the subject isn't madly popular in the tea room!' Draper's quieter voice seemed to carry much more weight.

'You're too damned pessimistic, Dan!' Harbin's voice explored the higher decibels. 'Remember, they'll be thinking about their own property interest. Don't forget that!'

'Maybe. There's a rump of "predictables," Harold, but a lot are sitting on the fence.'

'Do what I do, Dan, remind them of their constituency chairman. That concentrates minds wonderfully!' The decibel level had dropped.

'What worries me is Blackstone.' Draper's voice seemed even quieter. 'It's a free vote. The whips won't be breathing down our necks, and if he speaks in that convincing way of his, well...' Draper paused. 'He could swing the House.'

'Hell, the way you're going on we'll all be weeping! I tell you, the leafy streets of suburbia will sink him.' But Harbin's voice had lost its edge.

'Dan's right, how do we stop him, I mean Blackstone?' Kingsway snorted.

'We can't, short of putting a bag over his head.' The decibels had risen again.

Suddenly Kingsway wasn't so confident. Blackstone *was* the problem. He had to be stopped, and Kingsway knew he had to act. He was completely focused, as he always was when someone, or something, was threatening his business and his hard-won gains. His will was like a locomotive on a railtrack. It was straight ahead and nothing to the right or to the left. No wishy-washy ifs or buts. Yes, he'd bottle up the girl, and screw this boy-scout Blackstone to the floor. Hell, what did they expect him to do? Sit back and applaud! But these innocents were not to know.

*

Apart from the anti-Blackstone headlines, the main story in the press was the troubled state of the supermarkets. If fact, one giant was in merger talks with a major rival. World food prices continued to climb and customer resistance was hardening, so profits were eroding with alarming speed. Home agriculture had been neglected and the spectre of food shortages had begun to raise its head. But in the Capital the main preoccupation was Tuesday's tube strike.

Everything that could go wrong was going wrong. The country's state was like a witches' brew, with fresh ingredients daily added to the bubbling mass. Yet even his most dedicated critics couldn't blame the PM for every ill, but they did criticise his assumed inaction. 'What was he doing about it – nothing!' was the usual mantra. Blackstone's 'If' card, as he put it, was tested frequently. There was one piece of cheery news, however; the innuendos aimed at Jake had been withdrawn, but in the most elaborate convoluted way, no doubt, to make it lawyer-proof. The ruse had failed.

The media's treatment of the unofficial strike leader stretched Blackstone's patience to the limit. Here he was, little more than a wrecker, using the strike weapon unofficially on two politically sensitive days, and receiving kid-glove treatment on a prime-time slot. It was difficult to know whether to laugh or weep.

Thankfully the North had simmered down again. For this, Winston took the laurels. Both sides trusted him, and that was half the battle. Blackstone had a brilliant team, and he knew it. He was especially grateful to Bill Jones and Willie. He smiled. With Patricia at his elbow, Willie *had* to toe the line. But that was wishful thinking. Willie was his own man.

Chris and Sam Redwell were working well together, and the wildcat union leader would find that out in not too many hours. Common sense and decency weren't dead. The government were trying to ease the common lot. Why were they striking, the ordinary chap would ask? If Chris were right, it was the wildcat leader who'd be up the creek without a paddle.

189

Blackstone's eyes wrinkled with humour. Chris and Janet Simmons were still together. On the face of it, an impossible union, for Janet was upmarket, but they seemed to have transcended such so-called trivialities.

Blackstone knew he really hadn't focused on the healthcare problem, and it was a problem, Janet's problem. New treatments and new drugs meant new expectations. Costs were rocketing and, of course, people were surviving longer. The sums simply did not match. That's what their initial row had been about, but Chris had been persuaded. Janet's modest fee proposals for minor ailments had received his backing, even though he knew it was the thin edge of the wedge.

Would the Chancellor still hold firm? His past performance was not encouraging. Alexander felt he would. Maybe they had judged James wrongly. He had been subject to the experts on his staff, and few ministers, with any sense, dismissed their highly qualified advice lightly. They had told him that the move was ill-considered and he had hesitated, a not unnatural reaction, but hopefully the weekend at Chequers had won him over.

Charlie Cox wasn't one of his immediate circle, but he was a solid and reliable man. He would need these qualities, for education was a priority once the tax shift was under way. He stopped short. Blackstone, you're assuming things. Thursday was drawing closer. Just tomorrow and Wednesday and then it would be judgement day!

Chapter Thirty-Three

On Tuesday morning the Governor of the Bank of England made a statement to the press attacking the tax-shift proposals as dangerously destabilising. The statement was uncompromising, and its delivery had the finality of a deathblow: it was difficult to believe the timing was simply accidental. For Blackstone, it was a devastating blow, as the Governor of the BoE was usually careful of his words. There was little doubt that MPs would be influenced; and the Chancellor, would he revert again?

Impulsively he rang Alexander Collingwood, but it was Anna who answered. She was indignant.

'It's like assassination, Henry, and theatrical in its timing, though maybe a day too early.'

'Maybe he's been dithering and finally made his mind up. As an honest public servant, he could be genuinely concerned. We mustn't rule that out. Is your father in?'

'He's right beside me.'

'Good, I would like him to speak to the Chancellor.'

'I'll hand the phone across.'

'Alexander, could you speak to James and keep him on the path. This BoE thing may get to him. Listen, I can't speak now for I'm meeting some energy experts in the next minute or so. Give my love to Anna.'

'I will and I'll phone the Chancellor right away. He gave me his private number.'

'Before you go, do you remember the trouble with organised protests in the constituency?'

'Yes.'

'Well, of late the "nasties" have been joining in. Daubing paint and all that sort of thing. Unfortunately someone or ones broke into the constituency office and ransacked the place.'

'Probably looking for embarrassing confidential info they could splash across the press.'

'That's what I told Sir Robert. I also told him he was much too boring to have any juicy secrets, and he guffawed with great gusto.

Alas, that's not the end of it. Sir Robert had two of his windows broken. He didn't tell me, but I was contacted by a mutual friend. The police are on to it, of course. So, Alexander, things are hotting up.'

'Yes, the finishing line is getting close!'

∗

The Energy meeting was not an easy one, for no matter what avenue they explored they met a wall of difficulties. Nuclear was horrendously expensive. Oil was uncertain. Gas supplies, subject to a growing reliance on imports. That left coal, which was a native asset, but most unpopular with the carbon-sensitive lobby. There were wind and wave power, and the other alternatives, of course, but the output, relative to development costs, was problematic. Decisions had to be made. They needed time, yet need was shouting that there was no time. Blackstone listened, but said little. Was the ever-upward graph of energy need a sign of progress? Did it have to be like this? he asked eventually. There were nods around the table, but no one answered.

The Energy meeting took most of the morning. Ted Banks, the Industry Secretary, was also present. It was a highly concentrated discussion, and the lunch break, when it came, was welcome. Blackstone found the debate disturbing when it came to stocks. Gas reserves were good, but were they good enough considering the high reliance placed on gas-fired facilities, and oil stocks were much lower than he'd thought. He recalled a talk on Benjamin Graham's 'Ever normal granary'. It was to do with reasonable price stability and protective stockpiles, but his memory was vague. Maybe it was something Alexander could explore.

∗

In the afternoon it was the Commons and the first debate on the issuing of interest-free credit. The Chancellor had promised to introduce it, and no doubt he would. James was like that. He might vacillate, and waver like a reed before the wind, but when he finally gave his word he kept it. Even so, his swings of mood didn't engender confidence.

Blackstone talked casually to Collingwood, who was seated on the benches reserved for advisors. They were on the floor of the House, and when the Chancellor entered the chamber Blackstone joined him; then after some brief words they walked in tandem to the despatch box.

The Chancellor's statement was brief and to the point. He assured Members that the interest-free credit would be closely monitored and that any commercial laxity would not be tolerated. He also reiterated that the credit would be used strictly for infrastructure projects, and essential ones at that. He sat down and immediately the questions started.

'Will the Chancellor assure us that no grandiose prestige projects will be contemplated?'

'The Honourable Gentleman has my complete assurance.'

This was followed by supportive comments from the MPs whose constituencies were the first to benefit. Then inevitably came the voice of opposition.

'Chancellor, this so-called free credit is unsecured. It is highly irresponsible and it undermines the banks. I'm appalled by the complacency of the House!'

'The Honourable Member will have heard many times that the credit is secured by the infrastructure that it will promote. Bridges and roads are fairly solid stuff, a lot more solid than the dodgy debt packages that we've heard so much about. Indeed, it seems to me that the banks have done a pretty good job in undermining themselves! Consequently, it is my strongly held belief that credit should be confined to productive enterprises which, of course, includes infrastructure.'

Blackstone smiled; James had got the bit between his teeth.

'Sir, this slur, this abuse of parliamentary privilege is intolerable,' the MP exploded, jumping to his feet. 'The City should be supported, not undermined, and especially by the Chancellor!'

'Of all people, the Honourable Gentleman should know that I have solidly supported the City in these difficult times, but I do not support irresponsible loans and the speculation of bankers mesmerised by glittering profits.'

The MP, Basil Crankshaw, jumped to his feet again and the Speaker caught the PM's eye.

'The Prime Minister' he boomed.

'We all know how passionately the Honourable Gentleman defends the City's interest. This is appreciated. We have heard the Honourable Gentleman; he has made his point forcefully. Let me assure him that the measure before the House has been exhaustively debated in Cabinet. The Chancellor tirelessly supports the

City's interest. I can assure you he wouldn't let us get away with any quick-fix solution!'

'What about the tax shift then?' It was Harbin's loud aggressive voice.

Blackstone smiled.

'Let's leave to Thursday what belongs to Thursday,' he answered evenly, and then he took his seat to knowing smiles on either side.

The vote in favour of the credit issue was overwhelming, but realism tempered any sense of celebration. Thursday's battle was yet to be joined, and the outcome was far from being certain.

The Chancellor turned towards him on the bench.

'Alexander phoned this morning. Told me to keep some arrows in my quiver for Thursday. I think he may have thought the Governor might have pushed me off the track, but he shouldn't have troubled. I know the Governor well; Joey Archer likes a drama, and the bigger the better!'

Blackstone nodded, but held his peace. There was a lot more to James Jamieson than met the eye: a lot more. What a strange game it all was.

*

Four hours later, when Blackstone was busy with the energy report, the phone rang. Only priority calls were put through at this time. It was Chris.

'*PM, turn to channel one. It's Hanwall, and you won't believe it.*'

The screen flickered into life, and there was Sir Harold with his graceful wife.

'*This isn't easy, but I feel compelled to speak. I've been wrong. I've been totally blinded by what I felt was an attack on my legitimate rights. The government's proposals were, to me, legalised vandalism. How dare they undermine my age-old sanctioned claim to property. Well, I listened to all our Prime Minister has had to say and indeed to what Jake Hud proposed. Mind you, I've been less than polite in my reactions, but I couldn't find the slightest whiff of party political posturing. This was a principle they were putting forward, not an interest group agenda – there was nothing-in-it-for-me in a sectional sense. So my thinking began to change. This wasn't painless. In fact, it was damned painful. The government's proposal is about*'

*what's-in-it-for all: what's-in-it-for the country. That is all I've
got to say.'*

'Well, well, well,' Blackstone whispered. He lifted the phone. It
was still live.

'Chris, that can't do us any harm!'

*'No, Sir, no harm at all. As Mabel might say, I think your
Guardian Angel has been working overtime.'*

Chapter Thirty-Four

The day following the Commons debate, the Lords added their seal of approval. At last Blackstone could lift the phone and give the go-ahead. Hugh Robbins, the father of his boy correspondent, had come into his own, and new hope would be shining in the North and in the West. It was only the beginning, but, at least, something was actually happening, and despite his growing pessimism surrounding Thursday's debate, he felt elated.

It was six o'clock when he headed for the flat, where unexpectedly he found Mabel in tears.

'What's wrong, Mabel?'

'Your lovely Anna. She's missing. A news flash on the radio!'

'What?' Blackstone was stunned. 'Why wasn't I told?'

'I don't know, Mr Henry.'

Blackstone stood without moving, trying to still the outrage and the pain.

'I think you need this, Prime Minister.' It was Mabel with a glass of red. Why was she calling him Prime Minister? She never did!

'Thanks, Mabel,' he acknowledged; a stranger's voice, he thought.

The phone rang. It was Jenny. But when she heard his voice she couldn't speak.

'I'll come down, Jenny,' he said gently.

What was happening wasn't really happening. On the surface a detached dreamlike feeling seemed to have possessed him, yet every detail was observed, as if by someone else. Again, the observation was uncritical and without a commentary. Phone call followed phone call. Then, at last, Jenny managed to get through to Alexander.

'Alexander, what happened?'

The security people are baffled. It happened in the super-market she habitually uses. One moment she was there, the next, gone! A highly professional operation, security maintain.'

'How are you coping? You can always spend the night here if you want.'

'That's kind, but I think I'll stay here. To be truthful, I don't think it's quite penetrated yet. But, Henry, they, whoever they may be, are trying to weaken you. That's the obvious reading of it all. It's political; the timing says so. Get some sleep tonight; don't let the bastards win! Anna's all right, why would they harm her? It's you they want to stop!'

'Alexander, you're being very rational!'

'As I've said, I don't think the nightmare's penetrated yet. Give me another hour!'

'Well, there's a bed here if it gets too hellish!'

'Thank you, Prime Minister.'

Mabel had called him Prime Minister, and now Alexander. Neither rarely did. The message was obvious.

He had barely put the phone down when it rang again.

'The US President for you, Prime Minister.'

There was a wait and then the voice came through.

'Henry, Gill and I are shocked. We've just heard the news. That sweet girl: it's hard to take it in. How are you?'

'A walking zombie, Andrew.'

'They're getting at you, Henry. They want you sleepless and confused, for the debate. That's the Ambassador's view.'

'My prospective father-in-law says so as well.'

'Take my word for it, Henry. It's a property tycoon: some fat-cat fella real jealous of his cream. They come in truckloads over here!'

'Yes, what you say sounds very feasible.'

'Listen, Henry, if you win tomorrow, and I do believe you will, I'll go on prime time. I mean it; it's a goddam promise! The memory of my grandfather and the principle he held so dear commands it! And, Henry, I'll do it for Anna. But don't you worry. She'll be back with you in no time.'

'Thank you, Mr President.'

'And, thank you, Prime Minister.'

There was a knock on the door; it was Jenny.

'Prime Minister, Her Majesty will be leaving the Palace in the next few minutes, so she'll be here rather soon. She has stressed that this is a strictly personal visit.'

Blackstone didn't react immediately.

'Sorry, Jenny, I got a little emotional. A Churchill moment, if you like. I'd better tidy up this place.'

'I don't think she'll mind, Sir.'

'No, I don't suppose she will.'

*

Blackstone managed three hours' sleep at the latter part of the night, but when he woke, the pain returned. Stoically, he acted out the morning routine, applying his father's discipline of attending carefully to every movement.

The papers were waiting on the table, and with a cup of tea to hand he scanned them quickly. Anna's picture graced almost every publication, and the leader columns were, without exception, sympathetic. The anti-tax-shift articles, though, had reached a crescendo. This was their final and absolute denouncement.

'Good morning, Mr Henry.' Mabel had arrived to prepare breakfast. 'I hope you got some sleep.'

'About three hours, Mabel.'

'Good, that's more than I expected. It's going to be all right, Mr Henry. A strange thing happened this morning when I woke up. It's never happened to me before, but it was like a voice, yet not a voice, more like a feeling. I knew Anna was safe and well. There was no doubt.'

'You're very fond of Anna,' Blackstone said quietly.

'Yes, Mr Henry.'

'Thank you, Mabel; thank you for that.'

Blackstone never dismissed such things, and especially coming from an open heart like Mabel's.

Then the phone calls came. First was Bill, then Willie and after that his sister Patricia ringing from Italy. Jake Hud was next. Marjorie hadn't slept a wink, he told him. Next Blackstone rang Alexander.

'Did you sleep?' he asked.

About two hours or so: plus dosing off a little in the chair this morning.

'Will you be able to come this afternoon?'

'Oh yes!

Blackstone then relayed Mabel's experience.

'There are more things in heaven and earth, Horatio, than are dreamt of in your philosophy.' [1] Collingwood muttered Hamlet's well-known words automatically.

198

'Well, Alexander, the light's flashing. There's another call.' It was Chris.

'Prime Minister, no word, I suppose?'

'No, Chris.'

'Well, Sir, I just think she's safe. Mind you, I don't know why. But there it is, that's how I feel.'

'Thanks, Chris. Mabel has said as much as well.'

'And PM, because of Anna, a lot of votes will swing your way. The idiot who dreamt this kidnap up has shot himself in the foot.'

'Maybe there's a group of them.'

'Doubtful, with a group, secrecy would be impossible.'

'Another candidate for Vauxhall Cross.'

'We're all rooting for you, Sir. And Anna, she's safe.'

Blackstone sat back.

Why had he not seen the glaring fact right from the beginning? Why had no one told him until Chris revealed the obvious? Perhaps they thought it was insensitive. That was understandable. He, of course, was too numbed by Anna's disappearance to see clearly. Then there was another question: why was the perpetrator of this damnable act so blind? Why had he not seen the obvious? Another, much more sinister answer, was that Anna had been abducted for a different purpose. He shuddered.

✳

Sir Frederick Kingsway had been snapping at his secretaries from early morning. His dark moods, of course, were not unknown, but this time he had plumbed new depths.

His secretary's phone buzzed.

'Mr Harbin is here, Sir.'

'What's he want? Send him in!' Anger and frustration seemed to colour every syllable.

The secretary didn't respond. Instead, she waved Harold Harbin through.

'What the hell's going on?' Kingsway grated. 'Where's Draper?'

'Organising a last-minute leaflet drop for the MPs'

'What the hell's that about?'

'He's trying to squash the sympathy vote!'

'Sympathy vote?' Kingsway asked, pretending not to know.

'Blackstone's girl!'

'They're all too hard-bitten, and keeping their seats is way ahead of Anna Collingwood. Suburbia will win!' Kingsway said confidently, masking his own frustration. Why had he not anticipated the sympathy swing? It was as if something had been blind deliberately, for a child of six would have seen it coming! He cringed. His own stupidity was a bitter pill. 'What's Dan saying on the leaflet?' he questioned.

'Sympathy for Anna, but no sympathy for the levy.'

'Good, I like it: short and sharp. Anyway, the girl will soon be free.'

'What do you mean? How do you know that?' Harbin's voice was like a ripsaw.

'It's common sense. These guys, whoever they are, thought they could weaken Blackstone. So the debate's the thing. Why keep the girl longer? Anyway, the idiots shot themselves in the foot. Why were they so bloody blind, for their stupidity could lose us votes. Let's hope Dan can stem the leak! But I can't believe there's a problem. As I said, suburbia is king. Those postage-stamp back gardens are our ally!'

'For God's sake, Freddie, don't say that in public – at least, not until after the vote!'

'Yeah, I'll be real careful, as they say across the pond! But I'm right; the MPs cannot bite the hand that feeds them, and that hand is the hand that tends the gardens of suburbia!'

Kingsway was himself again. He smiled. He'd played his cards like a croupier.

Chapter Thirty-Five

Despite the united support of the Cabinet and his friends, and despite the special reassurances of Chris and Mabel, Blackstone felt drained. No matter what he did, the greyness and the sense of sickness in his very being would not lift. Real grief must be like this, he thought. How many in the country at this very moment were in anguish at the passing of a loved one? At once compassion flooded through him, and it seemed as though his body tensions melted. What a blessing, just before being driven to the House.

Once amidst the bustle of it all, he felt much more himself. He made his way round to the main lobby. Sentimental perhaps, but he felt as if she were walking with him. We'll do this together, my love. He smiled. She would chastise him, of course, for being Platonically incorrect. Henry, we'll do it *as one*. It was as though he heard her voice and saw the characteristic movement of her head.

Nods of acknowledgement were frequent as he made his way towards the entrance to the Chamber. Dan Draper was surreptitiously handing out flyers. No doubt they were anti-levy. Just through the entrance, he turned to the right where Alexander was seated 'under the stairs' in the bench reserved for experts and advisors. Then, after a brief word, he made his way toward the despatch box. The House was packed, and as if by order all rose to their feet. There were no exceptions. Blackstone was moved. The House could be rough. Indeed, the members could be ruthless, but, in moments such as this, humanity ruled.

After thanking the House for their gesture of support and sympathy, Blackstone paused. This was it. Pray God he would be worthy of the moment, and it was a moment; the chance to lay the first foundations of economic justice. Not justice for the greatest number, or for the underprivileged, but justice for all.

'Mr Speaker, Rt. Honourable and Honourable Members, *poverty is not a normal state of society. It is a disease produced by the stupidity of men.*[1] These are not my words but those of a between-the-wars Labour MP. What did he mean by stupidity in this instance? Let me offer an answer.

'Currently, we allow location value, such as that present in the city centre and the high street, to be claimed by private interest. Let's put it another way. We allow publicly created wealth to enrich us privately. So what is, in fact, a naturally created community fund is not collected. Instead we tax earnings both corporate and individual, and you all know just how popular that is!

'Can I say it rather bluntly? We allow private interests to claim what they haven't created, that is the value created by the community as a whole, and because of this we tolerate the community taxing what they haven't created, that is our earnings. Now in my book that is fairly stupid.

'This is what the tax shift is about: the gradual shifting of tax on income to the collection of location levy. Nothing could be simpler. The trouble is the world we have created isn't simple: it's horrendously complicated, and no wonder. We've ignored the natural economic laws for centuries – and the result, a terrible grinding poverty pressing on the people, while their so-called betters wallow in abundance. Such a situation is *not* God's will; it is immoral!

'When the land, which is nature's gift to all, is claimed by the few, we create a society of haves and have-nots: those who own their property and those who pay them rent. It's as simple as that!

'Up until this week we have financed infrastructure improvements out of general taxation. Such improvements enhance community benefits. This we know, and if we're lucky enough to own a property in the area we receive a windfall. The irony is that the have-nots help to provide the windfall, for improvements are financed out of general taxation. However, on Tuesday we took one small step towards a new approach.'

'One step too many!' Basil Crankshaw shouted.

'The Honourable Member doesn't miss a trick! Now courting the risk of upsetting the Honourable Gentleman further, may I take a further step?'

'You may!' Crankshaw shot back, prompting laughter.

'The provision of interest-free credit for special infrastructure projects will be closely monitored. Clearly, the benefits arising will enhance location value in general. In the nature of things some sites will see their value soar. This is where the location levy comes into its own, for the community can recover at least some of the value it's created. Indeed, it is the perfect partner to the credit-funded projects, for the more we advance infrastructure services the more revenue we collect.

'What's the percentage?' someone shouted.

'Twenty percent at most.' Blackstone didn't pause. 'Mr Speaker, public sector expenditure and taxation resistance are head to head. It's a crisis that's acute, and using current models, there's no way forward. Honourable Gentlemen, this isn't mere rhetoric. It's a sleep-disturbing reality. We need fresh thinking, a new approach, and the tax shift is just that! What's more, the tax-shift isn't just another theory plucked from the swirling mass of complication. On the contrary, it's the living fact of nature's rule and visible to all. The community by its collective presence creates a fund. If we collect it, we obey the law; if we don't, we disobey.'

Suddenly Blackstone took his seat, and, at once, over a dozen MPs jumped to their feet.

The first questions were supportive. Next came a flurry of indignant opposition to the rape of private property. This gave Blackstone an opportunity to reiterate the principle. Then an MP that Blackstone rather liked stood up.

'Prime Minister, I have a lingering fear that this location levy will spell the end of patronage. Art in all its forms depends so much on wealthy donors. Will this levy kill the will to give?'

'We all know the Honourable Gentleman is a keen supporter of the arts, and for this we should be grateful. As to your question: location value levy is not a soak-the-rich impost. The same principle applies to the rich as to the less well-off. Indeed, some country estates could fare much better. When men are freed from the economic treadmill of our current system, art patronage could have a much, much wider spread.

'Honourable members, this is an exciting day. You have the chance to enter in the statute book the key to economic freedom. At present we are graced by civil freedom. Give the people economic freedom, too!'

Again he sat down.

Anna, he thought, you should be listening, for I don't know where this stuff is coming from.

'Can the Prime Minister give us an indication of the time scale that he has in mind for the location levy?' The MP's voice was measured.

'As quickly as possible: there really isn't time to linger. My Honourable friend, who is overseeing this tax-shift proposal, is best placed to answer you.'

Jake Hud stood up, and after a glowing tribute to the Prime Minister, gave a detailed survey of the tax shift.

As he listened to Jake's amusing account, he wondered why the rockets he'd expected still remained unused. Were they waiting for some coup de grace? But when Harold Harbin stood up after Jake sat down, he felt the time had come.

'Mr Speaker', Harbin's powerful voice filled the Chamber. 'After centuries of tradition, we are at last setting fire to our heritage, but in such a cloud of piety it would make a fellow weep. Observe any creature, see them mark their territory, and watch how fiercely they defend it. The urge to own our square of land is natural and fundamental, and those who go against it do so at their peril. If we pass this bill we go against the people, and, Honourable Members, that is dangerous. Ask yourselves, who will stand up at the hustings and say outright that they obeyed the people's will?'

Blackstone stood up, without any inner prompting how he would reply. Then he spoke.

'Mr Speaker, we are not animals. We are creatures endowed with the gift of reason. I would suggest that our constituents recognise the voice of reason when they hear it. They may not agree, but they will respect the MP who speaks according to his conscience.'

'Mr Speaker', Harbin reacted. 'The Chancellor has been very quiet. What has he to say?'

Blackstone stiffened. Harbin knew exactly where to strike. For God's sake, James, hold firm.

James Jamieson rose slowly. He always did. And the whole front bench sat frozen.

'Mr Speaker, the Honourable Gentleman has asked what the Chancellor has to say. The truth is, very little. Being Chancellor, of course, I'm surrounded by experts. They are most erudite gentlemen but when I broached the subject of the levy they merely spoke in sound bites. It was a "commie" thing. It was "old hat" and past its "sell-by" date. They knew the history of it all, but the theory was really of another age. One man told me that it was theoretically correct but unworkable. Now, I'm slow and stubborn, so I made enquiries, and, you know, it wasn't a "commie" thing. It wasn't "old" hat, and it wasn't past its "sell-by" date. It *was* theoretically correct, but the charge that it was unworkable was untested.

'Being Chancellor, I felt it my duty to understand this tax-shift measure, for Honourable Members, we're closing on the danger zone where we cannot meet commitments. This tax-shift measure is a godsend. I urge you to give it your approval. And before I sit down, I wish to acknowledge the courtesy and forbearance of the Prime Minister, who never once voiced impatience at my vacillations.' He turned to Blackstone. 'Pray God, Sir, that Anna Collingwood will soon be at your side.'

James Jamieson sat down to almost total stillness. Chris Crouch could hardly contain himself. They'd done it, they'd bloody done it, and James had put the icing on the top and the bloody cherries too! He wanted to get up and shout, but no, he sat, as if unmoved. The 'fat cat' who was holding Anna had shot himself in the foot, both bloody feet! He'll be on a bloody zimmer. Chris had no doubt about his reading of the kidnap. It was the feeling that he had, and when he had these feelings they were usually right.

Bill Jones was the next to speak. Then Willie Windbourne added his endorsement. The time had come for summing up.

'Prime Minister,' the Speaker called.

Blackstone rose. He felt exhausted; the tension prior to the Chancellor's speech had drained his meagre reserves.

'Location value is the natural fund of the community. It rises to its peak in city centres then diminishes in a concave arc to nominal values in the outer reaches. It's all so incredibly simple, yet application in the complicated world we have created is not easy, but, with our thinking firmly anchored to the principle, we can, at last, begin to root out poverty in what should be a land of plenty. For when the natural law's obeyed, nature gives us right of way. Today, by backing the tax-shift proposals, we have the opportunity of stepping down this road. Take it! Support the motion.'

Blackstone sat down wearily, and the Chancellor turned to him.

' "Nature gives us right of way." A wonderful line, Prime Minister.'

'James, you took the laurels. Your words were very apt.'

✳

When the actual figures were revealed, Chris Crouch was proved to be correct. A hundred and thirty abstentions and forty-two against. The rest had voted 'aye'. It was quite a victory, but there was no triumphalism. It was not a party thing.

The PM was chatting to the Chancellor and Bill Jones, but Chris, in his sure-footed way, intervened.

'I'll walk you out, Prime Minister.'

'Thanks, Chris.'

Chris's intervention was quite natural, and neither Bill Jones nor James Jamieson seemed to mind.

'She's all right, Sir.'

'Dear God, I hope you're right.'

Chapter Thirty-Six

The Prime Minister's car was waiting in the yard. There'd been a downpour, and the cobbled ribs were sparkling in the sunlight. The last few drops of rain were falling as Blackstone approached, accompanied by Chris Crouch and Janet Simmons.

They had said little since leaving the Chamber and it was only when Blackstone was about to go that Chris broke the silence.

'It was a triumph, Sir,' he said briefly, careful of the anguish that his chief had to be suffering.

'Yes, Chris: in the old days I'd been swanning round Westminster with someone telling me I wasn't God! Say, why don't you two come back with me to Downing Street? That's if you can squeeze in? Bill, James, Jake and, I think Willie, are gathering for a drink.'

'A pleasure, PM.'

Chris could see the Premier's bonhomie was studied. He wanted desperately to help this man, but what could he do?

'Will the Lords cause trouble?' Janet asked, as they set out.

'Some of the senior "Hereditaries" are for it. I think they feel the levy frees them from the burden of privilege. But, understandably there is powerful opposition in some quarters – all those family acres. I feel the levy would be much, much less than they expect. City properties, of course, would feel the pinch.'

'It's only a small percentage, PM,' Chris cut in, 'and, if they're burdened by privilege, they can always pass a little on to me!'

Blackstone smiled.

'Go for the new money, Chris. There's more of it!'

The short journey was soon over, and once in Number Ten they headed for the white drawing-room. The Chancellor and Bill followed seconds later.

'I liked your speech, James.' Chris said immediately. 'You left Harbin nothing to attack. Those sound bites and the way you picked them off, just like a clay pigeon shoot!'

The Chancellor chuckled.

'Will the Lords behave themselves? That's the question. What do you think, Prime Minister?'

'Janet asked a similar question in the car. All my sources say it's in the bag. Their Lordships can be awkward enough at times, but in this case they seem pragmatic. It's not 1910, and the large hereditary block's no more. And, as I said to Janet, the hereditary element isn't so fiercely adamant as one might have expected. Of course, the tax shift will help, for direct taxes will be reduced. Ah, here's Jake. Jake, what do you think about the Lords? Will we have trouble?'

'They don't want to stir the pot! They've been "reformed" enough!' Jake said bluntly. 'And, even if they are a little tardy, it'll give us more time with this valuation survey.'

Blackstone's weariness was obvious in his lack of a response, and Chris felt he had to act.

'Pardon my presumption, PM, but I think you ought to have a rest.'

'You could be right, Chris. Yes, half an hour would be useful.'

'Don't worry Sir. Janet and I will look after things.'

'Sorry, gentlemen, I'll disappear upstairs for a while,' he apologised as he made for the flat. Suddenly he remembered Anna's father. 'Chris, contact Alexander Collingwood, find out how he is and where he is.'

'Done, Sir. Janet and I will follow you upstairs in a moment. You'll want a cuppa when you've rested.'

'Thanks – and Chris, Special Branch, what are they doing?'

'Yes, Prime Minister.'

*

The PM was wounded, and Chris Crouch felt a strange fragility. Yet, in tandem was enormous strength. The sensitivity, and the force of will together in one breast: the power to lead the state, and yet to weep. Stop blubbering, Crouch. He smiled knowingly, for he knew the common sense reality that he'd served so long was breached. Another world had been revealed. He stood still, his eyes unfocused. Please let his earlier feeling be correct. He looked upward. Please, if you are, and whoever you are, let Anna Collingwood be safe. Chris still stood, as if rooted to the spot, his strange involuntary behaviour like a stranger's will.

*

Dark clouds were gathering. Where were they not gathering? the policeman thought flatly. Maybe there was going to be another downpour. Well, at least the waving placards had gone – and the chanting! They'd been a fairly decent lot. Of course, they had every right to protest; it was a free country. Even that bunch of weirdos who had 'stopped by' for an hour or two, had 'moved along' without protest. A cab drew up outside the gates of Downing Street. It was a frequent happening – probably a regular, the Officer thought. It was still light, but the cabbie had his sidelights on. A passenger got out, a woman, her face shrouded by a scarf. She didn't stop to pay the driver. The policeman, alerted by the scarf, had instant thoughts of human bomb fanatics. He approached cautiously.

'My name is Anna Collingwood. I wish to speak to the Prime Minister.'

Yeah, he thought. Tell that to the bloody fairies – the perfect dodge to get her right inside. Maybe she *is* Anna Collingwood! She speaks well. That bloody scarf's the trouble.

'Could you remove your scarf, ma'am'? he asked correctly.

The woman immediately obeyed.

'My God! Come through ma'am. I'll escort you to the door. You had us *all* very worried!'

✳

His head was much too fuddled and confused to worry, Blackstone concluded vaguely as he lay down to rest. Nearly forty minutes later he woke up, not quite knowing where he was. He had slept deeply, and his mind was suddenly very much awake. Then he remembered Anna, and the greyness descended. He went through to the lounge, where Chris and Janet were helping Mabel with the supper things.

'Did you sleep, Sir?'

'I went out like a light.'

'Mr Collingwood is at home; we told him you were resting.'

The internal phone rang, and Blackstone answered it. It was Jenny.

'Jenny, are you still there? What's wrong? Have you lost your voice?'

'Anna – Miss Collingwood's here, Sir! She's – on her way.' Jenny was too emotional to be fluent.

When he put the phone down, she was there before him and

without the slightest hesitation they were in each other's arms. With one arm round her waist, and the other cupped behind her head, he held her close.

'My dear sweet love, what a blessing, what a blessing! It wasn't very nice without you, no, not nice at all!'

She murmured 'Henry.' That was all she said.

'What happened dear? Did they treat you badly?'

'It wasn't too terrible. They held me in a caravan, which was locked up in a shed. I was treated well, and the cooked food was hot. I was even given a radio, but the battery soon gave up. You might even say they were polite, and I never felt I was in danger. It seemed obvious they were trying to get at you.' She paused briefly. 'But, later, later. Henry, let's not spoil the present with the dreary past. Father!' she exclaimed, suddenly remembering.

A discreet cough issued from the kitchen.

'My ministerial car will soon be on the way to collect him, ma'am.' Chris used his best upmarket voice, and Anna laughed.

'Chris and Janet have been ministering angels,' Blackstone said quietly.

Mabel then appeared, weeping unashamedly, and Anna embraced her.

'I was right, I knew you were safe,' Mabel managed to say.

'Anna, the PM won the day, did you hear?' Chris interjected.

'Yes, the cabbie told me. Henry brought tears to his eyes, he said, and the Chancellor put the icing on the cake. It's a miracle. Father will be over the moon! He's worked so long for this without a sliver of success. General apathy, professional disdain, and hard self-interest, were as triple walls. Then Henry Blackstone rode over the hill!'

'Tilting at windmills!' Blackstone joked.

'No, PM, with the cavalry!' Chris countered.

'Henry,' Anna's voice was tentative. 'I'm suddenly feeling tired: the elation must be wearing off. Perhaps I ought to rest, but I'm smelly. There was no water in the caravan. I really must have a bath, but I don't have a change of clothes.'

'Your father thought of that and has asked your friendly next-door neighbour to pack a case, so don't worry,' Janet interjected quietly.

'Anna, my love,' Blackstone said softly. 'My bedroom's through there,' he added, pointing. 'Janet will look after you.'

'PM, I've been meaning to ask you a question for some time.'

'It's not like you to hold back, Chris.'

'Don't worry, Sir, I wasn't being a wilting flower!'

Blackstone's easy laughter resounded.

'Well, what's the question. Don't keep me hanging out there, as our friend the President would say.'

'Why are we all so bloody friendly? Cabinets are not always models of harmony, to quote an understatement!'

'Good question, Chris; I think we shouldn't underestimate the power of the principle we've been serving. We all know it's natural and true, and we know it in our hearts. It's not just an intellectual theory; it's living knowledge. That is powerful.'

'Well, Sir, I'm not a Shakespeare waller, but I think there was *a little touch of Harry in the night.*'[1]

*

After an overnight stay at a central London clinic, where she had a thorough check-up, Anna returned to Downing Street the following day. Special Branch officers interviewed her, but she had little to offer.

Apart from the chloroform swab pressed over her nose and mouth during the initial capture she was not treated roughly. And, although the solitary confinement nature of the caravan was frustrating, she had been fed and treated well. Her captors had even given her a radio, but the battery faded all too soon. She never saw their faces or was allowed to see the street or any of the surrounding area. They had covered the windows from the outside, so when the caravan was driven away for her release she saw nothing of the district where she had been held.

'When they opened the door, the light was blinding. They must have seen that, for they didn't rush me. "Good luck, Miss," they said and that was that. They had stopped near a rather bleak-looking park. I walked towards what I thought was the main road, and tried two payphones on the way, but they were out of order. Then a cab appeared. That *was* a piece of luck. The cabbie seemed a down-to-earth chap and I instinctively trusted him. So I told him who I was, and that I had no money. "Don't worry, Miss," he said, and then he started singing the praises of the Prime Minister. When I offered to get his fare at Downing Street, he said, "No way, it's on me, Miss." Mind you, it wasn't a short journey, for it took almost an hour. I memorised his number. Here it is.' She handed it over. 'I know the Prime Minister would like to speak to him, and I'm sure Downing Street could find him – but you must have ways and means, as they say.'

The two officers laughed lightly.

'As good as done, Miss Collingwood. It looks as if your captors were ODCs and pretty professional. We will be lucky to find them. They can get caught on other jobs, of course, and then things like this come out. Thanks, Miss Collingwood.'

*

'Henry, what's an ODC? Anna asked when she and Blackstone were relaxing after lunch.

'An ordinary decent criminal, dear!'

'That describes my captors to a tee!' she said with some amusement, while snuggling close on the sofa.

'Why do people take that route?'

'There seems to be a weakness in the human and in some cases it gains the upper hand. Times of crisis, such as now, don't help. Henry George himself was reduced to begging at one desperate stage, but someone helped and he didn't cross the line.'

'Yes, Father told me the story.'

They sat in a contented silence for some time.

'Christ said: – *ye have the poor always with you.*'[2] Anna said suddenly. 'What's it mean Henry, for it's been used to justify the *status quo?*'

'Yes, by those who ought to know, or to have known, better. How could Christ have meant his words to serve the gross inequities that our current system has evolved?'

'I'm sorry; Henry, but you haven't answered the question! What does the passage mean?'

'If my memory serves me right, a woman approached and poured an alabaster box of very precious ointment on Christ's head. The disciples saw this as a waste. It should have been sold, they said, and given to the poor. This incident is recorded by St Matthew, and there is a similar incident in St John when Mary anoints the feet of Jesus.[3] My reading of this, for what it's worth, says the women in both incidents were serving the truth, that is Christ, and by doing so served all. But, my dear, don't take my word as gospel, for there'll be volumes written on the subject. Yesterday, I trust *we* served the truth and by doing so served *all.*'

'I'm very fond of you, Henry Blackstone.'

He kissed her lightly on the forehead.

'My dear, don't you be running off again, for my tender constitution couldn't stand it!'

'When's Father arriving?'

'He should be on his way. A car was sent some time ago. Then it's Chequers.'

'So the miracle has actually happened!'

'Their Lordships have yet to give us their approval. All my information says they will. After all, it's a money bill, and with the majority we achieved, they would be very loath to cause a stir! The parliamentary battle may be won, but the application is another matter. Sometimes I feel we're dealing with two nations – the ones who have and those who don't – two nations, who often are in conflict. We all can vote, but if we vote in ignorance, we forge the chains that bind us. Anna, if this principle is to survive the test of time the people need to hold it in their hearts and see it as the natural way of things.

'Presently, there's still much work to do. We need time, but we do not have that luxury, for the present state of things demands a remedy. Jake says he still lies sleepless in the night wondering if the whole thing's going pear-shaped.'

'And you?'

'Yes, at times, but exhaustion usually wins!'

'Are we going to church on Sunday?' Anna asked.

'Yes, but why do you ask?'

'I just feel we should.'

References

Chapter 17
1 Thomas Jefferson, quoted by Jeff Randall, *Daily Telegraph* article, September 26th 2008.

Chapter 18
1 Plato, *Phaedo*, Random House, Vol. 1, p.456.

Chapter 22
1 Shakespeare, *Richard II*, Act 2, Scene 1.

Chapter 26
1 Brian Hodgkinson, *A New Model of the Economy*, Shepheard-Walwyn, 2008, p.15.
2 Robert McGarvey, *The Growth Conundrum*, The Economic Research Council, Vol. 39, No. 3.
3 Henry George, *Progress and Poverty*, Book V, Ch. 2, J.M. Dent & Sons Ltd, Everyman's Library, pp.201-2.
4 Compiled by Dr Mark Hassard, *The Prosperity Paradox*, Chatsworth Village Pty Ltd, 2000. Passage taken from book cover.

Chapter 28
1 Psalm 111, v.10.
2 Shakespeare, *Richard II*, Act 2, Scene 1.

Chapter 29
1 *The Philosophy of Edmund Burke*, Ann Arbor: The University of Michigan Press, 1960, p.74.

Chapter 30
1 Plato, *Timaeus* (28), translated Desmond Lee, Penguin Classics, p.40; first published 1965.
2 Psalm 37, v.7.
3 Winston S. Churchill MP, *The People's Rights*, Jonathan Cape, London; first published 1909, reset 1970, p.117.

Chapter 34
1 Shakespeare, *Hamlet*, Act 1, Scene 5.

Chapter 35
1 John Stewart, *Standing for Justice*, Shepheard-Walwyn, 2001. Passage taken from book cover.

Chapter 36
1 Shakespeare, *Henry V*, Act 4, Chorus.
2 St Matthew 26, v.11.
3 St John 12, v.8.